A
Lakeside
Reunion

A Lakeside Reunion

C. Chilove

FOREVER

New York Boston

Copyright © 2023 by C. Chilove
Cover design by Adrienne Krogh
Cover copyright © 2023 by Hachette Book Group, Inc.

Forever
Hachette Book Group
1290 Avenue of the Americas, New York, NY 10104
read-forever.com
twitter.com/readforeverpub

First Edition: April 2023

Forever is an imprint of Grand Central Publishing. The Forever name and logo are trademarks of Hachette Book Group, Inc.

The publisher is not responsible for websites (or their content) that are not owned by the publisher.

The Hachette Speakers Bureau provides a wide range of authors for speaking events. To find out more, go to www.hachettespeakersbureau.com or email HachetteSpeakers@hbgusa.com.

Forever books may be purchased in bulk for business, educational, or promotional use. For information, please contact your local bookseller or the Hachette Book Group Special Markets Department at special.markets@hbgusa.com.

Library of Congress Cataloging-in-Publication Data
Names: Chilove, C., author.
Title: A lakeside reunion / C. Chilove.
Description: First edition. | New York : Forever, 2023. | Series: Shores of Dora
Identifiers: LCCN 2022053131 | ISBN 9781538705629 (trade paperback) | ISBN 9781538705636 (ebook)
Subjects: LCGFT: Romance fiction. | Domestic fiction. | Novels.
Classification: LCC PS3603.H5647 L35 2023 | DDC 813/.6—dc23/eng/20221123
LC record available at https://lccn.loc.gov/2022053131

ISBN: 9781538705629 (trade paperback), 9781538705636 (ebook)

Printed in the United States of America

LSC-C

Printing 1, 2023

For Marilyn Eunice, my mother,
the Mount Dora girl who gifted me a history and
experiences that allowed me to
imagine the Shores…

A
Lakeside
Reunion

One

CHAREESE DEVLIN GLANCED up at the old bed and breakfast that had been in her family for generations. She'd spent the better part of her adult life pretending Hill House didn't exist because it seemed easier to forget. So why was it her first stop after passing the town welcome sign for Mount Dora? She hadn't worked through the answer to that question yet.

Perhaps she never would. Only, she couldn't deny how looking upon the place that held many of her childhood memories had quieted inner deliberations of life, love, and career woes.

A sigh escaped her as she turned her attention away from the top of the hill and headed back to her rental car. She slid into the convertible and pressed the button to let the top down. For a second, she considered tying the pink scarf peeking out of her purse around her hair, but then decided to just be wild and free. This would be the only time she could let go on her summer vacation because she knew that for the next month her life would be full of the restrictions and expectations she had shunned. She swallowed the bitter taste she associated with the Shores and locked her emotions away as the engine roared to life.

The warm, humid breeze licked her skin, and she pressed the gas as she rode the curves along the old highway. The view of the sun shining down, creating a sparkle effect onto Lake Dora, was spectacular, perfect…everything she remembered. Her gaze shifted to the houses neatly tucked among the hills as she sniffed the blooming magnolia trees, and for the first time in ten years she missed the place she vowed never to return to.

Never had been rigged. A daydream severed by a mother who remained caught up in the old guard and appearances. Hence, the Lakeside Debutante Ball she would attend to officially watch her sister, Alexandria, debut into society—just as she and four generations of the women in her family had.

Chareese shrugged off the encroaching pressure and turned the music up in the car. She had less than seven minutes before she turned into the driveway of her parents' summer estate. This was her last time to enjoy the vacancy of not having to battle against the mental games of which her mother reigned as queen for the next month.

The ringtone of her mobile blared from the passenger seat. She eased off the gas, hesitant to answer in case it was a work call. After seeing the number belonged to her longtime friend Carrah Andrews, she quickly tapped the hands-free button on the steering wheel.

"Are you here yet?" Carrah giggled into the line. "I've waited for a summer like this forever, Reese."

"Almost to my parents' house. Pray for me." She chuckled.

"Does Genevieve Devlin not know about your haircut? Or is she still upset that you haven't accepted the promotion to fashion art director?"

"I'm sure those are both reasons for her to find fault as normal. But, before being offered the promotion, I was told I have the 'look' corporate likes. That comment still doesn't sit well with me, and my mother believes I need to get over it. Except, I can't. I'm more than just a look. What about my work, innovation, and the Ivy League education she paid for that got me here?" Reese let out a long sigh while turning onto Lakeshore Drive, the only street that meant something in the Shores of Dora because it signified a family's wealth, power, and prestige in the South. "Don't mind my rant. I'm certain she's more concerned with us making it on time to some cocktail party this evening than lecturing me on my career decisions. You know my mother does not believe in being fashionably late."

Carrah let out a hearty laugh, which forced Reese into one as well. "Good luck, and by the way, it isn't just some cocktail party. Judge and Mrs. Caldwell are hosting this evening. Everyone will be there." Reese pressed her lips together tight. She knew not everyone would be at the judge's house. The circle was small, select, and unfriendly to outsiders. "Oh, I almost forgot. I received an invitation to Gavin's Back to the Shores party tomorrow night. Said he wanted to take it back to when we were kids. It's an old-school nineties theme at the roller rink, and I want you to go with me."

"I didn't get an invite."

"Reese, the last time you came here for the summer we were seventeen. No one expected you to come back to the Shores. I would've been surprised too, except I knew Alexandria was making her debut, since my mom is the committee chair. You had to come. It's tradition, and we both know how our families are when it comes to tradition."

Reese held her tongue. Tradition had shown the ugliest side of her family. The beautiful French country estate coming into view hid their ways well. It was the prettiest container for the uppity Black elite who refused to be stained by those not like them.

"Well, I just pulled up. And you know it would be unladylike of me to enter the house jabbering on the phone. I'll see you at the judge's house tonight."

After ending the call and gathering her belongings, Reese entered her family home. The sweet smell of butter mixed with vanilla and maybe a dash of lime wafted to her senses. Her stomach growled, and she dropped her bags before proceeding into the kitchen. A smile stretched across her face upon seeing the golden goodness displayed in the center of the kitchen island. The warmth radiating from the key lime pound cake let her know it hadn't been long since it came out of the oven and that her mother was somewhere in the house.

Resisting a slice of her favorite sweet treat, Reese set out to find her parents and sister. Surprisingly, she was pleased to see that not much had changed in their summer home except for new curtains in the parlor. She passed her father's study, which was empty, yet she could tell by the lingering odor that he had recently enjoyed a cigar. Just as she was about to venture to her parents' bedroom, muffled voices came from upstairs. She quickly took the steps two by two, feeling winded once she reached the top, and continued down the hall toward her sister's room.

"Chin up." Reese slowed when she heard her mother's stern voice. "Relax your shoulders and smile. A debutante must always present herself, Alexandria."

"Wow, I think I heard that same line ten years ago." Reese stepped into the doorway of her sister's room.

"Reese!" Alex jumped into her sister's arms. "How was Paris? OMG, I can't believe you came." She squeezed Reese tighter. "I know how much you hate the Shores."

Technically, Reese didn't hate the Shores. She hated the reality of how it dictated her life because some families were thought of as better, and how years of generational bias determined relationships, connections, and who you were allowed to love.

"I wouldn't miss your debut, Alex," she said, looking down into her sister's dark brown eyes. The same eyes she saw in the mirror every day. She hugged Alex tight, her way of saying sorry for bailing out on family summers, and wishing their relationship was stronger.

"Alexandria," their mother corrected her. "Now isn't the time for pet names, Chareese. I too am pleased that you found time to visit with us this summer and attend the ball. Most past debutantes flock in annually to show their support and respect for the traditions that set us apart from the rest—not to mention nourishing connections we've forged over the years with other families." Genevieve Devlin tossed a dress on Alex's bed and then turned to peck Reese on each cheek.

"Oh my goodness...you cut your hair!" Genevieve's hands grabbed Reese by the shoulders and turned her around in slow motion.

Record time for the *oh shit* moment. Reese would deal with it. She'd had plenty of practice. Besides, this was one time her mother wouldn't make her feel bad. For the last few months she had been struggling to find herself. The long hair she'd worn for years was her mother's look, not hers. The bob cut she now rocked seemed more of who she was...or rather who she wanted to be. It was chic, pretty, and still long enough to be tucked behind her ears. Nothing like the close cut her mother's reaction exaggerated it to be.

"It's so wild." Her mother's thin fingers began raking her hair. "Did you bother to comb it this morning?"

Reese cleared her throat. She was hyperaware of her mother's hesitation to embrace the woman she had become and refused to show how much her disappointment still stung. One day she would please her. "I let the top down on my rental. The plane had been so stuffy."

"Humph, I see." Her mother stood back, continuing her analysis. Reese did the same, admiring her mother's rich, golden-brown skin, jet-black hair, and stunning features that had crowned her Miss Florida and landed her in *Jet* magazine as a Beauty of the Week once upon a time.

In the looks department, Reese and her mother were near twins. Beyond appearances they were like oil and water.

"Well"—her mother's cheeks filled—"I like the hair." Both Reese's and Alex's jaws dropped to the floor. Surprise was an understatement since their mother believed hair was a woman's crowning glory. A lighthearted chuckle that Reese had not heard in a long time escaped Genevieve. "Come here, both of you." Her mother's arms wrapped around them. "I finally have both my girls home for the summer."

"Mother, you act as if I never come home. I saw you in March."

"You haven't been here, to our summer home, in ages. There was always a class, an internship, a promotion. Now, when everyone asks your father or me about you, we can say you're here." She kissed Reese's forehead.

"Speaking of Dad, where is he?"

"There was an emergency at city hall with your uncle Quincy and Hill House." She sighed. "Things have been tense between your father and uncle the last few months due to operational issues with the inn. Not to mention the money that must be spent to bring the house up to code. The city is particular about the downtown district and Quincy…well, the house needs some work. Quincy isn't your grandmother, and you know how your dad is about the family business. Especially since that bed and breakfast gave his family everything."

Reese nodded, accepting why her dad wasn't home like he said he would be. Something serious had to be happening, because Kent Devlin always attended every recital, graduation, promotion party, and anything else in between.

She then wondered about Hill House. She hadn't been brave enough earlier to pull onto the property, so she'd acted like the tourists who came into town and admired it from afar. The bed and breakfast had been in their family for over a hundred years, and like her father, she had spent time at Hill House learning the family business. She remembered her grandmother teaching her to bake oatmeal raisin cookies for guests, and meeting famous Black politicians and celebrities clad in designer digs that sparked her interest in fashion and design. Except, if she was honest, for the last few months she often found herself reimagining the latest designer printed fabrics on chairs and windows instead of people.

"Hate to break up this little reunion, but we need to get ready or we are going to be late for the five to seven." Alex grabbed the dress her mother had laid across the bed.

"Are you serious, Mom? Y'all still call it that? Most people would simply say *cocktail hour*."

"We are not *most* people." Genevieve stuck her nose up into the air. "The la cinq à septs are how all of us reconnect once we arrive for the summer. We've built businesses, friendships, and relationships with these people who have been in our sphere for decades."

Reese began moving from the room. She wasn't about to start with her mother on the parties her friends threw that were only meant to exclude while reveling in the gossip of well-to-do Black folks.

Genevieve rushed from the room, tugging Reese along. "We've got less than an hour to be ready before your father gets here to pick us up." Her mom paused in the hallway. "Dress to kill, Chareese. It's been a long time. You know they will be watching. Let's give them something to talk about."

Two

TIME HAD NOT changed tradition in the Shores. Reese didn't like experiencing the emotions she'd dealt with as a teenager: antsy, anxious, and dreading an evening that on the surface appeared to be full of rekindling of old friendships but was really full of inspection that led to criticism. Make no mistake, the annual evening soiree at the Caldwells' was where you learned the good, bad, and ugly of the Southern elite. By the end of the night, it was known who was graduating, divorcing, engaged, or making major career moves...and all that gossip was heavily discussed like a scandalous article in the newspaper until everyone left town. Reese knew her return would become a hot topic.

Too bad I didn't find a way out, Reese thought to herself as she sat in the back seat of the chauffeured car across from her mother, who wore a dress made for the red carpet. Reese didn't miss the way her mother scanned her with approving eyes. While flattered, it reminded Reese of why she had avoided ten years of scrutiny. She didn't miss summer after summer of being dolled up before climbing into her dad's fanciest car to make their way to Judge and Mrs. Caldwell's estate.

Reese shrugged off unasked-for thoughts and decided to re-call happier times in the Shores. There were sundae parties at Miss Mabel's ice cream parlor, nights at the roller rink, picnics after church, and fireworks over the lake on the Fourth of July. A small smile curved her lips as she thought back to those times when friendships mattered. She also recalled how when her grandmother was alive she made the sweetest strawberry shortcake to eat while watching the evening sky light up on the Fourth.

Back then, as she watched colors burst in the air and fall over the water, she had no idea that the people her parents called friends held influence over her life and who she loved. It wasn't until one night long ago, when they traveled along the road that they were on now, making their way to the Caldwells' annual soiree, that her father began explaining the rules.

Kent Devlin had started by asking if she had heard of Madam C. J. Walker. Of course she had. Black history was three-sixty-five and always woven into the historical thrust of Jack and Jill activities. After all, Jack and Jill was the gathering place for Black children of affluent families who wanted their children to remember where they came from while exceeding societal expectations and becoming future leaders. And yet, at age ten, Reese didn't know that when Madam C. J. purchased her New York mansion in 1917, the *New York Times* wrote, "No woman of her race could afford such a place."

She now knew that her father's question was not impromptu. If he had made it home in time to leave with them, he may have very well reminded her that a public show of wealth garnered too much, and not so good, attention. For Madam C. J., that was exactly what happened. Therefore, it became the first rule she'd learned of the Black elite, a social stratosphere she straddled but was born into and was expected to uphold. Sentiments that were expressed in that old article died hard, especially in the South. Fear of what happened in the nineteenth century to Daniel Murray and the original Black elite taunted her parents and other prominent families who were determined to keep their status. They never wanted to endure the nightmare of one day being held in high regard and the next deemed as a second-class citizen.

"How long will we be here tonight?" Reese turned away from her mother and gazed out the window as the chauffeur turned down the long cobblestone drive lined with ancient oaks that Judge and Mrs. Caldwell used to hide their palatial estate from passersby.

Only friends knew how people in the old guard moved. Invitation-only events were strictly enforced. Although, Reese often rejected hers. And like the Caldwells' mansion was removed from public view, she'd retreated from this life because it had taken everything she ever wanted.

"Why, Chareese? It's not as if you have anything else planned. You've been absent from this scene a while now and invitations for you come few and far between." Her mother cleared her throat. "You need to mingle and show your face. Our friends ask about you often. You know it's hard for my crowd to keep up on social media. That's for you young folks."

A small smile curved her mother's shiny red lips. "I also hear that Reginald, Christopher, and Gavin will be present this evening. They are all single and have done very well for themselves. It would be best for you to become reacquainted."

Reese recoiled. This wasn't the time for her mother to rehash the matchmaking schemes Reese and all her friends had been subjected to when they were prepping for prom or debut. The boys, now men, her mother spoke of were friends that she still shared her life with via social media. There was no need to reacquaint. "Not interested. Reggie, Chris, and Gav are like my brothers. We've played since we could walk…Here every summer learning to canoe and climb trees. I don't see them in that way, Mother. You know that."

"Perhaps you should. Friends can make the best lovers, darling." Her mother blew out a long, exasperated breath. "It's always a debate with you, Chareese, and they are exhausting. Just know by the time I was your age, I was married."

Reese fixed her mouth to respond but was nudged hard by Alex. Thankfully, the car finally stopped in front of the thirty-five-room lakefront mansion. Everyone knew the property had not been obtained or maintained on a judge's salary. It came from generations of wealth. The Caldwells had been farmers of sugar cane and made a living growing and harvesting the crop on their land. They were still one of Florida's leading producers.

"Gavin Lancaster is a chocolate dream, and so is his brother, Xavier. You don't know how crazy you sound, sis," Alex piped in as she checked her lipstick in the mirror one last time before sliding to the open door. Reese shrugged and exited behind her sister. She didn't do playboys, which both Gavin and Chris unapologetically were. "And everyone has been vying for Chris's affections since he got all big-time with his celebrity clients and opened a West Coast office for his firm. They are both indeed suitable matches as our parents would say."

The sisters chuckled, watching as their mother stepped from the car in her full regalia. This might be a party hosted by Sissy Caldwell, but Genevieve Devlin always managed to become the center of attention.

"Hush you two. We are about to go inside. Remember, if they ask about your father or uncle, simply offer regrets and let them know unexpected business pulled them away for the evening."

Her mother led the way up the steps and through the doorway where an oversized crystal chandelier greeted the trio upon entry into the foyer. Standing just under it was Zuri, the Caldwells' oldest daughter. Zuri was three years older than Reese, and was a pretty, curvy girl with long copper-colored hair that appeared as though it had just been curled with marcels. Her ebony skin had always been in such contrast to Judge Caldwell's that some ignorant people whispered she wasn't his daughter. Yet, with even a little study, anyone would see that Zuri had her father's keen nose, hazel eyes, and plus-sized stature.

"Hi, Zuri!" Reese leaned in, accepting her old friend's embrace. "Your dress is beautiful, and so are you."

"You just made my night. That's a big compliment considering it came from one of the fashion industry's movers and shakers. Mom and I saw the write-up of you in *Exposé Mag.* Everyone is so proud of you."

Reese knew the smile she forced didn't reach her eyes. She hoped it didn't appear fake as she stood back admiring the dolman sleeve drape dress that flattered Zuri's full figure. Maybe not the shade of orange she'd have selected; however, it was exactly the style she would drape the socialite in. Most intriguing was that the dress was by one of the hottest new designers Reese was eager to feature in *Haute*, the magazine she busted her ass for and where she was still considering a promotion to art director.

When word got out that *Haute* wanted to name her art director, the fashion world went crazy. It was the reason *Exposé* came after her for an interview. Only, she'd made it clear to the lifestyle magazine that the topic was off-limits for the write-up. The circumstances surrounding her position at *Haute* were still a sore subject, and she didn't care for public opinion on the direction of her career. Reese knew she never wanted to be given something because she had a palatable look for corporate America. Nor because she'd socialized in the right circles thanks to her debutante pedigree.

Reese wanted her advancement to be a reflection of her work, but the comments uttered as the promotion was being offered made her second-guess her contribution to the magazine and her career path. Never mind that lately her creative juices often floated from denim and red bottoms on a model to crushed velvet and lace on a queen-sized bed. "Thanks, Zuri, that means a lot."

An awkward moment of silence fell over them before finally Zuri blurted, "How'd they get you back?"

They both chuckled. It was a fair question. Only her parents and Carrah knew why she had been a ghost in the Shores, and it would stay that way. Luckily, she managed to slip out of the dark shadow the question cast and gestured to Alex. "My baby sister accepted her invitation to debut this summer. I couldn't miss it."

"Enjoy it"—Zuri tugged Alex into a strong hold—"I know I did…and so did you, Reese. I remember attending your debut. It was all the rage with you, Carrah, Quinn, and Ava debuting at once."

Reese forced a smile. Every single person's recollection of that night was different. If her parents told the story they would say it was the night she almost ruined the Devlin legacy. Her deceased grandmother would remind Reese that she had been two steps shy of being disowned. And…she used to wonder what Duncan thought. But now wasn't the time for that. "Speaking of Carrah and Quinn, have you seen them? I know Ava hasn't arrived in town yet."

"I've seen Carrah, she arrived a little while ago." Zuri pointed to the other side of the grand staircase behind her. "You know she likes to hang around the parlor until the guys give her a seat at the card table."

Reese thanked Zuri, watched Alex join a friend, then took a deep breath and ducked through the crowd. She had to escape even if it was only for a minute. Over the years she often wondered how people didn't see the turmoil she wore that night. Her debut had been the beginning of the misery she kept bottled inside.

Duncan…

She pushed another unwanted thought of him away. For ten years she had left him and everything in the Shores locked away. She could do it again tonight.

"Chareese Antoinette Devlin." Reese's steps halted before she rolled her eyes and turned to see her old friend. She loved the big, bouncy body curls Quinn rocked as she strutted toward her like the models Reese put on the runway.

"Why are you using my whole government name, Quinlyn Marie Hightower?" Reese giggled as Quinn shushed her.

"I can only imagine the eye roll you gave." The two shared a long, tight hug before Quinn hooked her well-toned, brown arm in Reese's. "Still short."

Reese smacked her teeth. "Tell me again why tall people like you wear heels? You're a giant."

Quinn threw her head back in laughter. "Gawd, I've missed you here. Come on, we've been waiting for you. Carrah's in the parlor starting stuff. She managed to get on the spades table and is giving Reggie hell."

Hearty, full-bellied laughter escaped them as they scrambled down the hall like they used to when there was a secret to share. It was just like old times and in that moment, Reese missed the camaraderie and comfort she'd experienced during the summers spent with people she'd known all her life.

To be fair, Reese's absence over the last ten summers in the

Shores did not make the friendships she'd forged with Carrah, Quinn, Ava, and others null. They all kept in touch; even if it was a quick text or a social like as they led busy lives in high-profile jobs. But it was different, almost disconnected. The bond they shared during the summers was unmatched. They had been like sisters, inseparable, and maybe one day she would forgive herself for diminishing that connection. Maybe this summer could restore it.

Reese and Quinn stopped outside the double oak doors of the Caldwells' parlor. Hearing the trash-talking mixed with laughter from the other side gave Reese a bit of a buzz. She giggled, turning the glass knob and pushing it open, knowing she would see Carrah in action. In true form, her petite, honey-skinned friend stood slamming a card down on the table, creating chaos since she loved to antagonize the guys with her potty mouth and high card-game IQ.

Reese stepped inside the lively room with Quinn on her heels. She saw Gavin, Chris, and Dex, as well as other familiar faces that had always been part of her summers as a child. She even recognized some of the younger siblings who had finally grown up. As a teenager she used to wonder why she got a buzz-like feeling when she arrived in the Shores and prepped for this annual gathering. Now as an adult, she finally realized, while moving about the room and extending hugs and greetings to her long-lost friends, that the feelings she experienced then and now came from the excitement of seeing everyone again.

She recalled lock-ins, Sunday dinners, Dorian's Cove, her first kiss...Duncan. She didn't bother to look for him, because he wasn't allowed to attend. The McNeals were not a family of status. According to Genevieve Devlin, and the lot in attendance here tonight, Duncan's family didn't belong. It was still a bitter pill to swallow.

"Well, if it isn't the Fashion Extraordinaire." Gavin wrapped Reese in a bear hug and squeezed her tight. "The cat finally did her job and dragged you back in."

"Hmmm, well if that's what you want to call it." She giggled and focused on the table where Carrah sat diagonal from a man she didn't recognize, along with Reggie and Chris. "The Andrewses and the Chennaults still don't miss a chance to compete, huh?" She gestured at Chris and Carrah.

Gavin erupted in laughter. "Nope!" He heckled the table good-naturedly before turning back to Reese. "How long you here for?"

"About a month." Once upon a time the slow pace and tranquility of the small town helped her find herself. Reese hoped her break in the Shores would allow her to reset and determine a path with the magazine.

"You seen Dunc?" He gave her a knowing stare. Forget being subtle. He let it all hang out, and it was clearly intentional based on his smirk.

"No."

"You can't ignore him forever, Reese."

"Maybe not forever, but at least for my first night back in town." She hooked her arm in his. "Now come on, let's watch Carrah kick everyone's butt on the card table."

Three

HELL WOULD FREEZE over before Duncan McNeal allowed the city planning and zoning committee to squash his plans for the youth village. He yanked off his tie and threw it onto his empty passenger seat before thrusting his car into park. His hands gripped and then relaxed around the steering wheel several times as he took deep, measured breaths.

Damn the Devlin family and the committee members they had in their back pockets. His money might not be old, but it was green and he wouldn't allow the old guard to turn their noses up at him and ruin something special. It had already happened once, and he refused to allow them another victory.

Not when he'd done everything right. He beat the odds and became the first in his family to graduate college. His prestigious Ivy League experience gave him a top education, membership inside the oldest Black fraternity, internships, and investors that believed in his redevelopment strategies for urban areas. Hence, he now sat as the CEO for his own urban planning and design firm, raking in millions annually.

Duncan had come a long way from being the boy on the

other side of the tracks. He never again had to see his father work three jobs to help make ends meet or his mother in the maid's uniform of Hill House Bed and Breakfast. In fact, he would not see another person lift a finger to do work for Hill House, because he had shut it down the second the ink dried on the bill of sale three months ago.

The bed and breakfast was his fair and square. Quincy Devlin had come to him hard up for cash after realizing Duncan had acquired tax liens on the old property. Patience had been a virtue, and watching a Devlin man scheme to avoid public ridicule for mismanaging his inheritance seemed like the beginning of revenge even though it wasn't. Duncan had been given a once-in-a-lifetime opportunity to reach back into his community, and soon the old Hill House Bed and Breakfast would be a youth village designed to give other underprivileged kids hope for a better future.

Before he could act on that last motivating thought and call his inside person to set up a dinner with the mayor, the ringtone of his phone surrounded him through the radio speakers. Business could wait while he had a conversation with his mother.

"Hey, Ma," he answered. "I'm already here to get Destiny from ball practice."

"That's not what I'm calling about. Is everything okay, Duncan? One of my girls from the restaurant said she served at a party last night for the old judge and there was much talk about what you were trying to do with Hill House. And I just heard the hearing didn't go as planned today."

Pearl McNeal always had a way of knowing when her son needed her. As a child, Duncan thought his mother was psychic. By high school he realized it was her intuition from the close bond they shared.

"The city is debating the land use of the inn. Its proximity to downtown is concerning for some residents, which is why the rezoning permit was not granted. Not an uncommon roadblock when there are wealthy, vocal residents calling the shots to preserve the ways for those who have always had," he mocked before a hushed curse escaped under his breath. "Minor setback, that's all." He sighed, unconcerned with revealing how the pressure of this project was affecting him, because this was his mama, the woman who had sacrificed everything for him to attend UPenn and make something of himself.

"I know this project means a lot to you. You've become a role model in this community for our young men. However, I need you to remember that when you leave and go to one of your other offices or visit projects that keep you gone for weeks on end, we are still left here. The Devlins have a lot of power...they have for a long time. Even if they are only here at Maypole and gone just after Labor Day." She paused for a few seconds.

"And don't forget your sister is participating in that debutante ball. Genevieve Devlin is on the ball committee. I don't want to make things difficult for Destiny. Your sister is excited about this opportunity, and so am I since she's the first in our family to ever take part in something so high society."

The tremble of his mother's words confirmed his worst fears. She was still afraid, ashamed for rising above the station in life people deemed her worthy of. A pang lanced Duncan's heart. He knew all too well what it was like to be in the firing range of a powerful, well-connected family. He'd seen his mother and grandmother worked weary to the bone for pennies on a dollar and stripped of their pride by Constance Devlin, the matriarch of the Devlin family. And then, the old woman had attempted to blacklist his grandma and mom after they responded to the demand for the food they cooked at Hill House and had begun selling hot plates to raise money for a restaurant.

During those humble beginnings, Duncan disliked running orders for the people who came to the rear door of his parents' old home. He especially hated those times when chitterlings and rutabagas were on the menu, because the lines were long. Soul food or "down-home cookin'" as his grandmother used to say, always appealed to Southern folks eager to get back to their roots. People came from neighboring towns to get a taste of what the women in his family prepared, and it severely strained the relationship between them and Constance.

So much so that Miss Constance reduced their work hours and then finally fired his grandmother. The last straw was when Constance forbade her granddaughter Chareese from seeing Duncan. It was a friendship that had existed since she was seven and he was eight, but was no more after a summer ten years ago.

He didn't want to wander into that dark memory of the first summer he came home from college. For everything that Chareese Devlin had pretended to be with him, she had revealed herself to be another rich, selfish girl who believed she was better than everyone because her family had a few more generations of freed people. Ten years had not changed his view on her or gotten rid of the scars she'd left upon his heart.

"Never again will we let those people dictate our lives. Destiny was invited to the ball because of our family's accomplishments and her stellar academics. She deserves to be there as much as any of those other girls." He glanced at his watch, deciding to table this conversation. "Let me go inside and get her. She should be done now."

Duncan popped the button open on his collar and exited his sleek Porsche Panamera. Since launching his project on the youth village, he had been in the vicinity of the Lakeside Inn more times than he cared to count, and he didn't mind. His love of architecture and old buildings lulled him into the Victorian era whenever his sights were set upon the bright yellow building with ornate gingerbread carvings that framed its oversized verandah. The white rocking chairs that sat on the porch beckoned him to enjoy the view of Lake Dora, but not today.

He entered the hotel, commanding the attention of all he passed, and strolled down the halls to the main ballroom. He still couldn't believe his baby sister was participating in the coveted Lakeside Debutante Ball. In a few weeks she would be presented into society beside the crème de la crème of Southern families. The McNeal family name would again be elevated.

This was another step along the path he'd carefully crafted that would ensure Destiny had the right network for college recommendation letters, membership inside the right social organizations, and ultimately a clerkship, since her goal was to become a federal judge.

"Duncan." His sister waved to him in the near distance. "Hurry, there's someone who wants to meet you before they leave."

He obliged, always a sucker for his sister, and picked up the pace. "It better not be a boy, Destiny." He chuckled, amused at seeing her eyes go big.

"No, it's one of the committee members." Her dainty, dark hand reached for his and tugged him inside the room. "Mom messaged me and said you were on your way in. She and Dad never seem to…you know, want to come in. They still feel like we don't belong," she whispered, fanning Duncan's anger over his parents' wayward thoughts. "I want these people to meet you and see what my brother, the *local*, has become. You know I'm proud of you, Dunc."

He looked down into his sister's heart-shaped, mahogany face and witnessed her hopeful dark eyes glitter with pride.

"Don't stop believing you should have everything. We may not have been born with silver spoons, but I got enough bread to afford a closet full."

"Who's your guest, Destiny?" A youthful, feminine voice spoke behind Duncan's back, catching his sister by surprise.

Destiny stepped to the side of Duncan as he turned to greet a pretty, brown-skinned girl with long hair about Destiny's age. "Alex, this is my brother, Duncan. Duncan, this is one of my fellow debutantes, Alexandria Devlin."

Duncan extended his hand to exchange pleasantries. It wasn't this girl's fault he didn't like the Devlin family. However, he knew they bred their children to behave a certain way. One day he would counsel his sister on befriending the enemy. "Nice to see you again, Alexandria." The girl's hesitation to shake his hand was masked by her firm grip and good eye contact. It was obvious she was already being groomed to run a boardroom. "Last time I saw you, I believe you were five or six, French braids down your back with bows, and you were chasing butterflies in your grandmother's herb garden."

"Oh my God, seriously," she giggled, "that seems forever ago." A bright smile filled her cheeks as her curious eyes scanned him. "So that means you know my mother, Genevieve"—she pointed to the left—"and my sister, Chareese, over by the window." Alexandria waved, prompting Reese to wave back.

Duncan felt like he'd just stepped inside the ring without gloves, unable to defend against a punch in the gut. His brows stitched together as he recognized the moment Reese realized who he was. The energy in her wave faded along with her smile. She stopped talking to the woman at her side and stared. He stared harder, watching as she began to move across the room toward them.

Duncan's mind flew back in time. He remembered them

riding bicycles as kids, jumping hand in hand from the old wood dock into the lake as teenagers, and then tasting butter pecan ice cream on her lips after their first kiss in Miss Mabel's Sundae Shoppe. Memories of the cute, short girl rocking a puff and gold hooped earrings couldn't compare to the woman she had become.

The seriousness of her face emphasized her almond-shaped eyes, high cheekbones, and full lips he'd kiss once more if they weren't so poisonous. The short haircut was unexpected. Yet, it communicated class, style, and sophistication, which was everything Reese Devlin had been raised to be.

As she drew closer, he focused on the way her brown skin glowed against the teal dress she wore. His body temp spiked. Damn that dress. It accentuated her perfect hourglass shape while hugging her thick thighs and invited erotic fantasies to fill his head.

"Duncan McNeal," she gasped, then took another step forward as if contemplating what should come next. To his surprise, one arm wrapped around him, and she pulled him in. A scent much like a blooming lotus flower invaded his senses, making him forget what he had vowed to do if this moment ever presented itself. "Been a long time," she whispered in his ear.

He closed his eyes, refusing to let his mind play tricks on him, and recalled the way Reese's father had burst into his parents' home. The man issued threats before promising to ruin Duncan's life because he wasn't good enough for his daughter. A *have-not* was what Constance Devlin proclaimed him to be that night she followed her son, Reese's father, inside.

Duncan had then watched in turmoil as they scolded Reese for making a mockery of her debut and the match they had secured as her escort. Instead of standing up to her father and grandmother, Reese admitted that Duncan was an experiment meant to defy Daddy before being shoved out of the house and into a car while promising never to see him again.

"Ten years." He pulled back. There was so much to say, and yet nothing at all. The fact that she never apologized in all these years, as if that last summer didn't exist, reaffirmed what they shared was fake. Except, his heart sped up. Heat spread across his body like a wildfire, wanting him to remember something different.

Duncan's eyes darted around the room, documenting wealth and prestige being passed down from mother to daughter. He glanced at his sister. For her he would keep his shit together. But then, his gaze darted back to Reese before landing on Genevieve Devlin. The hurt and rejection he had experienced at their hands made him more determined to rid the Shores of Hill House and replace it with something that wasn't a shrine to their legacy of elitism. Therefore, he cared not to engage in societal niceties.

"Ready, Destiny?" he asked, never breaking eye contact with Reese. Fuck the memories creeping into his head.

"Yeah." Her reply was low.

"Good"—he turned on his heel—"I have more interesting people to see."

* * *

Gavin jinxed her last night. There was no ignoring Duncan McNeal. Reese reached out and caught him by the arm. He stopped, and his eyes went to where her hand was wrapped around him. A bold, unforgettable scent of amber infused with sandalwood taunted her sensibilities and made her lightheaded as she took a step closer. "It's good to see you again, Duncan."

He tugged his arm away from her grip, then turned to

face her. Men shouldn't be beautiful, but Duncan McNeal was. He was the ultimate pretty boy, standing a good six two with smooth, dark skin, clean-cut with jet-black waves, and a goatee that so perfectly outlined his face you would think the angels painted it.

The rumors were true. The world had been kind to him. The evidence was on display with the Armani suit clinging to his athletic build, the Chopard watch at his wrist, and bespoke shoes completing his sexy ensemble. A part of her felt weird cataloging his style, only that was the world she worked in. As a fashion editor Reese set the tone for the vibe or story she wanted communicated through colors and styles. She could source anything, and influence men's and women's apparel. Therefore, she could tell by the way Duncan dressed that he was a man who knew his wealth yet appreciated his beginnings.

"You can't expect me to say the same, Chareese." He turned and left the room.

Her stomach fell into a bottomless pit and her heart was right behind it, crumbling into pieces. Not only did he dismiss her, he kept it formal by using her full name. Why did she wish he'd said her name the way he used to? If only she could turn back the hands of time.

"That was rude as hell." Alex came to her side, sticking her nose in the air. "He knows who we are. He said he last saw me when I was five."

Reese opened then closed her mouth. Memories of that summer always defaulted to pain, and it was too much to explain. The age gap between her and Alex often revealed itself at the most awkward times.

Back then, Alex was busy dressing Barbie dolls and chasing butterflies. She could not have cared less about why Reese rebelled against their parents' and grandmother's choice of escort for the debutante ball. And to this day, Reese harbored resentment for being forced to perform the ceremonial waltz with someone she barely knew instead of being allowed the choice to walk alongside the boy she'd secretly loved since she was thirteen. It was obvious her parents never explained anything to Alex, because then maybe she would see that the world they lived in was gray and laced with innuendo, not black and white on her elitist throne, judging Duncan for his actions.

Reese huffed, "Snooty much?" She side-eyed her sister, who was still blinded by the privilege their parents gave to them. Duncan knew exactly who they were and what they were capable of, and Reese had been complicit in her betrayal of his heart. "Not now, Alex."

"I'm serious. You don't deserve to be treated like that."

"Actually, I do," Reese admitted, submitting to the heartache and regrets of the past before she walked back to mingle with the remaining debutantes and their mothers.

Four

"I'M GLAD YOU were able to pull yourself together, Chareese. It would have been embarrassing for the debutantes and their mothers to see you act less than the young lady I raised." Reese ripped her gaze away from the sunset outside her window and looked over at her mother in the driver's seat. An uncomfortable silence lingered as she watched her mother pull up into the driveway, then park in the garage. "I understand that young man has done well for himself. However, we don't spend our time mourning things that were never supposed to happen."

"His name is Duncan." Reese popped the car door open, hopped out, and slammed it shut.

"I know his name. I can't forget it. Your absence every summer hasn't let me," Genevieve snapped.

Reese started to formulate her defenses as she followed her mother and sister to the side entry door. Her mother wasn't finished. She'd gone into battle enough times to know this was the opening Mommy Dearest had been waiting for since last night at the Caldwells' when Reese scoffed at every eligible bachelor Genevieve tossed her way. Only Reese didn't need to hear her mother's antiquated views of relationships and dating as a way to preserve or build family legacies.

"Son of a bitch!" Kent Devlin shouted from his office as they walked into the house. "Is that what you've heard? I can't believe this. We had the council in our pockets. Why is the mayor considering an override to the committee recommendation?" Her father blew a long, exasperated breath. "This could've all been avoided had you swallowed your damn pride and told me everything."

Her father's voice became muffled, making it hard to understand what he was saying or who he was talking to. Curiosity got the best of the Devlin women. They followed their mother's lead to the other side of the house and down the foyer to her father's study. Reese recognized the voice of her uncle Quincy coming through a speaker phone before her father barked more ridicule at his older brother.

Once the voices went mute, Reese knocked on the door. The late hour they'd arrived home last night from the party coupled with the early debutante breakfast stalled them from seeing each other, and she was excited to finally see her father. He was her go-to person for career and financial advice, and he kept all her secrets. Unlike her mother, he found ways to respect and support her decisions even when he didn't agree. The road back to where they were had not been easy, but somehow they had found a way back to being appreciative of each other. Even after he dictated who she was allowed to give her heart to. Maybe their relationship was his way of apologizing for how he'd handled things so long ago.

"Come in." Her father's aggravation was tangible, until his eyes landed on her. His smile stretched ear to ear, brightening his bronzed complexion as he made his way around the desk and scooped Reese into a bear hug. "My Reesey Pie! It's been a long time since you've been in this house. Glad to have you home, buttercup."

She kissed his cheek. "Same, Daddy. Maybe I shouldn't have stayed away so long," Reese lied, a little. There was a part of her that missed time with the people she'd spent so much of her childhood with, the house she called home May through August, and time at Hill House. However, that other side that didn't miss the baggage that accompanied the Shores simply wanted to keep the peace. She didn't want an awkward conversation that would rehash the anger and emotions that had kept her away.

Reese stepped out of her father's embrace, admiring how time remained still on everything except a small patch of gray hair. It was the only part of him that revealed he was well past fifty.

"What did your mother say about this new hair?" He winked.

"Actually"—Genevieve moved to his side and pecked his lips—"I like it."

"I told Reese you would." He boasted another million-dollar smile.

Her mom's mouth fell open. "You knew about this? And didn't tell me?"

Alex rolled her eyes. "Come on, Mom, you know Reese is Daddy's girl. She'd still be your favorite too if she had pledged your sorority and not refused to date your bestie's son."

A chill quieted the room. Alex knew what she was doing. She always lashed out whenever she wasn't the one receiving attention. A problem Reese witnessed today as Alex interacted with the other debutantes during the breakfast and style seminar.

The pedestal Alex sat upon, courtesy of their mother and others from the ball committee, was unfair. Each girl deserved a chance to shine as they made their debut. Not just one, and not just because she had the right last name. And then Reese wondered, had it been the same for her?

"I'll always be the favorite. I was first." Reese winked back at her dad all the while ignoring the sourpuss grin upon her sister's face. "What had you so riled up?"

"Yes," Genevieve chuckled. "What did Quincy do this time?"

Her father's entire demeanor changed. His face grew tense and his eyes cold as he folded his arms and leaned back on the desk. A long, exasperated breath escaped him as if he was searching for words. Finally he said, "He lost Hill House."

"What?" echoed in the room.

"Three months ago." Her father's large hands clapped together hard enough to make the room shake.

Genevieve dashed back to his side and began rubbing his shoulder. "Kent...h-how did this happen and why haven't you said anything?"

"The same reason he didn't tell me—pride. Quincy never once told me he was experiencing financial troubles. Instead, he simply stopped paying the property taxes on Hill House, cut staff, and neglected upkeep. My brother intentionally kept me in the dark. And unfortunately, it's too late for me to act on his regrets. Duncan McNeal's urban planning and design firm paid the fines and held the liens. When things spiraled for Quincy, he went to Duncan and cut a deal." Her father muttered a string of cuss words under his breath.

"Wait, so you're telling me Duncan owns the first property acquired by our family?"

"Yes, Reese, I am. Unfortunately, that's not the worst of it. He plans to transform it into some youth village for those little ghetto kids. Does he really think upstanding residents of the Shores want those kids near the business district?"

"Dad, don't be so harsh." Reese crossed her arms. "Just because they aren't well-off doesn't mean they're ghetto."

"They are what they are. Even if they grow up and become

a millionaire." He gave Reese a pointed look. "You can take the child out of the ghetto, but can you take the ghetto out of a child?"

"You sound elitist," Reese scoffed, refusing to look at her father for a minute. She recalled what she had seen at seventeen when her father drew lines in the sand, boxing her in from those who did not exist in their class structure. For a long time, she hated him for taking away her blinders and forcing her to see that the Shores was divided by the haves and have-nots.

"Is there a way to stop this and get Hill House back?" Alex asked.

"I tried. The committee gave Duncan a hard time today, but based on what Quincy heard from Roland Hightower, I doubt they will block his rezoning permit request. The mayor has also threatened to override a denial. That boy is well-liked, connected, and has invested a lot into this community and not just during the summer months like us."

"What do you mean?" Reese's question was genuine. She'd spent years pretending the Shores of Dora didn't exist because she couldn't forget her grandmother's harsh criticisms. And, if she was being honest, because of Duncan.

He was in every memory she held of the lakeside town she once loved. When she first met Duncan at age seven, he was the boy she didn't like because he got to deliver the fresh-baked cookies from the inn's kitchen to the guest rooms. One day he snuck her a cookie, then showed her the ropes of the sweet treat delivery for the bed and breakfast, and they became inseparable every summer—until that night.

Reese came out of her contemplation only to find her mother eyeing her as though she had been a voyeur to her deepest, darkest thoughts. She ignored her mom and focused on her father. "Dad, are you going to answer me?"

Kent Devlin pressed his lips together as he stood a little taller, sliding his hands into his pockets. It was a thing he did when something deeply bothered him. "He"—her father cleared his throat—"Duncan has saved some small businesses, placed his corporate headquarters here, which has generated jobs, and found use for old buildings by creating a new yuppie-like district that tourists simply love. The mayor and many of the council are grateful for his efforts and that is a problem for the survival of Hill House."

Constance Devlin had always told Reese to be mindful of how she treated people, because the ones she stepped on to get to the top would bring her back down to the bottom. The irony of those words probably had her grandmother turning in her grave, considering the way she had treated Duncan.

"Maybe you could talk to him, Chareese?" Her mother's questioning stare disarmed her. "The two of you were friends."

Checkmate. Again, mind games with Mom. There was a never-ending battle Reese fought to withstand her mother's questionable motivations. She understood how important it was for her family to remain atop of society. Generations before her had done things right. They worked hard, married right, and saved so that preservation of the Devlin name endured. However, that callous attitude of using things and people as means to an end was wrong, and exactly the reason why she and Duncan no longer had any sort of a relationship.

"I don't know about that, Genevieve." Her father started shaking his head, then abruptly stopped. He must've realized the stakes. "When is the next time you will see him?" he asked Reese.

"Tonight," Alex exclaimed, eager to be part of the conversation. "You told us you were going to Gavin Lancaster's party with Carrah. Destiny mentioned that her brother was going too. Apparently he and Gavin are close friends."

"Now there's a boy from a good family who you should be spending your time with…but your mother is right. Maybe you can talk to Duncan, learn about his plans for Hill House, and if we have a chance at saving it."

Reese never dreamed this would be the summer she gave a final goodbye to Hill House, because in the darkest crevices of her mind she always thought she had time. For Hill House she would swallow her pride…talk to Duncan and forget she'd broken a friendship and shattered her own heart when she lied all those years ago and said he had meant nothing to her. Just maybe she could save the place she had neglected. It hadn't turned on her like her family had.

Four hours later, Reese rushed from her parents' estate in full nineties garb and plopped onto the passenger-side seat of Carrah's champagne Mercedes coupe. Excitement surged between her and Carrah as they embraced before becoming a mess of giggles. Last night all eyes were on them, so for appearances' sake, they'd maintained composure.

They had talked about this moment forever, and now it was finally happening after ten long summers. The only thing missing was their third amigo, Ava Hamilton, who was still on a photography assignment for her most recent project but was supposed to be home in time for the ball.

"How'd you pull that fit together so fast?" Carrah fingered the metallic purple leggings before tugging on the vibrant geometric leotard Reese had on.

"Mom knew about Gavin's party and figured once people knew I was in town I'd get invited so she gathered a few items"— she held up the pair of her old, white speed skates with hot-pink wheels—"including these." The unexpected smile tugging her lips vanished. Reese wouldn't mention that her mother had been plotting for her to attend the Back to the Shores party as a way to display herself as eligible to Gavin Lancaster. "I like the crop top. How'd you get past Camille and Melvin in those booty shorts?"

They erupted in laughter as Reese fastened her seat belt and Carrah drove her car through the circle. "They weren't home. Besides, I'm twenty-seven years old."

"And your point? I am too, and I still feel like a damn teenager whenever I visit my parents' house." Especially since she again walked on cracking, thin ice at the thought of engaging with Duncan. Only difference this time was that her family knew because it was for their benefit.

And they saw no consequence in asking her to carry out such a task. Unlike Reese, who knew being too close to Duncan could summon old baggage that was never properly packed away. His anger earlier revealed as much. However, sadly, she didn't have time to process the potential backlash since the fate of Hill House hung in the balance. The inn meant everything to the Devlin name.

"True," Carrah said in a Lil' Kim voice. "So let's live tonight. We're celebrating all those summers we missed."

Not more than ten minutes later, nostalgia filled Reese as she got out of Carrah's car and threw her skates over her shoulder. She'd lived for skate nights in the Shores as a teenager. It was a chance to see all her closest friends while avoiding the watchful eyes of their parents. Not knowing then that their parents were secretly plotting matches and organizing events to preserve generations of wealth, power, and prestige.

Inside, the same shiny disco ball hung high from the ceiling, spinning flashing lights that colored the faces of people she had once fellowshipped with in the name of Jack and Jill, or because their mothers were in the same sorority. Remember-me waves and hugs started the minute Reese and Carrah sat to lace up their skates.

After gulping the sweetest tea over summer hookups and

town news, Reese stood somewhat wobbly on her skates and began making her way to the rink floor.

"Oh. My. God! You really are here!" Peyton Daniels, another childhood friend and fellow debutante, left Quinn's side and yanked Reese into a hug. Their embrace was long, hard, and full of giggles. "Glad you made it back, Reesey Pie," she teased, being one of a few people privy to her nickname.

"Reesey Pie?" a deep, smooth tenor mocked.

Reese didn't need to ID the voice. She knew it was Duncan. In fact, she felt him zap some sort of strange, invisible energy into her body that tingled along her spine and forced the butterflies in her belly to float. She faced him, withstanding the way her heart collapsed.

The man was a perfect chocolate martini, delicious, sexy, and full of deep, dark desires. His raw masculinity called to her, whispering naughty thoughts reserved for silk sheets.

"You can't call me that." She folded her arms, attempting to subdue the impulsive urge she had to kiss his full lips. It was easier than saying sorry for how things ended, but mostly for throwing away years of friendship.

His questioning gaze lingered. He took a step closer, towering over her, and slid his hands into his pockets. "Why, still not good enough for you?"

Before Reese could answer, Duncan walked away. Her privilege demanded she know why he was eavesdropping, until Carrah pulled her from the middle of the main hall. It was then she realized he'd overheard their exchange while passing by. Regardless of how desperate she was to engage with Duncan, it couldn't be like this. So, she watched him settle in with boys from families her parents approved of since they shared common interests, were *like-minded*, and had summered in the Shores for as long as she had.

"Uhhh…" Carrah waved a hand in Reese's face. "Are you going to keep watching his fine ass or are we going to skate?"

"You think Duncan's fine? I thought he wasn't your type."

"Reese, that over there is a chocolate lover's dream," Quinn said, pointing to Duncan and his crew. "The whole group is foine! Rumor has it they are all excellent lovers. Just ask the last girl he was dating. The chick moved from Chicago to little ole Mount Dora to be with him. He quit her and she still stayed."

"Ooowee…now that's some powerful dick," Carrah blurted, unable to contain her giggles. "And of course I think Dunc is fine. He's just always had eyes for you."

Quinn rolled her eyes. "Right! Remember the letters they used to pass back and forth or how Dunc made sure he pushed her higher than us on the swings?"

Reese had a hard time laughing along with her girls. Their fond memories had not been banished like hers, and for once she found herself jealous that all of them had been able to preserve a friendship that had been forbidden to her.

"They *are* everything our mothers taught us to want for in a man." Peyton glanced over to where Duncan sat with his friends. "I'm sure a few of our parents' failed matches are between us. But you know it's hard to really think of the guys in that way. Don't get me wrong, they are all very well educated. We already know they are gentlemen who come from excellent families, and of course have deep enough pockets to keep a girl spoiled. It's just awkward thinking of them romantically since we've known them all our lives. And let's not forget what happens when our mothers get caught up in their feelings after bridge. Our relationships would have to bear those fallouts."

It was true. Which is why they fell over in laughter. Carrah, Quinn, and Peyton stepped onto the rink floor and took off, but Reese hesitated. She wanted to give Duncan a piece of her damn mind for the way he'd rejected her earlier at Lakeside Inn and then mocked her tonight.

There was nothing either of them could do to escape that cruel summer. It happened a long time ago. They were grown now, and they no longer had to live in the shadows of regret. Except, she knew they did. Still, she was determined to find a way back to restore some semblance of a friendship, and maybe in the process it could mean a second chance for Hill House.

* * *

Duncan watched Reese zip around the rink with her friends. She was even more beautiful than she had been in his dreams. However, it reminded him of Icarus flying too close to the sun. So, he vowed to look but not touch. His ego could recover. Not his heart…again.

"Damn, is that Reese Devlin?" one of the guys asked.

"Yeah that's her," Gavin answered. "She's been MIA the last few summers but popped up last night at the Caldwells'."

"After ten summers," Duncan offered tersely with his brow cocked. "Why didn't you tell me? Maybe I wouldn't have been so caught off guard when I ran into her earlier today at Lakeside Inn."

"Dunc, chill, frat. If I had told you last night when I first saw her, you may not have been ready for today. You didn't need the distraction while battling the city." Gavin smirked before taking a sip of his drink. "All of us know you've had a thing for Reese since the summer before you left for college." He nudged Duncan. "I hear she's still single. Moms was trying to hook me up, but I ain't ready to settle down. No matter how beautiful or accomplished the girl is."

"Same," Duncan gritted out, lying through his teeth.

He didn't mind settling down one day. His parents had shown him the definition of unyielding love through their marriage and commitment to one another. However, he knew he was not capable of giving that to any woman, which was why he preferred casual flings. After what Chareese did to him, he'd adopted his love 'em and leave 'em mentality. It got him by until his mind went idle once a blue moon and he thought of her.

Her sweet face, golden-brown skin, dark brown eyes, and luscious ass were poison. Those nineties lyrics from Bell Biv DeVoe about big butts and smiles had never been so true of a person. She had always been his justification for guarding his heart. And it wasn't fair because he deserved more. Seeing her now made him realize that he had been a prisoner to her betrayal of his heart and abandonment of their friendship.

And yet, something primitive and deep stirred within him. He recognized the anger but was surprised by his desire. He wanted her, and it would take everything in him to resist.

She zoomed past him again, bouncing to the Fresh Prince's "Summertime." Totally cliché, yet perfect for the moment because this summer in the Shores was turning out to be an aphrodisiac.

He severed unwanted thoughts, adjusted his skates, and hit the rink. Freedom rushed over him; the same he experienced as a child whenever his quads glided across the wood floor. He slowed, watching Reese skate to the middle of the floor with Carrah and Quinn while Peyton hung back in a corner. They created a circle, then grabbed opposite hands and linked together to form a skate ring. Girls who knew how to skate well loved to perform their little stunts for all to see, but this was advanced side skating and he doubted they had been in a rink practicing like they used to during the summers.

They began pumping their legs to create the centripetal

force needed to get around. He paused to watch, noting the increase in their speed. Once it seemed like they caught a wave of energy, their circle zoomed around the middle of the rink while they threw their heads back in laughter.

Only, the smile tugging at his lips fell when he saw Carrah's toe stop graze the ground. They struggled to hold on, but their speed spun out of control and split them apart. They each went flying across the floor, forcing everyone else to the edge. Without hesitation, Duncan cut across the rink. He knew he wouldn't catch Reese before she hit the ground, and he hoped she didn't hit her head. Skate injuries were ugly and more serious than people knew.

He got to Reese right after she landed on her butt and prevented her body from sliding farther across the floor and crashing into the wall. His arms wrapped around her waist, and he helped her up. "You okay?"

She nodded, moaning as she rubbed her bottom. "Floor is hard."

"Ya think," he chuckled trying hard to forget that sexy-ass moan that escaped those full glossed lips.

A half laugh escaped her. Embarrassment was evident by the flush staining her cheeks. "Thanks for helping me." She leaned to the side to look around him and saw Carrah and Quinn being scooped off the floor. "You did not have to considering…" She scanned his face before breaking out of his hold and skated away from him toward the carpeted floor bordering the wood.

"Reese," he called over the loud music, skating fast to catch up. He caught her by the wrist, then turned her to face him. He stood towering over her and looked down into her eyes. He saw what he'd seen all those years ago, what his world should be. "I'm sorry about earlier. It's been a long time and I wasn't prepared to see you acting as if nothing happened."

She opened then closed her mouth twice before she looked down to the ground and whispered, "Me either, Dunc."

A familiar old-school R&B joint started. Duncan chuckled then made quick mention of them watching the movie *Love & Basketball,* and the scene that had made the eighties tune by Zapp & Roger currently playing regain popularity when they were teens. The DJ announced couples skate and their eyes locked, holding on to some unspoken promise. Duncan didn't know if he wanted to be her man like the song said, but he wanted something. He'd missed their friendship and needed something to quiet the anger and betrayal that had stirred within him today from seeing her again.

"Skate with me?" He extended his hand.

She took it and they went back to the rink floor. Duncan held her tight, knowing if he had another chance he may never let her go. He became high from the familiar scent of lotus mixed with the sweetest citrus and the feel of her body against his. Their divided worlds collided. Money and power faded into his humble beginnings.

"I missed you," she whispered, pressing her body closer.

He knew he did too. Still, she couldn't know. Privilege had already given her everything. Therefore, this was one thing he would deny her for the hope that she might discover just how much he had missed her every summer since the last time.

Five

THE NEXT MORNING Duncan sat in his office staring at his computer. Last night he'd flirted with taboo, again. Why?

He pushed back from his desk and walked toward the floor-to-ceiling windows lending views of the boardwalk of Lake Dora. He took a deep breath, gazing out onto the water. The peace and tranquility of the Shores was why he had found it hard to put the headquarters of his firm in any of the other cities where he had offices. And maybe there was also a part of him that always hoped she would come back.

It wasn't because he wanted to reclaim lost love. Reese had severed that path when she tore his heart from his chest and stomped all over it many summers ago. Duncan simply wanted her to see that he wasn't the boy from the other side of the tracks, destined by her grandmother to become a nobody. He had accomplished a life he'd once dared to dream of.

So, again, why'd he flirt with taboo? Maybe it was the way his heart kicked and jumped when he saw her, or worse, that she'd made him feel things for a woman he hadn't felt since that summer. Regardless, that dance last night should've never happened. He'd be damned if history repeated itself.

He shook his head, cutting off thoughts of a love story that was doomed from the start…and clearly not in his best interests. He didn't have years to spend rebuilding the confidence he'd gained from his experiences outside of the Shores. The life he'd learned and leaned into after attending an Ivy where he joined the oldest Black fraternity for men that upheld scholarly deeds while advocating for the community emboldened him to build a thriving multimillion-dollar business.

Which was why he needed the city to approve his plans for Hill House.

He snatched his gaze from the window and returned to his desk. As he reached for his phone, the sound of his assistant clearing her throat gained his attention. He glanced over his shoulder to see Tasha standing in the doorway. The angst written upon her face made him go still.

"We just got news from the city." Her downcast eyes didn't meet his as she strolled into the office. His grip on his phone tightened as he thought of the hurdles he would leap over to make life better for youth in the Shores. He never wanted them to be labeled as nobodies. "You did it!" she screamed and began waving papers in the air.

"Seriously?"

"Yes!" She did a little happy dance before holding the letter of approval at eye level for him to read.

Duncan clapped his hands together, then pumped his fists into the air. He took the document from Tasha and read it three times before reality settled in. He closed his eyes for a second while taking a deep breath.

A giant smile spread across his face that seemed to light up the room and chase the threatening clouds of nostalgia away. He owned Hill House, and now he would turn the place his mother and grandmother labored over into a place where local kids and teens could be exposed to college readiness, leadership training, and community service. Having a better life would not be reserved for the Devlins and their kind of people.

"So you should know, rumor has it the Devlins are planning to launch a save Hill House campaign." Tasha's stubby fingers combed her shoulder-length hair. "I wouldn't put it past them to try and smear your name. You know how these people operate, Duncan."

He and Tasha were both locals and knew full well how the summer crew pretended that the Shores belonged to them. For years the Devlins, Chennaults, Andrewses, Pierres, Hightowers, and other wealthy Southern families used their clout to influence business, politics, and life in the Shores even when they were not present. If Duncan had anything to do with it, their reigns were over.

It was time for someone who gave a damn about the community to invest in it and its future.

"Let them try it. I'm sure they don't want people to know Quincy lost the bed and breakfast by gambling the equity away. If it wasn't football games and horse races, he was in the backroom at Maude's, overbidding his hand at the card table."

Tasha gasped, "Maude's... You said tax liens."

His lips pressed tight for a second before he said, "He had those too." Duncan fidgeted with his cufflinks. He'd known about Quincy's weakness since he was in middle school. His father and other men from the neighborhood had often bragged about how they'd taken the rich boy's money on poker night when he visited the Shores outside of the summer months, to get away from the wife he hated and visit his mistress. "I'm sure the liens were a result of how he gambles his money away."

Duncan just never thought it would benefit him in a way that could further elevate his name, and the community, while sticking it to the family that had brought him pain as they were forced to realize who and what he had become.

"Clearly he didn't care about that stuffy old place, then."

And neither did Duncan. He shrugged, glancing back down to the document. "Under no circumstances are you to repeat what I've said here." She gave a quick nod as he moved back to his seat. "Thanks for saving me a trip to Mayor Fleming's office."

Tasha giggled, "I'm sure Denise Fleming would've welcomed your visit. She's supported all the moves you've made. My mom said she was in her office bragging that she didn't need to hire a city zoning and planning manager because she had you. The council still can't believe the spike in tourism amongst younger people. You've helped create something special here."

"We simply needed the right venues." Duncan winked. "Oh, and get Rebekah on the line. Let her know we got approval and that she can start PR for the acquisition now. Two steps ahead is the only way we come out of this on the right side."

* * *

Reese paced the hallway outside of her father's study. Since news broke that his attempt to persuade the city to revoke Duncan's rezoning permit for Hill House had failed, her entire family had been on edge. Although, she had yet to determine if they were upset about Duncan owning Hill House and his plans for it, or the embarrassment they suffered from their inner circle.

Given that her mother had conveniently bowed out of a ladies' tea with the ball committee, she was leaning toward shame.

Regardless of the reasons, Reese refused to let her grandmother's legacy become an afterthought. Her mind trailed back to the time she sat next to her grandmother at her sewing machine. They had just come from a picnic where one of the inn's guests wore a gingham dress. Both Reese and her grandma had admired the print in a pretty shade of blue. It had inspired Constance to pair a yellow gingham fabric with a coordinating paisley for a spring tablescape.

Now, in reflecting on that experience, Reese realized that she had witnessed the intersection of fashion and interior textiles. But she'd been too young back then to appreciate it. Fabric, sewing, fashion, and interiors all blended together now. She would never have a chance to thank her grandmother for the gifts of interest she'd bestowed. However, she was starting to understand why for the last few months she seemed uncertain and uninspired with fashion. Much like how the gingham dress led her grandmother to create a tablescape, fabric now whispered to Reese to create coordinating pillows for a sofa instead of pants for a blouse.

Reese had tried to disregard the impulses of her subconscious. It would be selfish to jump ship in a different direction after all the money her parents had spent on her education. Not to mention the connections they'd helped her establish so that her career remained fast-tracked. Only, one day, about a year ago, she noticed that she had been cataloging the many boutique hotels she stayed in across the world for work. Luxury textiles, bold colors, and aesthetics she would kill to influence like she did styles within the fashion world, and it forced her to acknowledge that she wanted to explore something different…something that made her more like her grandmother than she cared to admit.

Except her heart had remained hard as stone for her grandmother. Constance had been the matriarch of the family, controlling everything everyone did by dangling their inheritances as rewards. Reese often wondered if her father's actions that night ten years ago were his or his desire to capture what would be left behind. She would never really know, which was why she was still searching for a way to forgive her grandmother for driving the crusade that pit her family against Duncan's and made Reese a black sheep.

But...maybe it was time to let go and forgive, because her grandmother deserved more than having her life's work stripped away. Reese stopped pacing. She was no longer a child who had to stand by and watch the adults make decisions. She had opinions, ideas, her grandmother's creativity, and money to help. She raised her hand to knock on her father's study door.

"There is only one person that can stop this nightmare, and I hear you were in his arms last night at the roller rink." Reese lowered her arm, then moved away from the door and down the hall to see her mother slumped against the corner of an archway. She'd never seen Genevieve Devlin so defeated. "You were all anyone was talking about until this morning. I could strangle Quincy." An audible breath of exasperation blew past her mother's lips as she closed the distance between them. "We hid the gambling addiction and how much he loved women who were not his wife. But this business with him losing the inn is out in the open for everyone to see."

"Is that why you've decided not to attend the tea with the ball committee this afternoon, or are you bothered that I was in the arms of the boy from the wrong side of town?" she asked, purposely taunting the elite status that held her mother's ego hostage.

"Unlike you, Reese, I care what people say about this family. I'm only ignoring the gossip of you couple-skating with Duncan McNeal last night because maybe it can benefit us."

"What?"

"Don't be coy, Chareese. The boundaries your father and grandmother set all those years ago became void the second you saw each other." She stepped into Reese's face. "I saw the way Duncan looked at you yesterday at the Lakeside Inn. There is something unfinished between you two. You can change his mind. And I'm not asking this time, I'm telling you to do so."

"Change whose mind?" Her father's voice startled her for a second before he came to stand beside her mother. Neither Reese nor her mother offered a reply. "Can one of you answer me?"

Genevieve cleared her throat. "Duncan…No man looks at a woman the way he did Chareese yesterday and wouldn't contemplate selling his soul. She could persuade him to reconsider. That is if she wants to help this family."

"Finding out what he has planned for the house is different than changing his mind, Genevieve. I don't approve of this. I didn't want Reese mixed up with him back then and I sure as hell don't now." Her father abruptly turned on his heel.

"Your unwillingness to let go of the past is why your mother left it to Quincy the first time." Genevieve raised her voice, effectively halting his return to the study. "I will not stand by and watch this happen again. I'm sorry, Kent, but we have to do something or we risk losing the B and B forever."

Forever was a long time. The thought of the Shores being without Hill House tugged Reese at her heartstrings. She didn't care to use her feminine wiles to reel Duncan in. However, they were once friends. Maybe that connection was a viable option. So just like all those years ago, she knew she had to cave to preserve her family's good name. After all, she was a Devlin, and contrary to how she disagreed with aspects of her family, it was her name too.

"I have to go. This may be my last time to see Hill House before Duncan does whatever he is planning to do to it." Reese turned away from her parents and began down the hall.

"I have spent my life giving you and Alexandria the best education, experiences, friends—"

"That you have, Mother." Reese raised her voice a decibel before turning to face her parents again. "But you've also taken. Have either of you once stopped to imagine what now would look like if you had not ruined my friendship with Duncan?" She watched as fleeting glances passed between her mom and dad. They were still too hell-bent on preserving the old ways. Therefore, she would not get an apology, because that would be an admission of their wrongs.

"Your silence was expected." Reese's fists clenched at her sides as she gulped down anger. "Now, I'm leaving to go play nice and beg someone we treated really bad to be my friend again for the hope of maybe saving our family's legacy."

Reese resumed her departure. She strode down the hall and through the house, grabbing her purse and keys, and then walked outside to her car. She sucked down the fresh air, no longer suffocating from her mother's unreasonable expectations. Except, her mother was right this time.

She climbed into her car and started the engine, suppressing memories of last night. Even though she truly missed Duncan and wished things were different, she knew those old, lingering feelings that surfaced couldn't mean anything since her family wanted something in return. A conversation with Duncan was their only option if she didn't want to watch him erase the legacy her grandmother had built from the ground up.

Six

REESE PULLED UP the long driveway and followed the bend until she stopped in front of Hill House. A smile stretched across her face thinking of the times she would hop out the back seat of her parents' car and then dash through the front entry doors to find her grandmother when they arrived in town for the summer. So much had changed since then.

She reclined in her seat, determined not to let tears fall. The origins of Hill House had given her family everything and had become a point of pride for people of the Shores. In the decades that allowed racial bias to be tolerated, leading to segregationist Jim Crow codes in the South, Constance Devlin envisioned more than the rooming house she'd inherited. She wanted a place with high-end accommodations that catered to Black politicians, activists, and celebrities, since white establishments turned them away. Thus, Hill House Bed and Breakfast was established, the only place in the South for the Black elite to rejuvenate. As time passed, the bed and breakfast became renowned for its food, service, and celebrity clientele.

Black guests from well-to-do families began visiting each

year to rub shoulders and build connections with other elites. The popularity of Hill House lured more people to the lakeside village and paved the way for the Shores to become the most exclusive summer colony. Visitors had discovered a community that did not overtly subscribe to discriminatory practices.

Memories sat in the corner of Reese's mind as she gazed upon the old, pale-blue house. Suddenly she missed those days when she sat on the wraparound porch, tracing the lacy gingerbread that adorned every gable, eave, and doorway. Reese had always thought Hill House was special because it had two porches, one up and one down, and much more millwork than any other house its age in the Shores. Her grandmother confirmed her suspicions one day when she explained the inn's unusual architecture was steamboat gothic, modeled after ships that used to travel along the mighty Mississippi River. Despite the obvious signs of poor upkeep, the home still exuded the charm of a bygone era.

Reese popped open the door, swallowing the emotional attachment to the property, and exited her car. She walked the length of the courtyard, noting further neglect. Family legacy was always supposed to come first. And so she wondered, and not for the first time today, how her father had sat by and watched his brother squander their family's pride and joy. More than that, she'd replayed her mother's words several times and still didn't understand what she'd uttered about Grandma Constance not leaving the inn to her father because he wouldn't let go of the past. She may never get that answer.

Her attention shifted to the sound of tires rolling along the semipaved drive. A flashy black sports car came to a stop behind her rental. Years of conditioning had her ready to get to the porch and welcome Hill House's newest guest. But then she remembered, the inn no longer belonged to her family and she didn't have the responsibility of greeting anyone. She returned her attention to the verandah that could also use a fresh coat of paint.

"Mr. McNeal," a young brunette shouted, waving from the window of a news van that pulled in from the service entrance.

In slow motion, Reese turned and watched Duncan get out of the flashy car. His smooth, dark skin popped against the light gray suit he wore. He reminded her of the gorgeous male models she directed at photo shoots. Only difference was that the sight of Duncan caused her heart to beat triple time. Unconsciously, her teeth clipped her bottom lip while she admired the way the suit fit his athletic build as he strutted to the other side of the car, carrying swag that any man would beg to own.

He wasn't supposed to be here. True, she planned to find him and have that conversation that would likely bring up what would never be forgotten. But not now. This stop was her simply wanting to say goodbye to a place she loved. However, since he was here, there was no point in postponing the inevitable.

Just as she was about to move toward him and challenge his notions on taking her family's crown jewel, a tall Black woman rocking a gorgeous twist out emerged from the passenger side of the car door he held open. Ego deflated. Courage lost, and something…something she couldn't put her finger on that swirled around inside of her began to fade. The sight of Duncan smiling down at the woman the way he once did at her forced her to acknowledge that there may not be possibilities to mend fences.

The news reporter zipped past Reese to where the couple stood discussing something. Reese bet they were talking about the house, since the woman gazed fondly upon it and then at Duncan with what looked to be more than appreciation. She noted how long it took them to acknowledge the reporter while wondering if his passenger was the one Quinn had mentioned.

If so, it was utter realization that last night had been a figment of her worst imagination. The way Duncan's eyes had peered into hers as he held her on the rink floor was false advertising. The bridge her father and grandmother had burned with the McNeals seemed to be beyond repair. And she sure as hell shouldn't have told him she missed him.

"Chareese." Duncan waved from where he stood at the front of the car. He failed to contain the shock on his face as he walked between the pretty brown woman and news reporter to where Reese stood at the side of the porch.

"Hello, Duncan," she managed to say, despite the erratic beats from her heart that made her body quiver. She wished he weren't so damn fine.

"Rebekah"—he glanced to the woman who had arrived with him—"you and Miss Kirkland can go inside and get situated. I'll be there in a few minutes."

Both women nodded and then disappeared into the house. Duncan slid his hands inside his pockets before he claimed another step and closed the distance between them. His scent of amber infused with sandalwood and maybe a hint of vanilla was delicious, strong…and everything she was not allowed to have. She needed to remember that or risk being hurt again.

"I expected your father, considering his most recent machinations. Maybe even your uncle, but definitely not you." He stared into her eyes, searching for answers she would never reveal. "Are you here to do their bidding?"

"I'm here because I had hoped you had more compassion than what it sounds like you've bottled up." She looked to the ground and couldn't help noting the expensive loafers that matched his loftiness. Without him realizing, he'd slid into a world she'd been desperate to leave ever since she was forced to pretend he didn't exist. "Do you realize how much of my life was spent here?" She gazed up and around the grounds.

"How could I forget? We met here, chased each other in the backyard, raced up the stairs—"

"Then why are you doing this," she hissed. "I know you hate me. Could you maybe think of what this place means to the Shores?"

His stance turned bone rigid. The relaxed expression on his face became pinched. "What do you think it means? Your lens is clouded because it belonged to your family. I can assure you the relevance of Hill House in this community has changed over the years. Maybe you don't know because you've been gone."

"My grandmother attracted people to the Shores with Hill House. It's a thriving summer colony because of all the work she devoted to this community."

"I guess the world goes round because the Devlins say so? You all think everything that is good happens because of you. Do you know how much your grandmother took from the community to—" His lips pressed together and he looked off for a second. "You have no idea how incredibly spoiled and entitled you sound right now, Chareese."

A tremble slid over her body. The way her name rolled off his tongue contradicted his obvious annoyance with her visit. She thought about how she'd always gotten butterflies whenever he called her by her full name.

"Have you once stopped to consider how your absence from this town has left you disconnected? The inn hasn't brought near as many guests as it used to. There are repairs that need to be done before it turns into an eyesore, and for the record, it hasn't always treated employees fair when it comes to pay."

There were obvious signs of wear upon the inn. The other accusations he tossed into the universe were too much to contemplate while her family's legacy was dangling by threads. "If you just give it back we can make everything right, Duncan."

"Unbelievable," he huffed, "I guess the more things change the more they stay the same. Excuse me, I need to get inside." Duncan brushed past her.

"Wait." She caught him by the arm, halting his steps. "Just tell me you're not planning to tear it down."

He began shaking his head. "Has the time away made you forget? I love old buildings. Windows, balconies, columns"—he paused—"this woodwork that adorns Hill House, are all reasons that I fell in love with architecture and studied it in school."

"I remember." She rushed the words. "We used to ride our bikes around town cataloging various styles of the old homes." Her head lowered as she let go of his wrist and took a step to close the distance between them. "I meant what I said last night." She breathed a sigh of relief when he didn't move away. "I missed you."

"Last night was a mistake." He then turned on his heel, went up the steps, reached for the front door, and went inside.

Seven

"DUNCAN," REBEKAH, HIS public relations director, called out as he entered the house. She pranced in his direction, then abruptly stopped at the edge of the foyer. "Are you ready for the interview or do you need more time?"

Duncan continued pacing inside the vestibule, attempting to pump brakes on the emotional rollercoaster he thought he'd escaped earlier only to get back on seconds ago. His head tilted to the ceiling as he took in another calming breath.

"I need a minute," he confided. "The Devlin family…The woman outside was Chareese Devlin."

Damn her. He'd managed to remove Reese from his head after it had been consumed by her for most of the morning. However, the pop-up visit brought back the haunting attraction he'd dismissed last night. He didn't have time to chase things that were never meant to be caught. Besides, he needed to focus on the zoning approval he'd received from the city and move forward with his plans.

Despite her thinking his motivations were born of hate, he knew why he was doing this. The historic reasons that had made

Hill House prominent were no longer relevant. Society had evolved. The Black visitors who came to the town had more lodging choices, and social mobility had created the summer home phenomenon.

However, there was still an entire class of people from marginalized backgrounds that deserved an opportunity. A needs assessment had revealed that it was necessary to focus on educating and preparing underprivileged youth to become college bound or career ready.

His idea of a youth village was the only way to prepare kids in this community to finish high school, go to college or get a trade, and become future leaders that would also reinvest in the Shores. He had dreamed of paving a way forward since the morning his parents loaded their old minivan with his belongings and drove him up the eastern seaboard to college. This was his chance. He wouldn't let anyone stand in the way. Not even if the heart of his soul said something else.

"Oh, I had no idea." Rebekah's heels clicked against the wood floor as she moved fast to look out the front window. "She's leaving now. Do you think they are going to be a problem? Should I get a no trespass permit for the property?"

"No!" he snapped. "It's complicated. Chareese is an old…friend." He wouldn't do that to Reese no matter the pain she lanced across his heart. "Give me a few more minutes. This interview is important. We need to control the narrative and explain the plans for this place, or we face backlash built from assumptions."

Rebekah's eyes narrowed at him for longer than needed before she nodded and turned to walk back down the hall. Only after she was gone did Duncan realize the mistake in telling an ex-lover that his relationship with another woman was complicated. His head was a mess. He'd pondered more whys and what-ifs since he ran into Reese yesterday. He really was in no mood to be interviewed for the paper. However, the history and influence Hill House had had in the Shores and across the nation were not to be trifled with. He needed to control the narrative of the acquisition and show the benefits of an urban plan that was designed to revitalize sectors of downtown.

His analysis showed that commercial and nearby residential property values would increase. A greater sense of community would be established through a youth village that would help promote diversity, inclusion, and engagement of teens with local business leaders and owners. If a child could see it, then they could achieve it. He just had to convince the public that Hill House would be better served as a youth village.

Duncan started down the hall to the sitting room where his PR director and the news reporter, Ms. Kirkland, were waiting. For a second, his mind drifted back to a time when the old house was warm and inviting. He stopped and stared at pictures of the famous people who had visited the Shores.

Chareese had been right. Hill House had brought people from all across the country to their small, lakeside town. And part of that lure had been the reputation of the Southern cuisine his grandmother and mother cooked and served.

His gaze flitted to the pivot door at the end leading to the kitchen. He could almost sniff the buttermilk biscuits his grand-mother used to bake for guests from scratch and taste the raw honey that usually accompanied them.

Abruptly, Duncan severed thoughts of the past and began envisioning the future. The old house had over nine thousand square feet and could easily accommodate a small library, computer lab, dance room, and other engaging programming that would ignite youth interests in entrepreneurship, financial literacy, and civic duty while preparing them to be college bound. After all, this would become his legacy.

Therefore, he rejected the emotions his heart wanted him to feel and moved through the old bed and breakfast to where Rebekah and the reporter stood entranced by the memorabilia that littered the walls of the sitting room.

"Thank you for taking this interview, Mr. McNeal," the journalist said, offering a kind smile as Duncan entered the bright sitting room. "Since the city made the hearing public record, we've been following the story."

Duncan nodded. "Apologies for the delay, Ms. Kirkland. I appreciate you wanting to speak with me. I know this place." He scanned the room they were in, noting that it had probably gone untouched since Quincy stopped being able to pay staff six months ago. "It holds sentimental value for many. That's why it's important for us to be as transparent as possible with our plans. Shall we sit?"

The reporter lowered into a wingback chair. Duncan claimed the twin across from her while Rebekah made strides to the window. He never should've mentioned Reese. A year after their breakup and Rebekah still showed envy over another woman's name escaping his mouth.

"You mentioned that you know this place," the journalist started. "Is it because of its history in the Shores, or do you have a deeper connection?"

Duncan crossed his legs and relaxed in the old chair. Once upon a time he would've balked at telling a stranger that his mom and grandma were the help. He still had to swallow the bitter taste of growing up poor. His socioeconomic status at age fourteen dictated that he work odd jobs that kept him from meeting friends at the lake and being able to hold the girl of his dreams. He'd had no choice if he'd wanted to help his parents keep the lights on at home. As a teenager he was burdened with grown-up problems. He now had a chance to remove that load from other youths so that they might enjoy their childhoods.

"I spent time within these very walls as a boy." The journalist perked up, but Duncan ignored her. "My grandmother, Suzette McNeal, and Constance Devlin were friends, and she worked here preparing the meals. My mother joined when she was of age, and I would come see them or assist with small chores to help make ends meet at home."

"I had no idea. Such humble beginnings," she gushed. "Is that why you purchased this property? Are you considering updating Hill House and continuing operations as a bed and breakfast?"

"Great question." He had pondered the idea of bringing the old house current. However, those notions only catered to the vengeful spirit that stirred whenever he thought of his mother and grandmother, and all they suffered with Constance Devlin. "I have no interest in the hospitality industry. However, I do enjoy tinkering with underutilized structures and land use to create environments that benefit communities. In this case we are looking to develop a high-performance learning environment. It is something our community needs, and that I believe in."

"I'm sure I'm not the only one wondering why Hill House? There are other properties, such as the old bank, that have sat idle for years that could be revitalized?"

"The ability to convert this property into a space that meets our needs was far more cost-effective. Additionally, the location of Hill House makes it more accessible for youth that are from less affluent areas of town. There are additional benefits such as mentorships and internships that will be made available through a downtown partnership with local businesses. The engagement that is needed for youth in the Shores to develop the skills necessary to succeed at the next level is dependent upon these interactions."

"How do the Devlins feel about this? I mean this B and B was owned and operated by their family for decades."

"No comment."

The woman's pale nose crinkled at his hard edge. She adjusted in her seat, looked to his PR director, and then back at Duncan.

"What Mr. McNeal means is that we cannot officially comment on the position of the Devlin family," Rebekah jumped in, saving Duncan from making an ass out of himself.

"That's fair." She jotted down a few notes, then refocused on Duncan. "This is a classic rags-to-riches story. What does your mother think of you acquiring the business of her past employer?"

Duncan gripped the arms of the chair and prepared to stand. The question was triggering. It made him think of all the days his mother went to work, giving Constance her all to uphold the status of Hill House, only to be treated as an outcast. He would not exploit what his mother went through for media attention. The conversation was off-limits. There was no feel-good journalism in that tale. He would talk about the acquisition and goals of the project, only.

"The McNeals are thrilled that Duncan has found a way to repurpose the idle house," Rebekah piped in again, side-eyeing Duncan as he stirred in the chair and found a way to maintain his seat. "In fact, Mrs. McNeal will be donating meals from her restaurant to ensure kids are not going home hungry after attending programs. This is truly a venture designed to benefit the community."

An energetic nod came from Ms. Kirkland as her hand scribbled more notes onto a pad. "That's wonderful news. Last question, and I think it's the one the public is eager to learn more about. Are you planning to only convert the property, or will you demolish and rebuild?"

"A cost-benefit analysis favors conversion. Building a property from the ground up for educational purposes is extremely expensive." Duncan stood, ready for the questions to end, as he signaled Rebekah to grab the artistic rendering featuring the updates to the interior space. He wanted the reporter to deliver a message to the people that would gain public buy-in just in case the Devlins called in favors or aired their grievances.

"Here's a sample of the proposed changes." Rebekah brought the poster board over to her, holding the architectural drawings.

"Would you like a look around while we explain what has been envisioned?" Duncan glanced over at the plans, then to the reporter, and noted she had a smile upon her face.

The woman's nod gave him the approval he sought before the trio began moving about the space. Her comments hinted at admiration, and for the first time since he had agreed to have the media in his business affairs, he became comfortable. The praise he received during the tour warmed his heart and reaffirmed that the decisions he'd made had been right. Now was not the time for regrets.

Eight

TWO WORDS—RETAIL THERAPY. After leaving Duncan at Hill House, Reese craved the scent of new clothes. Maybe even a bag and shoes. A pair of Louboutins usually did the trick. It was easier to throw money at pretty things than to deal with the ugly, emotional stuff. Especially when it was unexpected.

She had left home prepping her mind to bid farewell to Hill House, not to be reintroduced to heartbreak. Had she known, she would've rehearsed words she knew Duncan needed to hear that might allow him to reconsider rebuilding their friendship. Certainly a conversation with Duncan should've started with an explanation for the years of silence, since she had skipped that last night and went straight to confessional. But none of it mattered. He dissed her and her peace offering from last night. If her parents thought she was the Trojan horse, they were wrong.

Reese glanced up into the fitting room mirror. Her impulses had been in overdrive as she grabbed every colorful piece off the rack, entered the changing space, and stripped down to try clothes on. Unfortunately, small-town inventory didn't exactly cater to her big-city, off-the-runway tastes, so it was taking longer than normal for her encounter with Duncan to fade away.

"Ma'am, how does everything fit?" Reese couldn't help the way her jaw dropped as her head recoiled from the formal address. Worse, the mirror had captured her reaction. When did she become a ma'am? "Do you need anything else?"

What she needed couldn't be purchased in a store unless people had found a way to bottle the antivenom for rejection. "The fit is good, thank you." Southern hospitality was real. She'd simply forgotten, or rather missed it from the time she spent in New York, Paris, and Milan, where it was rare to be acknowledged with such good manners. "Ehh...not so certain on the color scheme." She stepped out of the fitting room, tucking the chambray blouse into a paisley-printed skirt that was less than memorable.

"Mmm..." the young lady said before darting off to the other side of the store. "Yeah, I'm not feeling that either. I think there's something here that would be perfect for you."

Reese gave a nod of appreciation, then watched as the girl lifted a bold peacock-patterned skirt. The eye-catching blues and greens with hints of fuchsia and sparkles of gold sang that "buy it" song to her.

"Mmm, a Horace J. This was in his inaugural summer collection." Reese picked at the skirt, loving the lightweight fabric and color while knowing the fit would complement her curves as most of his pieces did.

"Yes, ma'am!"

"You don't have to call me ma'am," Reese said.

"I'm sorry, I can't help it." The girl giggled. "It's how I was raised." She passed Reese the skirt. "We've had this awhile. Most folks around here are a bit more traditional. You know, resort wear in bright colors that scream Lilly Pulitzer. I sorta figured you may be open to this piece after seeing your Birkin bag and Valentino sneaks."

A girl after her own heart. Reese knew from working in the fashion world that brand recognition was a blessing, but equally a curse. It was a rabbit hole that could make you snobby and stunt your finances, or reward you for being a brand ambassador who influenced the hottest labels and elevated platforms within the industry. She wasn't sure if the attendant was at that level yet, but she could tell the girl approached retail fashion like it was an art form.

Reese took the item and reentered the fitting room. She quickly stepped out of the drab paisley skirt and slid on the Horace J. pencil garment. Even if she hadn't stumbled across this skirt, she would've purchased the other and found a way to jazz it up. She couldn't present herself at the style seminar she was hosting for the debutantes lacking fashion sense. Nor could she go home to change. Her defenses were down, and she wouldn't know how to protect herself from her mother's reaction after explaining there had been no progress in changing Duncan's mind. She had no intention of using him as a means to their end. She could not betray him or his trust again.

Leaving Hill House today had been more bitter than an unripe mulberry from her grandmother's tree. Duncan's rejection had strummed the pain of her heart, which confirmed how she felt when she first saw him...the reasons why she'd stayed away summer after summer, avoided contact over the years, and refused to be complicit in her parents' schemes.

After all this time, something was still there. So, it was best she stayed away from home and questions she would answer with lies.

"How do you like that one?" the attendant called from the

other side, pulling Reese's mind from the ditch her thoughts were leading her to.

"Perfect!" Reese opened the door and walked out in the new outfit, then profiled to the side in the winged trifold mirror. "What is your name?"

"Jasmine," she responded with a bubbly smile.

"Well, Jasmine, I just need a chunky necklace, maybe a bracelet, and shoes to match. You think you have anything I might like?"

The girl winked. "I got you."

Reese followed Jasmine to the back of the store where they made random conversation while pairing shoes and other accessories together to complement her last-minute ensemble. She noted how the young woman's face lit up when they talked about the latest fashion trends. The girl reminded Reese of herself when she used to fawn over outfits that the celebrities who visited Hill House flaunted at dinners, picnics, and events. Back then Reese imagined dressing those guests up for award shows. Many of her ideas were inspired by the emerging styles chronicled within the pages of *Essence* magazine that she'd cut out and paste onto poster board.

"Have you considered a career in the fashion world?" Reese sincerely inquired.

Jasmine shrugged. "I don't know. The owner of the boutique has asked me the same question. It's just hard for me to get my hopes up when most colleges that have majors in fashion are far from here. My parents don't have that kind of money." An unexpected smile then surfaced on the pretty girl's face. "That's why so many of us are excited about the youth village my friend Destiny's brother has promised to build."

"What do you mean?" Reese quickly adjusted the cuffs on her new blouse before grabbing one last look in the mirror. She then scrambled to scoop up her belongings and meet her helper at the register.

"The youth village is going to prep kids for college. Destiny said there's going to be tutors, mentors, and scholarships. My parents can't wait to put me into whatever the program is because they see what Duncan has become, and how Destiny was invited to the debutante ball. The ball is sort of a big deal around here."

"Yes, sounds like it is," Reese begrudgingly responded as the girl finished ringing her up.

This made the second time today where she was reminded of her privilege. The first, of course, reared its ugly head at Hill House no more than two hours ago. Strike two was the realization of how she had taken the debutante ball for granted. She'd never once thought of not getting an invite because she knew she would. Generations of women in her family had been presented to society via the Lakeside Debutante Ball.

The event held esteem within the circles her family socialized in despite the chaos created in finding the perfect Cinderella gown, updo, and escort. Most girls bragged about how the experience helped them make new friends and build up confidence to face the world as an adult. They also enjoyed the volunteerism associated with meeting presentation requirements. However, for Reese, the experience had been the beginning of the painful end to her relationship with Duncan.

And yet, she wondered why it stung to hear the young lady share aspirations of becoming a debutante. Perhaps it was because Reese knew the contradiction of living in that Black world. She understood the expectation since she, and generations of women from her family, had spent their formative years studying the right foreign language, taking dance lessons, oratorical competitions, and, of course, engaging in academic rigor to prepare a celebrated curriculum vitae. It was necessary and quite boastful, but it demonstrated why a girl was selected to debut at the Lakeside Debutante Ball by age seventeen. Whereas the girls who existed outside the social constructs of the well-to-do crowd never had the chance. And that included the sweet young lady helping her now.

Just maybe the youth village was a genius idea. Duncan was extending something to enrich kids from around here. It was like the olive branch he offered last night when he asked her to dance. Only, Reese had taken advantage and shown up at Hill House demanding the whole tree.

Enough about Duncan McNeal, and so much for retail therapy. Reese handed over her credit card, accepting defeat. The man had single-handedly caged her into the shame she felt all those years ago for denying her heart because of status. And still, she didn't know how to set herself free.

"Thank you," Reese murmured as she grabbed her shopping bags, still cursing the failed intervention while proceeding to the door.

The second she stepped out of the shop and onto the sidewalk, a scent more familiar than that of Lake Dora begged for her attention. She peeped across the street to see that Uncle Willie's Sweet Shop had managed to withstand the test of time. She licked her lips as if she could already taste the caramelized sugary goodness and toasted peanuts of Mr. Willingham's famous peanut brittle. As her mouth watered, wanting to be reacquainted with one of her favorite childhood treats, her hips protested, knowing what too much of a good thing could do to the fit of skinny jeans.

Her feet grew minds of their own, carrying her across the street and inside Uncle Willie's. She sniffed the sweet cocoa from the chocolate melting into fudge. Bubbles of laughter escaped her as she saw the old-fashioned jars full of Lemon-heads, Red Hots, and sour pickles. This place was pure, sweet, and kind. Everything she'd found the world not to be after her grandmother ripped off her blinders and exposed her to the divide in the Shores. The haves and have-nots as Constance Devlin proclaimed that night and many after. Her grandmother never forgave Reese for ruining years of matchmaking that promised to further elevate the Devlins within the upper ranks of their elitist world.

"Is that Little Miss Chareese Anne?" The old, smoky voice of Mr. Willingham invoked childhood joy. She turned around and saw the gentle giant who had blessed the Shores with sweet things since she was old enough to remember wearing ruffle lace ankle socks. "Joyce, look who's rolled back into town."

His wife came hobbling on her cherry cane, eyes peering over half-moon spectacles. "Ohh girl, look at you! Lawd if Connie could see you now." The old woman extended an arm, pulling Reese into her chest. Licorice and butterscotch almost suffocated her in the warm cocoon. "We'd heard you had come to town. But then everybody started talking about Quincy losing Connie's place. I owe that boy a good whippin'."

Reese didn't know what to say, especially to one of her grandmother's oldest friends. She slowly peeled her way out of Mrs. Willingham's hold. A minute ago she felt young and care-free. Now, it was like she was back to figuring out a way to be friends with the person that ruined the play date.

"Get in line," she muttered.

"Ha," the old woman belted. "Who am I behind, Genevieve?"

"Touch your nose, Joyce." Mr. Willingham came to where they stood, cupped Reese's shoulder, and watched a contrite expression settle upon his wife's face. "It really is good to see you. What kept you away for so long?"

"Time for you to touch your nose now, Henry." The rose color staining the old woman's cheeks as she shook in laughter made Reese laugh too. And she needed it, needed the cheer and good vibes to suspend her thoughts on regrets of the past while she figured out how to go forward.

"It's okay. I'm here for Alexandria's debut. Although, maybe if I hadn't stayed away so long I wouldn't be coming back to Duncan McNeal taking over my grandmother's bed and breakfast." Reese sighed, leaving the small circle they'd formed to inspect the treats in the jars on the counter. "May I please get a pound of that peanut brittle, it smells delicious."

"One pound coming right up," Mrs. Willingham sing-songed, moving to the confections section.

"You know things changed on the Shores in the years you've been gone." The old man came to her side and handed her an empty brown bag to fill with her selections. "Your uncle and father never approached or appreciated that place like your grandmother. Hill House was her life. For them, it was an heirloom turned hobby. I'm not sure what Constance expected them to do."

"What she had managed to do. They knew how to operate the inn. We all spent time learning the business."

"How?" Mr. Willingham looked her pointedly in the face. "Your father was busy learning to perform brain surgeries while your uncle was on the Cape wowing them NASA folks with his genius for designing spaceships. All the while, the staff managing the inn had none of your grandmother's charm or business sense."

"You do though," came from across the store as Mrs. Willingham boxed up the brittle. "She told me that once."

Reese went still. It was hard to imagine her grandmother saying anything nice about her, since she'd practically disowned her after believing Reese had lost her virginity to a boy she believed beneath them. "When did she tell you that?"

The old woman grabbed her cane and came back to her side. Her attention fluttered for a moment as the bell rang over the door announcing another patron. After Mr. Willingham left to tend to their customer, she refocused on Reese. "Connie told me right before she passed."

Reese ignored the burning at her cheeks and avoided meeting the revealer of truth's eyes. Five years had gone by since her grandmother's funeral. She'd been in Paris at Fashion Week making a splash with the world's most notable designers and still too bitter from the way she'd been shunned for challenging tradition and accused of improper behavior with Duncan, so she didn't come. Why pay respects to a woman who wouldn't give her any?

"Well"—Reese regained her composure—"she never told me."

"Well, I'm tellin' ya now." If sassy had a drip. Reese huffed a chuckle. "Maybe try talking to Duncan. He's a very reasonable young man."

Reese snatched up all of her goodies and went to the register. "Can I check out now, please?"

"I…I'm sorry, Chareese," the woman apologized as she carefully made her way to stand behind the register. "I meant no offense. Duncan helped us keep this shop."

"How did he help you?"

The woman pointed to Reese's shopping bags from the boutique. "Not sure if you remember, but that used to be Sylvia's hat shop. We almost became a gimmicky national chain for bath products. Duncan stepped in with his urban design team and helped many of the shops on this side avoid Sylvia's fate." The woman looked down to the old-fashioned cash drawer and stroked a few buttons before she looked back at Reese.

"Duncan then invested in Henry's brittle. He helped with branding and gave it nationwide distribution. The college students he sends us through his internship program help with computer orders and other inventory. Now people from all over make it a point to visit this shop when they come to town. Duncan cares about what happens here and wants to see as much of what y'all grew up knowing remain. That's why he did what he did for us."

But *us* was the Willinghams, not the Devlins. Reese took it as a hint even though the old woman didn't know she was giving one. The Willinghams hadn't been the family to burn the bridge between themselves and the McNeals.

Duncan had no reason to care about Hill House's downward spiral. And why should he after her family attempted to dictate his social mobility because he hadn't had a Lakeshore Drive address. Karma had become his ally as he proved them wrong for proclaiming he was a nothing.

"No disrespect, Mrs. Willingham, but you do realize that he's turning Hill House into a youth village or something. Those actions don't lend to preservation." She exhaled a deep breath, settled the bill, and left.

Nine

TWENTY-SEVEN GIRLS from the South's most elite families stood in the ballroom sporting gaudy crinoline skirts over their clothes while attempting to perfect the side-step and curtsy. The pressure to perform was a living, breathing thing floating about the room, and Mrs. Inez Russell, the debutante drill-master, wasn't kind in her critiques. She hadn't been ten years ago, and the years hadn't softened the woman. Perfection on presentation night was all Mrs. Russell cared about.

Reese checked her watch, noting she had about twenty minutes before she was due to lead the style seminar. She took a seat in the back of the room and peered out at the sea of teenage girls. She remembered those days of mandatory curtsy practice. Of course, as she watched her sister, she knew that her mother had been coaching her.

Her posture was almost perfect, and the smile Alex maintained was the epitome of a beauty queen's. She shone like a bright star compared to the tall bright-skinned girl beside her, who was obviously a Taylor. Women from that family were gangly, uncoordinated, and had a hard time achieving Mrs. Russell's requests during debutante season.

Destiny was also having a hard time as she fumbled and fidgeted, crossing her legs and bending in high heels. At least they were not alone. Quite a few girls seemed to be having trouble executing the debutante curtsy that was the hallmark of presentation.

"Silence." Mrs. Russell's high-pitched voice carried across the room as the cane in her hand banged hard against the oak floors. "I see some of you think this is a game. Should you really feel that way, then please leave, because you are wasting my time." The old woman's dignified posture was finished, with her feet turned out heels together, a proper first position. Also code for *try me today if you want to.* "Chareese and Quinlyn," Mrs. Russell called without a look over her shoulder. "May you please meet me at the front of the room?"

Reese wiped her face clean of the pinch that had jacked up an eyebrow. She looked around and saw Quinn standing just inside the doorway. They made eye contact but dared not shrug. The old woman still had eyes in the back of her head, and the fiery personality they'd been introduced to long ago was not yet dormant. Therefore, they obeyed. God forbid Mrs. Russell report their failure to do so to their mothers.

As they made their way to the front of the room, the stern demeanor of the drillmaster evaporated. She had once told them they were her favorite debs. Perhaps it was true. The kind smile and wide-open arms she greeted them with communicated as much. After Mrs. Russell let go of Quinn, her frosty attitude resurfaced as she again began scrutinizing the current slate of debutantes.

"Chareese Antoinette Devlin and Quinlyn Marie Hightower," Mrs. Russell announced as if the girls were royalty of the highest court. "These two young ladies were a part of one of the most celebrated debutante classes in the history of the Lakeside Ball, and I had the distinct privilege of training them both."

Mrs. Russell continued elevating Reese and Quinn's pedestal as she raved over the educational and professional achievements they had made since their debut. Many of the girls seemed impressed with the strides the older debutantes had made. Only, Reese was certain her sister felt differently.

The way Alex's eyes rolled before a scowl marred her pretty face confirmed Reese's worst thoughts. Their nine-year age gap had always lent Alex to feeling like a mistake instead of enjoying her designation as the spoiled baby sister. It was unfortunate that her sister had not yet realized they weren't each other's competition.

"Which one of you will show these young ladies the proper way to curtsy?" Mrs. Russell stared at both Reese and Quinn.

Quinn pointed at Reese. Reese cut her eyes over to where her sister stood with folded arms denoting further dejection. However, she couldn't refuse Mrs. Russell's request, and Alex knew it. This was the world their mother had raised them to stand out in, and so, even if she wished to escape the spectacle presenting itself, the politeness she had to fake dictated otherwise.

"It would be my pleasure, Mrs. Russell." Reese turned on her million-dollar smile, then moved to stand front and center of the debutantes. "May I borrow a crinoline?" She stretched her gaze over to Alex, who excused herself from the room with haste.

Surely once Alex's actions got back to their mother, she would plead a case and become the victim of being overshadowed by Reese. It wasn't the first time, but it had never been so public or disappointing. Had it not been for so many of the other girls wishing to show Reese love as they reached to untie the drawstring closures at their waists, the awkward moment might have lasted even longer.

Before any of them could shed their hooped skirts, Destiny McNeal popped up next to her with the white, frilly mass in her hands. "Here," Destiny offered. "You can use mine." The girl's smile reminded her of Duncan's, and disarmed the many defenses she had begun constructing since he confessed their slow skate a mistake.

Reese accepted the skirt. "Thank you."

"Are you kidding," the girl gushed. "Your debut is still talked about…and I'm sorry about how my brother acted yesterday," she whispered.

They exchanged nods of understanding before Destiny reclaimed her spot. Reese then solicited Quinn for help in committing what she deemed a fashion faux pas of the modern era. There was nothing cute about the poofy white skirt that was loaded with frill and meant to alter a woman's shape just for a skirt to appear full.

However, the oversized garment had been an equalizer. Freed Black women had once found power in their ability to wear crinoline as a symbol of elegance, power, and proper dress. It was the one fashion statement that had not been relegated to race or class, and she planned to educate the girls on those facts during the style seminar.

Reese flounced the many layers of netting and stepped into the skirt. Quinn tied the drawstring, then went to stand beside Mrs. Russell. Southern belle fashion had been a hallmark of the Lakeside Debutante Ball for almost a century. Reese held her head high, honoring their traditions, and became the center of attention.

Reese took in a deep breath. She hadn't curtsied in a long while, and she would never forget the many lessons her mother and grandmother provided to ensure she had the most elegant curtsy for her debut. On an exhale, she straightened her back as she elongated her neck, pushing her chin high. She gracefully opened her arms as if she were preparing to port de bras, while transferring weight to her right foot.

She turned on the smile that had always given her everything she wanted, and began lowering herself into a pretzel-like seated position. All the while her posture remained impeccable enough to rival a lady being presented in a queen's court. Once her bottom hit her back foot, she dropped her head to complete the bow.

Applause, coupled with a few unladylike whistles, erupted in the room. Reese lifted her head, unable to contain the giddy feeling. She hadn't felt this good when she'd taken her own curtsy. She then began rising up with the assistance of Mrs. Russell.

"And that, my dahlings, is how you present yourself into society." Mrs. Russell's excitement was undeniable. "Marvelous, Chareese, you continue to make us all so proud." She kissed Reese on the cheek as she applauded her. "All right, ladies, that is all for today. You have a few minutes to get out of your crinoline, grab a snack, and then Chareese will begin the style seminar."

The young debutantes dispersed into various corners of the room. Reese made quick work of untying the ribbon holding the crinoline together around her waist. Before she could step completely out of the skirt, Mrs. Russell and Quinn came to her side, offering assistance. "Thank you." She adjusted her clothes. "I need to find Alex."

"She's right there." Quinn pointed to where Alex stood huddled up with the other debutantes. They were the same girls Reese remembered her sister hosting play dates with during the summer months. All were from families within their parents' inner circle.

"Don't mind Alexandria, Chareese. That sister of yours likes attention. If you give it to her now, she will continue to respond in the way she did today." Mrs. Russell was matter-of-fact.

Reese followed Mrs. Russell's line of sight, failing to contain the grimace etching away at her lips as she watched her sister. The last thing her family needed was gossip of a sibling rivalry on top of them losing Hill House. "My apologies, she knows better. I will speak to her."

"I have always appreciated your politeness, Chareese." Mrs. Russell pushed her nose in the air. "However, please do not apologize on Alex's behalf. Genevieve has taught her better than how she acted today. I plan to have a word with your mother a little later."

"To be honest, I'm not surprised," Quinn admitted. "Her attitude needs to change. Members of the ball committee have noted the behavior to your mother. Only, it's Alex, and she's a Devlin, and well…you know the rest."

Third strike. To hear a dear old friend note Devlin privilege knocked Reese down at the knees. "That's no excuse, Quinn. And since when did you become a part of the ball committee?"

"Most debutantes find ways to give back, Chareese. Quinlyn has been part of the ball committee the last two years, and we're happy to finally have you assisting in some way. Now, in addition to the style seminars you are hosting, we wondered if you would consider mentoring one of our rising stars?"

"Yes." Quinn put an arm around Reese's shoulder. "We were thinking you could spend time with Destiny McNeal." Reese drew back. "Hear me out. She's a brilliant girl with a bright future. The only issue is that because she is the first of her family to be a part of something like this, she lacks awareness of our customs."

"Correct, and in order for her to reach the potential expected of all debutantes at the time of presentation and beyond, she needs someone to help ensure she is prepared. Her bio, the dress, escort, and networking for her future."

Reese glanced over her shoulder. How could she say yes to mentoring Destiny when it seemed her own sister needed help?

"After seeing you and Duncan connect last night, I thought you would be a great fit for Destiny." Quinn nudged Reese. "Besides, your sister has your mother and doesn't see Destiny as competition, so she probably wouldn't be upset."

A lifeline was being extended. She wasn't sure if she deserved it or if she should even take it. Only, she knew this might be her last chance to get close to Duncan. She was desperate to see if the angst playing Double Dutch in her head was a figment of her imagination or meant to be. This was her way to find out. "I'll do it."

Ten

SWEET, TINKLING CHIMES began before strings from the harp. Reese preferred to be cooed into a conscious state, not evicted from sleep by an obnoxiously loud siren. She took a deep breath, wiggled her toes, and then opened her eyes to greet the morning before hitting the end button on her alarm.

Instead of easing from the bed like she normally would after silencing her wake-up call, she cuddled back under the covers. There was no five a.m. prep, photo shoot, or last-minute edits. Her head sank back into the pillow, and she closed her eyes.

"Reesey Pie!" her father called as he knocked on her door.

She yawned, fighting the sandman's pull, and managed a groggy, "Come in, Daddy."

Her father stepped in the room, dressed in his old college T-shirt, jeans, and a cap that represented the oldest and coldest Black fraternity. "Morning, baby girl. Want to join your old man for a ride? I'm going to the flea market. You used to love that."

A second, maybe two, passed for his words to resonate. She sat up in the bed and looked at her father. He loved venturing to Renningers, the old farmers and flea market that over the years had become known as one of the largest antique centers in the southeast. Since her mother never bothered to go, Reese and her dad would load up into his old truck, travel back roads, shop for knickknacks, and grab ice cream before returning home. Saturday mornings used to be their sacred time together. They had taken it away from each other and this was their chance to try again.

"Sure, Daddy." She pushed the covers away. "Let me wash up and get on some clothes."

A big, bright smile landed on his face. "I'll be downstairs waiting for you."

Reese moved from the bed. The sunbeams shining in lured her to the window seat in her room. She'd missed the sunrise, which had always been spectacular over Lake Dora. At least she was up early enough to hear the birds chirp while squirrels raced up the ancient oak. The natural beauty of the Shores crawled out of its slumber and greeted her in a way she would have never appreciated as a child.

Calm spread over her. How many mornings had she risen in her New York apartment and wished for this feeling? Too many to count…especially as of late. The city had been different from the landscapes of Ithaca, where she attended college at Cornell. After four years in the upstate college town with the prospect of putting her degree to good use, she'd wished for the energy and excitement in the heart of the Big Apple.

But now, she longed for something different and yet familiar at the same time. She didn't know exactly what it was. Only that she wanted a place where there was time to enjoy life and maybe even love without compromising professional dreams. Reese turned away from her view and padded to the bathroom.

Less than an hour later, Reese met her father in the fifth bay of the garage where he kept his classic 1966 Ford F-100 pickup. The Caribbean blue of the truck still appeared show-room ready all the while highlighting its vintage appeal. He got a kick out of driving it around town since her mother never allowed him to bring it to their permanent residence in Winter Park. In Genevieve's opinion, the truck wasn't ritzy enough for the posh central Florida suburb. Nor was it the kind of vehicle she believed one of the nation's top neurosurgeons should ever drive around in.

Life seemed to rewind as Reese climbed inside and sat next to her father. They took off, traveling toward the outskirts of town where the market was located. The roads were clear and quiet, and oddly her father was the same.

"Are you looking for something in particular today?" She decided to break the silence.

"Peace of mind." He glanced across at her. "Your mother is driving me crazy with everything that is going on."

"Mom can't resist inserting herself. She's a fixer, Dad." Reese huffed a laugh. "I used to think I got lucky that stuff always seemed to work out. It wasn't until freshman year of high school when I was passed over for first chair violin in the youth symphony that I realized Mom handled things."

"And handle things she did. Your mother took the gloves off for her baby." His chest puffed out with pride as a smile stretched across his face. "You know those people still fear her. They put on smiles when she attends events because she now sits on the board, but never again will they simply give someone first chair because their ole grandpappy donated enough for a theater to bear his name or thinks the community isn't ready to see a gifted Black girl as first chair in a youth symphony."

"Can we not bring this up in front of Mom? Me quitting the violin after high school is still a sore subject for her."

"Is it really? She hasn't mentioned it in a while."

"Maybe not to you, but it comes up here and there. Just like me not pledging her sorority, or her not understanding why I'm at a crossroads with the promotion that was offered." Reese sighed and slumped a bit in the seat.

"Chareese, I know your mother and she means well. She's placed you on a stage for success. From the best grade schools, dance and music lessons that started at age two, oratorical contest that began at ten, and acceptance into an Ivy League institution. She is your biggest cheerleader even if you two don't always see eye to eye." He paused for a second as though he were checking the temperature in the cabin. "Enough about your mother, I want to know why you're hesitant to accept the promotion to art director." He looked across at her as he slowed down approaching a stop sign. "Ever since you were old enough to hold a needle and thread you've been dreaming up the next couture dress. The *Paris* internship, *Vogue* apprenticeship, having the hottest designers eat out of your hands. Is this not what you wanted, Chareese?"

"What I don't want is to be a token, Dad." She folded her arms. They had somewhat had this conversation already, so why was he asking again? Perhaps to change her mind and have his investment in an Ivy institution pay off. "Everyone is big on diversity right now, and that's great but not the reason I should be promoted. I deserve to be the art director, for the reasons you just mentioned plus many more. However, I wasn't a choice until diversity became a buzz word and a company initiative."

Reese turned her attention to her window. As they began to move again she noted how the scenery she knew as a child was no more. Soon, the inn would be the same unless she found a way to have a civil conversation with Duncan. The thought, easy. The task, hard. It was no longer possible to hold back the years, and if she hadn't forgiven herself, how would he forgive her? Still, she had to find a way to at least make him rethink his plans for the future of Hill House.

"Your view on this is admirable. However, I feel like you aren't telling me everything. I would buy this token excuse had I not seen you take opportunities in the past that were equity building."

"Something was…is missing, Dad. The way I used to imagine and create has changed. I don't think about clothes and shoes, setting a fashion trend, or making some model look hot for a cover anymore."

"Do you need to go back to school? Many young people change careers."

Reese vigorously shook her head as her father pulled into the dirt lot of the twin markets. He had influenced her educational path years ago when he talked her into Cornell instead of UPenn for undergrad studies in fashion marketing, and then advised her on obtaining an MBA. She didn't need more academics to fill the emptiness she felt, even if his early advice had been instrumental in her current success.

But she knew he wouldn't let her out of the car until he got an answer. She took a deep breath and tried to remain un-concerned about whether or not he would accept her rationale. "I touch fabric and wonder the possibilities. I pulled out my sewing machine and made pillows instead of a dress. I even registered to audit courses on space planning and the history of interiors. Those were the only classes that did not have transferable skills from my degree in fashion design."

She closed her eyes, waiting for her father to respond. He didn't, so she continued. "I'm bored at my job, somewhat unfulfilled. At first, I assigned it all to not getting a promotion. Except, once one was offered I still felt off. Like a part of me was missing something. And honestly I don't think I really understood until I saw Hill House yesterday. So much of me is strangely eager to follow in Grandma Constance's footsteps and explore this other side that wants to create something more."

"It's not strange." He gave her a quick once-over before he cut the wheel and pulled into an empty parking space. "You two may not have made amends, but you spent a lot of time there with her. She's the one who taught you how to sew. You helped her change over rooms." He released a hard sigh then turned his head up to the ceiling.

He reached across the seat and clasped Reese's hand. "I understand now. Perhaps you will have the chance to experiment with this new interest. I submitted an appeal to the rezone permit McNeal was granted. Hill House's fate isn't sealed yet."

Her spirit relaxed a bit in gaining her father's support over her career woes. Yet, there was something inside still wrestling with why he had been idle and allowed Hill House to become neglected and fall into the hands of someone else. She could no longer resist asking. She had been asked to subject herself to emotional warfare to get next to Duncan and convince him to sell the property back; she deserved to know how things got so bad.

"Dad, I don't want to sound disrespectful, but how did it happen? I guess what I mean is why didn't you know the inn was in trouble?"

"For a long time, I was upset that your grandmother wrote me out of ownership for the inn even though I agreed and understood why. It was my choice to forfeit my share of Hill House to start the Neurosurgery Center. My anger over being left out made me blind to your uncle's games. Don't get me wrong, he did his absolute best to keep me in the dark with forged documents and fake accountants."

His sigh seemed to shrink his stature as his shoulder slumped. "That's the power of his addiction," he whispered. "I need and want to help my brother. Only I can't even look at him now." A deep thought seemed to grab hold of his mind before he snapped out of it and pulled the keys from the ignition. "Come on. Let's forget about all of that for now and have some fun."

They hopped out of the truck, ducked inside the market, and began exploring the aisles. Her father used to tell her that this was his way of time travel. As a teenager she rolled her eyes, believing her dad to be the king of corny jokes. However, now as she walked alongside him—seeing a pair of eighteenth-century Chippendale chairs hold graphic novels featuring Baby Yoda, and literary classics piled high with a remote-control car on top—she visibly saw eras of time blended together.

For a while, they remained empty-handed. And that was fine because they became full off of catching each other up and sharing perspectives on various topics going on in the world. Her father's quest for peace of mind seemed to have been found.

An exhibit for antique radios gained his attention, and they split up to treasure hunt on their own. Reese roamed around aimlessly searching without a clue as to what she was looking for and ended up in a used bookstore. The smell of old books definitely made her think she would find an old copy of *The Three Musketeers* or *Beloved*, for her mother to add to her collection of books by famous Black authors. But then she saw vinyl records, comics, kids' books, and some serial romance novels.

Reese realized anything she imagined could be within the oversized shop—which was good. She began pulling books from the shelf and reading their back covers. She needed a pleasant distraction after the heart-to-heart with her father. She'd never known he lost ownership of the inn. Nor did she know her grandmother funded the development of his world-renowned surgery center. Her mother's comments about him losing Hill House for a second time made sense.

"You've got to be kidding me."

Duncan? Reese froze for a second. She was not prepared to hear or see the owner of that voice so soon after yesterday's encounter. She peeked around a stack of old encyclopedias and saw Duncan standing at the counter.

"It's not even in a plastic sleeve. I'll give you twenty."

She covered her mouth, attempting to hold in her laughter over his incredulous tone. She got the sense that Duncan really wanted whatever it was he was bargaining for, and it made her curious about what he had his mind set on. Given that he wasn't one for literary classics and used to spend free time dissecting the superhero universe, she had an idea of what was up for grabs.

Luck was on her side. She hadn't had an idea of how she planned to connect with him after a not-so-great ending yesterday. Now, she had a way. Eager to reconnect, Reese grabbed a random book off the shelf and went toward the register. She was grateful Duncan's back was to her. After the way he'd dismissed her yesterday she needed a few extra seconds to find the right words to speak to him.

"Is it Hulk or Dr. Strange," she blurted, then noted the way his body tensed once he realized she was the voice behind him. She had never forgotten that many of the villains and heroes she knew were introduced to her by Duncan. It was one of the main reasons she stayed away from movies featuring Marvel characters. "My gut goes with Strange."

Duncan finally faced her and then leaned against the counter, sliding his hands into his joggers. "And why is that?" His face tight, way too serious.

Reese's heart started to race. She took a calming breath and told herself to focus on reconnecting and not his handsome face. The man put every male cover model she'd selected over the years to shame. "Because he was your favorite." Her sheepish reply seemed to soften his expression.

"Still is." He watched her for a second as she inched closer to the register, then he turned and handed the guy some cash. "And this kid is trying to milk me for it," Duncan chuckled.

"Am not, Mr. McNeal," the clerk snickered. "I'm the one who made sure we put it to the side for you."

"Hmmm, sure." Duncan extended his arm and took the book Reese was holding. "Add this too." He scanned the cover of the book before placing it on the counter. "Since when do you read horror stories?" His brow arched as he questioned her.

She didn't. It was a device to make it look like she wasn't trying to be all up in his business. *For appearances' sake* is what her mother would've said. "I needed something a little stronger than Harry, Hermione, and Ron."

"You're going to sleep with the light on tonight," he teased while collecting his change and shopping bag. "Appreciate you, Jake. I'll catch you next time."

Duncan faced Reese, then gestured for her to lead them out and followed without a word. Reese hoped his guard was down, given how casual he was today. Last time he had been all business in his suit with the media waiting to interview him.

"Don't forget to check out Loc's stand, Mr. NcNeal. I heard they came across some good books at an estate sale," the boy called as they exited the store.

"On my way there now," Duncan replied over his shoulder. "Thanks again."

"Mind if I tag along?" Her question seemed to have landed on deaf ears since there was no response. She took his silence as a hint and split to go in the opposite direction.

"Reese." His deep voice stopped her steps. "I didn't say no. Besides, aren't you forgetting something?"

She turned to see him a few inches away, holding the book in his hand. She went to him and took it. A giggle escaped her as she finally read the title. "You think I'll need the light on after reading *Interview with the Vampire*? We saw the movie when I was what—"

"Fifteen," they said together.

Their eyes met. It was one of the many times they had taken advantage of the summer movie fest and planned in secret to meet at the theater among all their friends. They would blend in for a little while and then slide into a movie together, share popcorn, and hold hands. The darkness concealed their otherwise public display of affection.

Not all of the history between them was bad. She had many happy memories that included him. They had simply been suppressed because it hurt to know there was someone in the world she had shared so many good times with, but couldn't be with.

She slid the book from his hand and cradled it in her arm. "Can we pretend that yesterday…and the last few years didn't happen?" She knew she was asking a lot. The look he gave would've killed under supernatural circumstances. However, all she wanted was for it to not be so hard between them. "At least while I walk with you to go check out this comic book."

* * *

Pretend like she never hurt him? He had not expected such a selfishly loaded question. And while he should have said no, a part of him wanted to be by her. The walk to the other vendor would be easier if they acted like what happened never did.

Duncan nodded and then watched a smile brighten her face. It almost touched his heart. The way it used to when they spent time together during the summer months.

"This way." He began walking in the opposite direction. Within seconds she was at his side. He dared not count the many times he'd longed for this.

"So...what book are you looking for?"

"It's not just one book. I'm looking for a few. Doubt I'll find anything. Although, sometimes I get lucky." He winked at her and didn't miss the way her cheeks became flushed. Did he still have that effect on her? She always got so shy around him. Especially after he got muscles and she filled out her bikinis.

There were so many questions he wanted to ask; like, How was life in the fashion world? Did she think of him the way he had thought of her? Is the life she got the one she dreamed?...Instead, he chose silence. The more he considered uncovering the ten years between them, the less inclined he was to hear her answers. While they had both grown up and seemingly led accomplished lives, Duncan knew he was not in the head space to listen, smile, or congratulate her on anything beyond a professional accomplishment.

Duncan continued leading them through the crowd, and after a few minutes of vigorous walking, they entered the shop. Unlike the last booth, this one was dedicated to comics. It had been a place Duncan frequented since middle school. The stories he'd read here gave him hope. They made him believe he could one day change his community for the better. Just like the heroes in the pages he read that gave their all to defend mankind.

"'Sup, Dunc!" Rahmel, one of the nerdiest comic gurus he knew, greeted him. "Dad's not here today, but he told me you were dropping—" The boy leaned to the side and looked around Duncan. A geeky smile stretched across his face. "You've never brought a girl here."

"Mind ya biz, Rahmel," Duncan chuckled, then looked over his shoulder at Reese. She was beautiful, spinning around in complete awe of the collection. It reminded him of when he took her to places on his side of town, like the old fishing hole or BBQ stand, as she discovered them for the first time. "Reese," he called, smiling when she looked at him, "this is Rahmel Lochlan. He and his father own this shop."

"Wow," she said, breathless. She then moved closer and extended her hand to shake the boy's. "Nice to meet you. This place is awesome."

"Thanks," Rahmel gloated. Duncan noted how the kid pushed his glasses up on the bridge of his nose and continued smiling at Reese. "Are you into comics too?"

"Not really," she confessed. "Everything I know I learned from him." She pointed at Duncan. He couldn't deny the pride swelling inside from knowing that he still held that special place. "Although, I do admire their costumes."

Duncan's hand covered his eyes. She hadn't stopped calling heroes' clothes costumes. "Reese, I've told you they wear uniforms not costumes."

She giggled, then tried pulling his hand down from his face. "Did I embarrass you?" She mocked him, laughing, then yanked his hand so hard that when it came down she bumped into his chest.

He wrapped his arm at her waist to prevent her from flying back. So many thoughts and emotions rushed over his body, confusing his mind. He was never supposed to be this conflicted over seeing her again. Life, and the hurt he had experienced, told him to hate her. Only, he couldn't.

"No"—he finally found his voice—"you're not embarrassing

me." However, looking into her big, brown eyes challenged his heart.

"Actually." Rahmel's voice pulled Duncan's mind from a path that could reminisce on the times they shared. This wasn't the time to forget those invisible lines that were revealed ten summers ago. He removed his arm from around Reese and faced the boy. Rahmel cleared his throat. "Suit or uniform...and sometimes *costume* is correct. We do have some here. Would you like to see them?"

Reese's eyes lit up. She clapped her hands, bouncing up and down like a kid entering a candy store, and followed Rahmel. They went into a part of the store that was off-limits to shoppers. The excess inventory should have been on display. However, space was limited and theft was easy in the flea market.

The tall, nerdy boy pulled at some sheets and uncovered a wardrobe of character suits. Reese rushed to them. Duncan had seen them already. They were used in the business pitch given by the boy and his father when they came to Duncan for help in obtaining retail space downtown. So far, they had lost three bids. However, Duncan was determined to help them. He knew a shop like this downtown near the youth village could be an inspiring haven for other kids, much like it had been for him.

"They dyed and painted the cotton to give it texture. That's why it looks like leather." She glanced up from the clothes at Rahmel and continued rambling on about sewing techniques. "Why are these back here? You should have them on display. Do you need help creating one?"

Duncan had fought it the last half hour or so, but now it was easy to pretend that none of the bad had happened. The old Reese was here with him, offering to help someone who needed it. Much like she had helped him when it came to learning social niceties to better fit in with other elite kids—with the exception of Gavin, as they had been friends since age five after meeting each other in Sunday school. The lessons she gave had actually prepared him for college life in the Ivy League.

The shock mixed with excitement written on Rahmel's face caused Duncan to burst into laughter. "You know how to make fashion displays?" Rahmel asked.

"I do!" Her enthusiasm seemed to fade a little. "It's one part of my job I still like."

The comment made Duncan wonder what she meant.

"We don't really have the space to display here. Hopefully soon." Rahmel gestured to him. "My dad is working with Duncan to get us in a space downtown. I'm sure we could use your help once we're in."

Duncan avoided her penetrating stare. He cared not to answer questions on his motivations because it was simple and mirrored the way he had been raised: Leave the world better than how he found it. And that meant giving small businesses in his local community a chance. Besides, she'd be gone once the Lochlans finally opened downtown.

"That's sweet of you, Duncan." Reese gave him a small smile, then turned back to the wardrobe. "I guess *suit* is a more appropriate name than *costumes* for these garments." She stuck her tongue out at Duncan, then winked at Rahmel. "Are these from the movies?"

"Some," Rahmel answered as he peeked over the wall they were behind. "I'll be back. There are customers out front."

Duncan watched as Rahmel left and Reese continued her examination of each piece of clothing that had been uncovered.

"Did you go see the movies?" Reese asked as she wrapped a crimson cape around her shoulder and began tying it at the neck. He nodded and started peeking inside boxes that were scattered across the ground. "Alone?" He paused what he was doing and concentrated on her face. It contained no humor, no shame. And she had no right to probe personal aspects of his life. "I mean, I'm just asking. It's an innocent question, Duncan. You used to like company at the movies."

Had he read too much into the questions? Perhaps, but he would never really know. Maybe she had thought about him the way he thought about her. It wasn't an all-the-time thing, but here and there she crossed his mind and he wondered what bastard got to hold her.

He felt the smirk play on his lips. He couldn't help the satisfaction he got in discovering a part of her wanted to know who had occupied his time. "Who goes to the movies by themselves, Reese?"

Her teeth clipped her bottom lip as she pushed a stray hair behind her ear. "I did…or I just didn't go at all. There were always fashion displays and shows to attend. Besides, everything eventually comes to TV." She snatched off the cape and scurried from the room.

It wasn't his fault. He wouldn't apologize for living without her. Still, he took off behind her. There were already more than enough regrets between them to last a lifetime. He didn't need to add any more.

"Reese," he called, seeing her dart out of the comic shop. "Chareese," he shouted over the crowd, then sprinted to catch her. He grabbed her by the arm, and she stopped. "What happened back there?"

She looked off. "Nothing. I—"

"Chareese." Her father's deep, authoritative voice made them both tense.

Duncan dropped his hand from her arm when he saw her father a few feet away. Disdain for him was written across the man's face and Duncan knew it was still because of the girl standing next to him. The acquisition of Hill House simply gave Kent Devlin a reason to fester in his hate of the McNeals.

"What were you about to say?" Duncan asked, ignoring the way her father motioned for her to come to him.

"Nothing," she whispered, then walked to her father and didn't look back.

Bitterness of all those nights ago rooted deeper within him. The same way she walked away now was how she did back then. She would always place her family and their status above all else, and he would never compete with it again. "So much for pretending."

Her steps faltered. She glanced over her shoulder, but it was too late. That cold, hard edge that had thawed today had begun retracing his heart.

Eleven

DUNCAN PUSHED THROUGH the side door of his parents' house and into the laundry room. "Am I late?"

"You would've been," his mom responded as she rounded the corner wiping a spoon on her apron. "But your father and Destiny aren't here." Her frown turned into a smile before she pulled him into a warm hug.

"Smells good." He rubbed his stomach before removing his suit coat. "Where are they? You know I don't like my food being held up."

She laughed, "I know, baby. Your father won't make it tonight, he had to stay behind at the restaurant for some late deliveries, and Destiny's at practice for the ball. She should be here soon."

"Speaking of the ball, how's that going? Does Destiny need anything?" He hesitated in asking his next question as he followed her to the kitchen. His mother wanted him to forgive and forget. Yet, he found that impossible considering his most recent encounter with Kent Devlin. Four days had passed since seeing him and Reese, and he was still shaking off the way the man redrew boundaries. "Are they treating her okay?"

"Duncan." His mother lifted the top of a pot, shaking her head as she stirred okra stewed with tomatoes. "They are not all bad. I know you saw and heard things back then that no child should have, but not everything is how it appears. You have to move on. Don't let the past dictate your future and ruin things you are destined to have."

Had she read the book of his life? He had yet to tell her how Reese kept inconveniently popping up around town, strumming the pain of his heart. The past had not ruined him. It had given him lessons that made him persevere and helped him realize people were selfishly motivated. Hence the most recent shenanigans of the Devlins to interfere with his rezoning permit.

He shrugged and slumped down onto a stool at the kitchen island. He was still licking old wounds of an ill-fated love. Therefore, he wasn't ready to talk about the one thing—person rather—who had him second-guessing everything. Somehow Reese slid past his defenses days ago in the flea market and gave him a glimpse of the friendship that should've been allowed to exist. She'd even made him wonder if something could be found between them after all these years.

"I thought we were supposed to learn from the past. My previous experiences won't allow me to trust certain people, like Dr. Kent Devlin. The man filed an appeal with the zoning review committee all because they are angry I own Hill House." He leaned into the counter. "Would he do the same if it were anyone else?"

Pearl sighed, shaking her head. "Who knows, Duncan. Point is that people fight back for the things they love. I have my own opinions of Kent, but I cannot sit up here and tell you he didn't care about that place 'cause it would be a lie."

"He loves legacy, Mama." It was Duncan's turn to sigh. He wished his mom understood the way he felt about the acquisition. "And I want to make a difference in this community. To whom much is given, much is required. Isn't that what you've always taught me?"

She nodded without offering a verbal reply. She might not want to admit it even though she knew he was right.

"It may not matter what I want to give back to the kids here anyway. Mayor Fleming has remained neutral, but you know they're all friends…have been for years. And if we judge on past behavior, then I'm not certain whose side she will take should it come to that."

"The right side," Pearl said, giving him a pointed look. "You think you've gotten this far in life because you've been on the wrong side of things? I thought I taught you better than that."

"You—"

"I'm home." Destiny's high-spirited voice flowed into the kitchen. "Mom, where are you?"

"Cookin'."

Duncan and his mother eyed each other. Destiny rarely expressed excitement unless it had to do with books, school, or her dreams of becoming a federal judge. The last time she had this much enthusiasm was earlier this year when she came from the mailbox waving her acceptance letter to Yale.

Destiny skipped into the kitchen, her smile contagious. "Smells good, Ma. What are you cooking?"

"Your brother's favorite." Pearl winked at Duncan. "Braised short rib, stewed okra with tomatoes, garlic mashed potatoes, and corn cakes."

Duncan licked his lips as he rose up from the stool. "I'm ready to eat now. We've been waiting on you."

"Not yet. There's someone here from the ball I want Mom to meet." Pearl's wide eyes revealed her shock as Duncan managed to contain his. "Please, Mom."

His mother began mumbling under her breath as she turned down the burners on the oven. "Why didn't you call? I came straight from the restaurant and started cookin'. I'm not dressed to be meeting people, Destiny." She removed her apron, balled it up, and tossed it on the counter before Destiny grabbed her hand and pulled her.

Curiosity filled Duncan, so he decided to follow them. This was uncharted territory with his sister, and he still hadn't had the conversation with her about frenemies since witnessing the camaraderie between her and the youngest Devlin. The age gap between him and his sister had left her oblivious to many of the misdeeds his family had suffered from people in positions of power.

Things had not changed until he became an inspiration to many by breaking the generational curse and becoming the first in his family to go to college, and then coming back to reinvest in the local economy. The launch of his parents' restaurant, creating a national brand for the sweet shop, and repurposing distressed businesses in the warehouse district had shown everyone his business acumen. Therefore, he was wary of people latching on to his family for the wrong reasons.

"Oh my goodness, Chareese!" His mother's words stilled his stride. The hallway seemed to close in around him as he stood there, uncertain about joining them in the front room. "It's so good to see you."

"You know Chareese, Mom?" Destiny's question was oddly annoying.

Duncan huffed. He knew his sister was too young to remember everything that had happened, since she was eleven years younger. But he'd given her bits and pieces over the years so her complete ignorance was inexcusable.

Asking their mom if she knew Chareese Devlin was damn

near insulting. His mother had kept a watchful eye on Reese every summer when she came to the Shores and ran around her grandmother's bed and breakfast like a queen bee. Too bad Pearl's kindness had only been met with contempt once Constance found out the meals being served at Hill House were also being cooked and sold as hot plates out of his parents' kitchen.

"I've known Chareese since she was a little girl. She and your brother were uh...they used to play while I worked at her grandmother's bed and breakfast."

"That was a long time ago." Duncan stepped into the family room. He folded his arms and then leaned against the wall.

Her beauty disarmed him just as it always had. Their eyes locked and he wished he could read her thoughts. He would never pretend again, so was she here to apologize for how she had walked away at the flea market or make more demands upon him? Did she miss him like she'd confessed, or was this about his sister? Honestly, he was afraid to ask.

If this was about the inn, they were on their way to becoming enemies. Her confession had been a good song, but not one he could listen to, because it would lead them to the same place that it had all those years ago—nowhere. And if this visit had to do with his sister, then he'd have to intervene. He'd done too much to ensure Destiny was nothing like the privileged elitist woman before him.

"It was," Reese affirmed under a hooded gaze. "I miss those times."

Memories burned in the corner of his mind and then pulled the strings of his heart as he stared at her. Their childhood friendship had been cute, tolerable as he had learned. But then teenage years rolled in, changing and shaping them into young adults. He'd tried to deny the way he felt about Reese as she blossomed into a woman. They were friends and he didn't want to make things awkward. Only, she'd felt the same until her father reminded her of why she wasn't supposed to.

"So what brings you here? I—"

"Ehem." Destiny cleared her throat and squinted her eyes at Duncan. "This is my guest, Dunc." She went next to Reese and smiled bigger than a kid in the candy store. "Chareese is here to help me. She was assigned to mentor me for the presentation and help build my profile. She's already introduced me to her friend and fellow deb Peyton Daniels, who is a corporate attorney and daughter of the chief justice for the Florida Supreme Court. I'm going to meet him later this week!" Destiny almost squealed as she did a little happy dance in the center of the room.

Duncan couldn't believe the good news Destiny was sharing. He'd spent his entire adult life making sure she attended the best schools and joined the right groups to make the sort of connection Reese had given her in one day. There were benefits to being born with a silver spoon that hard work couldn't replace. His sister had just witnessed the power of networks. And while he was grateful she had this opportunity, he still had questions.

"Mentor you for the ball? I thought you just had to dress up and get announced into society while we eat from five-hundred-dollar plates."

Reese snickered. "Oh boy. You really do make it sound simple."

"Right, I'd love to see him try the belle's bow." His sister cackled with Reese, and for some odd reason he was a little envious.

"Belle's bow," his mother asked. "What on God's green Earth is that?"

"You'll see soon enough, Mom. That's why Chareese is here.

We're going to practice my curtsy. Do you mind if we go out on the lanai for a while?"

"Aren't you hungry, don't you want to eat first? Chareese, you're welcome to join us."

Duncan watched Reese go stiff as a board. He knew the invitation was awkward, considering their misadventure on Saturday. Hell, it might even get her disowned. However, if she was willing to be here, he wouldn't deny giving his sister the best chance at entering a world he'd worked hard for her to be a part of. Irony would never be lost on Reese being the one that helped ostracize him for being too close to her guarded world.

"Thank you for helping my sister." Duncan managed to relax a bit after seeing Destiny so vibrant and capable of building relationships with people who could set her up for future success.

"Of course, Destiny is an amazing girl with big dreams. There is no doubt they will come true. I mean look at you." She gestured at Duncan. "You've always loved architecture and rebuilding things. Now you do it for a living."

A part of his heart smoothed over the crack Reese had put in it as he weighed her words. She was standing in his family's home as if it were her turn to gain his approval. If she stayed for dinner, her presence might tear down his defenses and make him incapable of pretending the laws of attraction had no effects on him.

Duncan cleared his throat. "My mom has cooked up a mean meal. I doubt you get any of this Southern cooking in the Big Apple. You should have dinner with us." Dammit, it was too late, the universe had won.

Twelve

REESE MOANED, SAVORING her last bite of stewed okra piled on top of the corn cake. "Oh my goodness, Miss Pearl, I've not had anything this delicious in a long time." The buttery crunch mixed with sweet yet spicy tomatoes in the okra made her want to hum.

Only she couldn't. Her mother had raised her to have impeccable table manners...and Duncan was staring. Reese had yet to determine if the way he looked at her was good or bad. She hoped good since that would make it easier for her to try engaging him again about Hill House. More than that, she didn't want Duncan to hate her anymore. She missed her friend. They used to talk about anything and share everything.

She wished they could turn the hands of time back and do it all over again. If she'd known that her heart would still feel tied to his after all these years, she would've fought harder to make her parents accept him. Instead she wasted years dating men that were too tall, too short, boring, unaccomplished, overzealous—not Duncan. What she had searched for in every other man could never be found because it was always in the Shores.

Her body temp spiked as their gazes locked across the table. Had he read her thoughts or heard the secrets her heart whispered to his? In this moment she didn't care. He was devastatingly handsome, and she wanted him to want her again.

Destiny's giggle forced them both to look away. "I think Chareese has the Itis." She giggled again. "It's Dunc's fault you had to eat so much. Mom thinks she has to cook all his favorite things the night he comes over for dinner."

"A man's gotta eat. Thanks, Ma." Duncan leaned over to his mother and kissed her cheek before he stood and began clearing his plate from the table. "I only get one meal like this a week, little sis. You get them every day."

Miss Pearl swiped at her son, blushing from his praise. Their relationship seemed to be loving, kind…easy. Nothing like the one she had with her mother.

"You do look full, Reese." His polite smile didn't reach his eyes. "But aren't you glad you got a taste?"

He turned away from the table and started walking in the direction of the kitchen. His sexy ass taunted her sensibilities and sent her mind straight to the gutter. She couldn't help wondering what he would taste like, as her eyes traveled his tall, muscular build.

"Chareese, can we practice tomorrow? I'm stuffed and feel like I weigh a ton. No way will I bow"—Destiny threw her hand up in air quotes—"'like a decent young lady.'"

The teenager imitating Mrs. Russell made her laugh while providing a much-needed distraction for her mind, which was being lured down a dark tunnel full of indecent things she wanted to do with Duncan. Time had not weakened her attraction to him. In fact, it seemed enhanced by the fact that they were no longer two innocents contemplating their first kiss.

Her mind floated back to their summer before the last, when Duncan was preparing for his senior year in high school.

She was sixteen and done pretending that she only wanted to be his friend. Except, her parents wouldn't allow her to date, and Duncan was busy completing college applications, doing community service, and avoiding her. Until one night at the drive-in movie he pulled her to the side and confessed his heart. He'd been distant for fear that his feelings for her may scare her away and ruin their friendship.

Reese had never been so happy and sad at the same time. Their years in the friend zone had taken precious time away from them being what they had always wanted to be to each other. And yet, they knew long distance would be hard, so they promised to wait for each other until she graduated from high school, before kissing under the moonlight.

Reese came back to the now, recognizing the taboo still surrounding them. She had to ask herself if this unnatural attraction to Duncan was part of her wanting to rebel against the elitist establishment. She quickly searched herself. The short answer was no. She didn't care if her parents wouldn't approve of him or the success he'd found, because she no longer needed them to travel along life's roads. And she was tired of being trapped in a world that dictated who she was supposed to be. Perhaps this too was at the source of why the art director position was no longer appealing.

"No problem, Destiny. I should be getting home. I've been gone all day." She took a deep breath as they all began to get up from the table. She was done following her parents' rules. "Where's Duncan? I'd like to tell him goodbye before I leave."

* * *

Dusk cluttered the sky as Duncan stood on his parents' lanai, listening to the world go still. A few moments ago, he thought he might reveal the secrets of his soul. The way Reese looked at him across the table reminded him of the time he chased his first kiss from her. Those innocent brown eyes had stared into his, stirring the chaos that he hoped would one day fade.

"Nice night." Her sultry voice jumpstarted the rhythm of his heart. "Your mom and sister told me you would be out here. If you want me to leave, I will."

He stopped observing the flickering little lights floating within the cattails by the shoreline of the pond and glanced at her for a second before turning back. "I always wanted to catch a firefly."

"Same." She came to his side. The scent of jasmine tickled his nose, then blended into something sweet.

"My parents wouldn't let me." His hands slid into his pockets, masking the nervous energy he felt racing through his body from being so close to Reese. "My father said it wasn't right to trap a living thing in a jar and watch it lose its freedom."

"Mine too. He said the old people in the Shores used to tell him that when he was young. Unfortunately, his worldly advice didn't always translate well to his parenting style." She blew a long, hard breath. "I'm sorry, Duncan."

He swallowed, then took the steps that led off the lanai and began walking toward the pond. The way things went down between them had haunted him, compelling him to overachieve. He'd proven he wasn't supposed to be a trapped firefly in the Devlins' jar. But—he paused because he couldn't keep running from her, never fully acknowledging the pain she caused. It would ruin him.

He pivoted, noticing she had followed him off the lanai. His eyes searched hers as if they were decoding the truths of her soul. "For what?" His question was point-blank and full of raw emotion that he tried but failed to hide.

"You were right the other day." She took a deep breath. "I had no business questioning your motivations or demanding you do something simply to please me…or my family. It was also selfish of me to ask you to pretend."

An awkward silence rested between them for longer than a few minutes. His reasons for walking away from her had little to do with the way she approached him at Hill House and everything to do with that summer ten years ago. Yet, it was possible that her perspective of what had happened back then was different than his. Maybe she saw no wrong since they were young and caught up in teen love. Only, he would never forget.

The hell of that night started when Reese called him. Her panicked voice came through the phone out of breath, begging him to meet at the old lighthouse. He'd dropped everything and left to find her.

She'd come to him a mess of tears, explaining that her parents had forced her to attend a pre-ball function with Drexel Collins, a well-to-do boy who had been chosen as Reese's escort for the Lakeside Debutante Ball. The boy took liberties, demanding more of her affection, and when he didn't get it, he groped her.

Drexel was so bold in his antics to make Reese more than the girl he was escorting, that he followed her to the lighthouse and proceeded to accuse her of being a tease, not knowing Duncan was there to defend her honor. The night became uglier when the boy realized Duncan meant something to the girl he wanted.

When Duncan refused to engage in the rich boy's pissing contest, Drexel spat ugly, false rumors about Reese before he walked into Duncan's face and tried to punch him. The only reason they had not ended up tussling in the grass was because her parents showed up and hauled her away. The Devlins later visited his house and issued the ultimatum that had become the chasm between them for ten long years.

"I don't want you to hate me anymore, Duncan." She exhaled hard, then stared off into the distance, forcing his mind to return from the hurt of all those nights ago. He wasn't ready to linger in the darkest part of his memory from that evening featuring her grandmother in his family's home.

The bitterness he'd held on to for so long broke away from his heart. He reached over and gently cupped her cheek to make her face him. Chareese Devlin was a magnet that drew him in, and he wasn't sure if he'd ever pull away again if he really let his guard down. "I don't hate you, Reese. I've tried, but I can't."

Her eyes closed. "Then why do you act like it?"

He shrugged. "It's easier," he said gruffly.

"Than what, being nice to me?"

"Than missing you. We were friends before anything else." His body tensed as though he was bracing for the pain of losing her all over again. "You took it all away."

She claimed the space between them until there was no more. In her eyes he saw everything he ever wanted, and then he felt it. Her lips pressed to his demanding affection. His will was being tested and he was done doing battle.

He stopped resisting what he'd been denied and leaned in, accepting her kiss. An unnatural heat shot up his spine, spread across his body, and made his heart race as her arms wrapped around his neck. His tongue tested, and then tasted her. She was sweet...addicting, he thought, as he pulled her in, deepening the kiss.

"I...I..." She was breathless. Her eyes remained closed. "Only in my dreams had I kissed you like this."

It was true for him too. Chareese Devlin had always been the girl for him. However, he wasn't about to say it or anything that could jinx them this time around.

Thirteen

REESE ROLLED TO her side, pulling the covers along. She blinked once and met the sunrays peeking through the sheer curtain panels, then closed her eyes again before pinching herself. The sting from her fingernails made her sit up in bed. Last night had really happened.

Her fingers pressed to her lips, which were begging to relive the moment Duncan's kiss set her soul on fire. When she had gone outside to say good night, her goal had been to make amends for their less fortunate run-ins the summer had so far produced, but there was no escaping the chemistry burning between them. The flame they had kindled all those years ago had been yearning for attention, and they'd both finally given in to what they most desired.

She'd spent years trying to fill a void and didn't understand why until last night. So long to treading in shallow waters. She'd dived headfirst into the deep end and wasn't sure if she wanted to come back up.

"Get up, Reese." Alex burst into her room and plopped her bottom on the bed. "You disappeared after practice last night then snuck in the house and went straight to your room. What's that all about? Scared I'm not able to handle you mentoring Destiny?"

Alex's sarcasm killed any regrets Reese may have had over spending time with Destiny to prepare her for the ball. Additionally, Reese wasn't in the mood for the early morning drama her sister came prepared to dish. The girl was definitely Genevieve's child, barging inside a room and attempting to make conversation after giving Reese the cold shoulder for a little over a week. It wasn't her fault the ball committee had paired her with Destiny.

"My door was closed, Alex. You're supposed to knock." Reese fell back into the pillows, blowing out a hard breath. She had to deny the less-than-innocent actions her fingers were eager to explore between her legs as she wondered what it would be like to wake up beside the sexy Mr. McNeal. "And why wouldn't you be able to handle me helping Destiny? If you had a problem with it, you should've said something last week when we were paired."

"I don't care about you being with her," she snapped. "I have Mom, and like you, I've trained for this moment my whole life. I'm so unbothered by you engaging in charity," she finished in her mean-girl tone.

Reese looked over to see Alex picking at her nails as she stared at the ceiling. That attitude would cost her one day. "Destiny isn't charity, Alex. Why would you say that?"

"She's not like us, Reese."

"Stop. You sound like Mom…and Dad." She sighed, still in disbelief over her family's determination to exist within a caste system in the Shores. She wondered when they would learn that barriers formed around social stratification were meant to be broken. Duncan's ability to acquire their family's prized possession and the fact that so many people admired him and invited his sister to the debutante ball poked holes in their problematic views.

If there was ever a time to call Alex out on her jealousy it was now. Destiny was the kindest, most pleasant, beautiful girl she had met at the ball rehearsals. Reese was happy to help and excited to give back in a way that uplifted another young woman. Sadly, she much preferred to be Destiny's mentor than her own sister's.

She would never speak those words out loud. However, she did need to defuse the teen girl drama unfolding. Only, it involved telling Alex that working with Destiny was a way to get close to Duncan. Reese didn't have the heart to utter something she didn't believe. Destiny was her cover, but not for reasons that would have made Alex less jealous. In fact, her sister's mean-girl spirit whispered sabotage. No way would she confess that mentoring Destiny gave her access to rediscover what she and Duncan had lost.

"Destiny deserves a chance to debut properly too, Alex."

Alex rolled to her belly and looked up at Reese with a frown. "Are you kidding me? Mom said that Destiny's mother and grandmother worked as maids for Grandma Constance well before they got that restaurant. She's the first in that family to be invited to the ball, and everyone knows the McNeals are locals. Oh, and yeah, she's using a cousin as her escort. The boy has a different last name, but he has two left feet. Her waltz will be hard."

Reese didn't cower at her sister's sinister smirk. Not having the right escort for the Lakeside Debutante Ball was like Florida not having sunshine. There were balls that preferred debutantes use male relatives. Not this one. Society wanted to see credentials, networks, and social status. Parents wanted to brag about them. In the end, an escort revealed much about a family's connectedness.

Cringey, but it was how things had been for decades and there had been no precedents for change, despite how much Reese had tried to break away from tradition when she debuted. She froze, attempting to stop her thoughts from drifting back in time. But she couldn't catch them. *"No, Chareese."* Her mother's *pointed stare made her nervous, but she kept her head held high. "Young men like Duncan McNeal are only meant to be friends. Remember that and don't ask me again. He isn't suitable for your debut into good society. No one will take it serious."*

"Why?" Reese shouted. *"Duncan is kind, super smart, and he—"*

"Cannot. Escort. You. For the last time." Her mother's stern words made her recoil. "Your grandmother warned that the two of you were spending too much time together during our summers. I let it slide because…" Her mother's breath hitched and then she began to pace. "How did I not see this? Oh my God. You are not to see him again this summer. Do you understand me?"

Reese shook her head. "You can't tell me that. He's my friend."

"Are you sure he isn't more?" Her mother's icy tone chilled her to the bone. "And don't let your father find out."

"Find out what," Kent asked as he entered their bedroom.

Neither Reese nor her mother responded. They stood staring each other down, animosity swirling in the room making it difficult to breathe. Her father asked again, and this time her mother responded without breaking eye contact.

"Chareese has asked that Duncan McNeal be her escort for the debutante ball."

"Absolutely not." Her father came to stand between Reese and her mom. "You and that boy have spent too much time around each other." He turned and pointed at her mother. "This is your fault, Genevieve."

"It's no one's fault. I should be allowed to walk out with whomever

I choose. A debutante ball is meant to celebrate a young lady entering society. I've done everything worthy enough to be presented. The guy who escorts me does not define me or my accomplishments." She palmed the tears from her cheeks.

"The McNeals do not carry enough prominence." Her father's hands clapped together. *"For Christ's sake he lives in East Town and his mother is a maid. You will debut with the young man your mother and grandmother have selected for you. Stop being so damn ungrateful."*

Reese released a sob. *"I am not ungrateful. I deserve a choice, and I chose not to walk with Drex."*

"Then you have chosen to pay your college tuition, car insurance, and all those other fancy things you have that Duncan will never be able to afford…"

"I-It won't be hard." She took stuttering breaths, struggling to recover from the darkness of the past. That night had shaken her to the core. The madness began with a misogynist putting his hands on her before attempting to fight Duncan. After which her parents found her and took her back to the function she'd snuck away from to go be with Duncan. "I'll teach them to waltz."

"Make sure she knows her brother's money isn't hers, and it won't buy her a curtsy on presentation night. You've got a lot of work to do." Alex snickered as she sat up, rambling more on what she perceived as her fellow debutante's shortcomings.

Reese made mental notes to practice the waltz. Maybe even call in a favor to find Destiny a suitable escort. They were already planning to perfect her curtsy. The other frivolity Alex mentioned had nothing to do with meeting the ball's expectations.

It was all about her sister's snobbery. An attitude Quinn and Mrs. Russell had taken issue with. The very same one Reese often overlooked because they were siblings and Alex often felt that they were competing for favor with their parents.

"Did Mom and Dad send you in here?" Reese needed Alex to state her reasons for barging in so she could address them and her sister could leave. The longer Alex lingered, the more Reese feared she would say something she wouldn't be able to take back.

Her sister shrugged and slid off the bed. She moved until she was standing at the bay window with views of Lake Dora. "You know I wanted your room so I could have this view…they wouldn't let me though. Summer after summer this room remained empty like a shrine while our parents suffered their regrets over whatever it was you did."

Reese had done nothing but love someone her family deemed beneath them. It was clear they never told Alex the true reasons she had stayed away from the Shores for so long. Perhaps they feared Alex too would rebel. Although, if Reese had to bet money, it was because they didn't want to relive the disappointment of her choices and how it strained their relationships.

A few minutes passed before Reese sat upright in the bed again and watched her sister sit in the window seat. That same dejected expression she'd noticed upon Alex's face the day she'd showed the debs how to curtsy had returned. If Reese didn't know any better, she would think that life had been unkind to her sister. Only, it was the opposite. Alex got everything at everyone else's expense without consequence.

"I didn't do anything," Reese gritted through her teeth. She wanted to tear Alex's condescending nature to shreds. She fought hard to suppress the hurt and shame she'd felt acting as a bystander while her grandmother and father berated Duncan and his family in their own home before making Reese agree that he was a mistake. "I couldn't have cared less if they'd given you this room." She kicked the covers away, hopped out of bed, and started to the bathroom.

"Of course not. You don't care about anything with this family." Alex stood, glaring at her. "If you did you would've made some sort of progress with Duncan. Maybe try seeing him today. How hard is it to flirt? We lost Hill House! Dad is devastated and Mom is too embarrassed to show her face around town so she's declined RSVPs to annual outings."

Reese huffed, folding her arms. "Mom should reconsider her friends."

"That's messed up, Reese. And here I thought I was the selfish one." Alex stormed across the room to the door.

Her sister's young mind was clearly delusional on the ways of the world. "Do you really think smiling in a man's face gets you what you want? If so, you've got a lot to learn, little sister."

"Tell that to Destiny since she's who you're mentoring." Alex cut her eyes back, then opened the door and slammed it shut on her way out.

Not one bone in Reese's body had the urge to go after her. Like their mother, Alex had a gift for bringing out the worst in people. The memories she triggered of Reese arguing with her parents, being pulled away from the boy she'd loved, and then disregarding her heart were the very reasons why she had avoided the *I'm sorry for back then* conversation with Duncan last night.

Reese was sorry for what happened all those years ago. Yet she didn't see it as her fault. Like Duncan, she had been collateral damage of her family's so-called pride. Being trapped in her father's hold had suppressed her freedom to love whom she wanted. The possibility of Duncan not agreeing that she too was a victim of her family's ideals was too great, and right now she wanted them to focus on moving away from her mistakes in the past.

She shrugged off the exchange with her sister and headed to the bathroom. For a second she stared in the mirror. Yeah, she was lying to her family to avoid judgment. And maybe she should've declined being Destiny's mentor instead of using it as a way to gain proximity to Duncan. The method to her madness could easily produce another bout of heartache if she wasn't careful. Which was why Alex's reckless conviction that Reese did not care for the family was an insult.

The vibrating sounds of her mobile redirected her attention to the nightstand by the bed. She lifted the phone from the table and read Did you have sweet dreams?

Every ounce of irritation that her chat with Alex had provoked melted away. Her cheeks began hurting from how hard she smiled. Slowly, they deflated as she lowered to the bed. She now realized their kiss brought confusion.

Her and Duncan's lips meeting in his parents' backyard was never part of her plan to get past his defenses. In fact, she had intentionally nixed any notions of flirting or the use of her feminine charms for his attention. She just wanted a chance to get close enough for them to engage normally before trying to talk about Hill House.

Yet, it was clear that what they had once lost wanted to be found. A moment like the one they experienced last night subdued the past and quelled the aches of her heart.

I did. What about you? she texted back.

The palm of her hand covered her face. Her reply was so boring. She didn't know what to say. She definitely wasn't ready to talk about how wet her panties got from the way he held her last night as his body pressed against hers.

The phone vibrated again and she peeked between her fingers to the screen.

I'm going to remain a gentleman and keep those details to myself. Breakfast? If you haven't already eaten.

Remain a gentleman. He need not. Her mind had caught up to her body and she welcomed any unholy act that involved them doing what lovers do.

Can I meet you in an hour? Just waking up.

His response was an address. The man made her feel like a foolish, crush-struck teen. Not ideal, since her aim was to gain forgiveness and rediscover their friendship. Still, she couldn't help the excitement eclipsing her confusion over wanting him but needing to rescue Hill House. Without further delay she sprang into the bathroom. First, she would focus on getting past his defenses and preserve what was left of hers, since he had weakened them well over twenty-four hours ago.

Almost an hour later, Reese traveled at a turtle's pace, searching for the children's library that sat on the outskirts of downtown. Duncan's follow-up message had been clear in explaining that the restaurant was across from the library. However, everything she remembered was gone. The old redbrick building that she frequented for story time as a child had been stripped down to a tan color. The small park beside the library had been replaced with bistro tables and chairs, while many of the once shabby houses had been converted into posh shops. There was even a boutique hotel.

Uncertain if she had come to the right location, she prepared to make a U-turn, until she spotted Duncan's sleek black sports car. She quickly turned the wheel and pulled into a parking spot. She glanced around in awe of the yuppyish vibes she never thought would exist in the Shores, and then began making strides to the white cottage house with green shutters and a whimsical sign that read MAMA'S PLACE.

Reese inhaled the rose scent from the bushes at the front

steps while telling herself to keep it cool for the thousandth time. Once she felt like her head was on her shoulders, she pulled on the door to enter the restaurant. The aroma knocked her back to her childhood.

She recalled the times she'd worked in the kitchen of the inn pulling breakfast pastries from the oven. Reese thought she would never smell breakfast at her grandmother's again. This moment changed that. Maybe she wanted this scent to flood the halls of the old house again. How much had she taken for granted? She pondered Mrs. Willingham's words of being the one her grandmother believed capable of running the family business.

She had to find a way to preserve what her grandmother gave to the Shores so that a new generation of vacationers could have the Hill House experience. She had to get the bed and breakfast back in the Devlin name.

"Good morning, Chareese!" Destiny stood in front of her at a hostess stand with a bright smile. Reese returned the greeting as she admired the space that was the epitome of a *Southern Living* magazine cover.

"I didn't know you had a job. Your debutante application didn't have that listed." Reese had put her foot in her mouth again. Maybe the girl hadn't wanted anyone to know she was working. After all, all of the other participants were legacies and too caught up in their generational wealth to think of gaining an ounce of responsibility from holding a small summer job.

Destiny held her head up higher and maintained her smile. "Since this is my parents' restaurant, I don't really see it as a job. More about supporting my family and learning the business." Reese couldn't find the words. She was stuck between celebrating one of Duncan's dreams of having the family restaurant come true, and relief that she got lucky with Destiny's reply. She gained more respect for the girl and for Duncan. He had done everything he ever said he would do. "My brother is expecting you. Follow me."

As the two moved through the restaurant, it became apparent to Reese that Mama's Place was popular. There were young families, older citizens, and no racial divide. The diverse atmosphere reminded her of the cafés she frequented in the city.

The number of full tables really stood out when she saw some of her parents' friends. Their trip to where Duncan sat was interrupted with hugs from Mrs. Hightower and Mrs. Daniels, praising her for the style seminar she did with the debutantes. Friendly hellos came from just about everyone before she got wrapped up in a conversation with the town historian, who also happened to be her old friend Ava Hamilton's father.

"Everyone's happy to see you. Dunc mentioned that you hadn't been here in like ten years." Destiny extended her arm, showing her to Duncan's table, which was perfectly situated beside a window.

He liked windows. When they were younger, she joined him on bike rides where he would explain how windows defined the style of the houses they passed. It was the design element that made him fall in love with architecture.

Reese nodded. "Yeah, it's been a while."

Duncan stood as they approached, displaying his chivalry as he pulled a chair out for her. Her heart swelled and then became light, as though it were floating at the sight of the dark king. His thoughtful actions revealed how long she'd been deprived. Only, she found it hard to enjoy the moment because she'd just now realized they would become the subject of town gossip, so she bottled up her happiness.

"Still worried about what everyone thinks?" His deep voice gained her attention, but it was the sarcasm that severed her thoughts.

"No," she lied. "Why would you say that?" She stiffened in her chair, fidgeting a little before reaching for a glass of water.

Duncan rested back in his chair, studying her. It reminded Reese of the first time she came across *The Harp* by Augusta Savage. Hours had come and gone as she'd sat decoding how Savage reinterpreted the musical instrument to feature African American faces as if they were singing James Weldon Johnson's "Lift Every Voice and Sing."

Their eyes finally met. "Then why did you clam up? If you prefer, we can go."

"I didn't clam up." She looked around, noticing that all eyes were still on them. "I just know how things are."

He chuckled. "Small-town gossip. You forget I've lived here all my life. Including the months when all of you were gone." He then leaned forward with a full smile upon his handsome face. "Come closer," he whispered, and she tilted into the table. He reached across, took her hand, and kissed it. "Now they really have something to talk about. Who knows, before noon, word on the street may be that I sat across from you with hungry eyes and then kissed you in the middle of the restaurant."

Duncan winked and then sat upright in his chair, while she squirmed in hers. It wasn't fair that he could do this to her—make her want him in a matter of days when she hadn't seen him in years. More than that, she hated that he made her miss—no, regret—the years they were apart. Regardless of what would be said about them being here today, she knew her mother would dismiss the rumor mill and accept Reese's actions as duty to the family's best interest.

But it wasn't fair. She shouldn't have needed a cover to avoid criticisms. Not when she was a grown woman fully aware that she felt something for the man sitting across from her. Something that she believed wanted another chance. Allegiance to her family had only brought her pain. She had to listen to her heart this time. She wasn't here to manipulate him into selling Hill House back. She came because she wanted them to find each other, again. Unfortunately, just like with her sister, she still couldn't tell her mother the truth.

A nervous laugh escaped her. She quickly reached for the menu to shield herself. Her jumbled mind blurred the words. She had no idea whether she was going or coming.

"You can't hide from me, Reese," said the sly fox to the little hen.

And she didn't want to. She glanced over her menu to see him twist his lips in a panty-teasing sort of way that made her so hot she almost used the menu to fan herself. She cleared her throat. "Mind telling me what's good?"

* * *

You, he wanted to say. How could he resist after he'd tasted her sweetness last night? "Depends on what you feel like. Savory, sweet, light, heavy."

"How about good."

He nodded, then signaled for the server to come over. Once he put in their order, he pushed the menus to the side of the table and focused on her. He wanted to know how she was doing and what she had accomplished. He still hadn't forgotten her comments about only liking one aspect of her job.

"So how's life been? I heard you were in New York, and I know that you followed your passion for fashion, as you used to call it. What don't I know?"

Her smile was like the sunshine. It brightened his day and made him feel like he had a fresh start. He had always thought she was beautiful, but now ten years later he saw that the woman across from him wrote the very definition. He would never not want her.

"I'm still in New York." She tried to smile, but it never fully formed. Strange, uncertain energy surrounded her. "I was recently offered a position as the art director of my magazine. Still debating if it's what I want."

"Sorry, but isn't that the dream? All those little dolls you used to make clothes for and then dress up with written summaries of their outfits." They burst into laughter.

"You remember that?" she asked, unable to contain her giggles.

He nodded. He'd never seen someone who loved clothes more than Reese. She was the only girl he knew that took sewing lessons, named ensembles, and imagined dressing people for a living. "That is the kind of job you always wanted. So what is there to debate?"

She frowned, releasing a long sigh. "I want a promotion because I'm the best at what I do, not because I'm Black."

If he could've told her one thing right now it would be to keep following her dreams. Yet, the seriousness of her expression gave him the sense that he needed to say more since she had shared a personal aspect of her life. "So, you're not thrilled to be the poster child of diversity for your magazine?"

"No." She shook her head. "Not if the work I've done means more because I'm a minority woman rather than a gifted creative."

Duncan had not followed her career, but he'd heard of her work and knew the genius that created extraordinary fashion campaigns that influenced what people wear. "Have you considered that it is because you are both?" He took a sip of orange juice, watching as she contemplated his question. "You work for a world-renowned magazine. They wouldn't make you a director if your work was mediocre. So what if they want you to influence diversity? Use the platform to bring change. Hire more minorities to help get their feet in the door, influence media to where Black and Brown faces are not the exception in ads, and make sure you promote designers of color. You can make this work for you."

She sat a little taller in her chair while fingering a tear from the corner of her eye. He had not meant to upset her. He simply wanted her to be her best self.

"Classic Duncan." She smiled. "You always knew how to turn my gray skies blue." She huffed a chuckle. "Remember when you used to help me get out of afternoon greetings at the inn to go tubing on Lake Gertrude? I would get so upset that I was stuck inside while my friends were all out having fun without me. Thank God you were always there to bust me out."

"Those were the days." He couldn't control the happy thoughts he'd conjured as he reminisced for a second about the times they'd hung out on the shores of Lake Gertrude. Some days it had been full of water sports, and some they sat on a dock while he cast a fishing line. "I think your grandmother just wanted you out of her hair some of those days."

Reese laughed louder and Duncan joined in. "Perhaps. She said I was a busybody. Thanks, Dunc, for then and now." She cleared her throat. "Sooo…enough about me. I hear you've been helping a lot of people. I went to the old sweet shop and Mrs. Willingham told me what you did for them and all the other businesses on that side of the street." She paused, scanning him. "I also know you're working on the comic book shop, and I even met a girl working in the boutique that used to be Ms. Sylvia's hat shop who is excited about the youth village. To be honest, she made me a bit excited for it as well. You were always good at making good things happen for everyone."

Her words tore down more of his defenses. He hadn't

expected recognition or acceptance from her, given the current property he was converting had belonged to her family.

"I'm just glad a need will be met. There's a lot happening in the world. I didn't want this community to be left behind. Besides, opportunity shouldn't be tied to birthright."

Reese reclined back in her seat. It was possible he'd touched a nerve. Maybe he'd meant to. "Did you consider any other buildings or just my grandmother's place?"

Trick question. She played her hand well. The one thing she didn't know was that Hill House had never been his first choice. He was an architect and therefore on many occasions became a preservationist. The steamboat gothic style of the inn was a lost art form that he believed should remain for people to see. So yes, he had considered many other buildings, because initially his team thought it would be a place they would demolish and then have new construction. He'd never tell her that though. Her family could try and take advantage of his weak spot.

"A youth village has been on my radar for a while. When I determined that my firm's headquarters would be here, I began searching for a building to repurpose for the village. Hill House presented itself and fit the specs of what we were looking for. I hope that answers your question."

She nodded with understanding before her shoulders slumped. He sensed defeat that for some reason didn't settle well with him.

"Once you finish your village, I'd like to recommend a teenaged girl named Jasmine. Apparently she's one of Destiny's friends who also has a passion for fashion." Reese managed to smile. "She deserves a chance, and I'd like to help give her one."

Before he could say anything, the server came over and set their food down. Except, he no longer had an appetite for food. He wanted to devour Reese Devlin for sabotaging his heart.

Fourteen

DUNCAN GLANCED DOWN at his watch before collecting his notebook and making his way to the meeting room. Once there, his line of sight went straight to the four projects displayed on the whiteboard in the front of the conference table. The Brooklyn Heights project in Jacksonville was on schedule, there was a minor delay with the warehouse district in Atlanta, permitting for West Hyde Park in Tampa had become a bitch, and then there was Hill House, which had finally received the green light. Only, he now had reservations about moving forward.

An hour ago, Reese had been in his arms for a quick goodbye hug after surprising him at breakfast with understanding the need for the youth village. He hadn't wanted her to leave. Worse was had it not been for his parents' old-school beliefs on public displays of affection, he wasn't sure he would've been able to stop kissing her in their backyard last night. The emotions of his heart were playing games with his head.

"Morning, Mr. McNeal," a few of his employees chimed as they entered the conference room all at once.

Duncan cleared his throat and moved to his seat at the head of the table. "Good morning."

"Sorry I'm late." Rebekah rushed inside the space. "There's something you need to see." She placed her tablet in front of Duncan and maneuvered it until a video feed began to load. "I just got off the phone with my contact at the local news station. This isn't good."

Duncan watched as Hill House came on the screen. Justice Blake, the local news reporter and longtime resident, began talking about the house's history and importance in the Shores as the camera zoomed out and then refocused on him standing beside Kent Devlin on the front lawn of the inn.

"Over a century ago, the Devlin family came to Mount Dora and settled along these shores. The travels that led them here exposed them to the treatment of Black women, men, and children in the South. They realized there should be a place with wholesome accommodations for people who looked like me." The reporter's head turned, and he gestured to the inn in the background. "What they did was establish Hill House, a place that became known as a safe haven for Black travelers in the South."

He then turned to Kent Devlin. "It was a rooming house first, isn't that correct?" asked Justice Blake.

"Yes, it was. However, as time passed, my mother took up the mantle from my grandmother and envisioned so much more, hence Hill House Bed and Breakfast was founded. For decades the inn has helped the local economy with creating jobs, holding events, and bringing in tourists. Most important is that it is a symbol in this community of progress during dark times in our history. Why would we let one man's ideals of so-called urban revitalization alter the landscape of this place we all know and love?"

Duncan scoffed at the backhanded remark. He wished he had been there to give Kent a rebuttal and further highlight how his plans for the old inn would benefit many more people than some high-priced hotel.

"I urge all of you to write the council, call the mayor's office, and demand we preserve what Constance Devlin left to the Shores. What she gave us should be above one man's glorified recreational center."

Duncan slammed the cover down on the tablet. Kent's arrogance was palpable, and perhaps, had he been managing the bed and breakfast, Duncan may have never had the opportunity to acquire it. None of it mattered anymore. The man's disrespect was uncalled for, and Duncan didn't appreciate the way his character was being assassinated.

He had not preyed on Quincy's botched business acumen or gambling addiction in order to purchase the tax liens for the purpose of owning the house. No, his original goal had always been to bargain for a seat at the table they commanded. The Devlins were a part of the little cabal that influenced what happened within the city. Many of the projects Duncan had worked on to reinvigorate the town had to have their approval because the mayor failed to make decisions without their input. However, a shift in priorities occurred once Duncan realized investors were trying to find ways to gain access to the Shores. He became more concerned with ensuring the property didn't fall into the hands of developers seeking to turn the Shores into a hot, new resort destination.

Nervous at what Quincy would do if he became too desperate, they struck a deal. Duncan settled all of Quincy's outstanding gambling debts and then received the deed to Hill House. The news failed to mention how the Devlins had mismanaged so much of the business's money that they had not been able to pay their employees or vendors. He could tell that story and show what thieves the Devlins were along with exposing how the inn's guest volume had been on a constant decline for the last few years.

Except, he wouldn't because it wasn't his style. Duncan pushed the tablet away and reclined back in his chair. He hadn't expected Kent to hit back so hard. "It's a smear campaign. I won't allow these people to tarnish my brand. Rebekah, when is the interview I did going to drop?"

"Well…that's the other thing." She collected her tablet and claimed the seat on his right. "I've been told it was put on hold."

"He's friends with Mr. Sampson," Duncan mumbled, rubbing his hand over his face.

"Who is that?" Rebekah asked.

"Lloyd Sampson owns the town paper." Duncan stood and moved to the front, all the while ignoring the grim faces of his employees. "This isn't the first time we've faced challenges with a project. I'm certain it won't be the last." He scanned each of the projects on the board. "I'm going to pump the brakes on Hill House for now. I still want updates on the other three."

Before he could transition to a project manager, the door to the conference room opened and his assistant, Tasha, barged in. "Duncan, your father's here. He says it's important."

Duncan petitioned a few minutes from everyone and left the room. He found his father in his office, pacing. This wasn't good. Only serious matters brought David McNeal to this side of town, and Duncan was certain this was about the news clip he'd just watched. He closed the door behind him, then stood in silence, waiting for his father to speak.

"I thought your mother was pulling my leg last night when she mentioned that Chareese Devlin was at our home." His father stopped wearing a hole in the rug and stared him down. "This morning I couldn't believe my eyes when I came to the dining floor and saw you sitting with her having breakfast like old friends. Have you forgotten?"

Duncan glanced down to his feet. The pointed question

began to unravel the seams he was attempting to mend between himself and Reese. "I have not."

His father huffed. "Then why does it seem like I'm the only one who remembers being in our living room ten years ago when Kent and Constance came to put us in our place after you almost got into a fight over Chareese? I told you purchasing that inn was a mistake. You didn't listen."

"Pop, if I listened to you every time I made a business decision, I wouldn't be where I am today." Duncan's hands slid into his pockets. He looked into the face of the man people deemed his twin, the only exception being the salt-and-pepper hair on his father's head.

"Duncan, I put you on the path of least resistance. I sacrificed everything for you to get outta here and make something of yourself. I will not stand by and let that girl ruin you again."

"It's not like that, Pop." Duncan looked away, trying hard to control the anger his father fanned back to life.

"The hell it is! My mother and wife were almost blacklisted by those people. We struggled to sell meals out of our house that would keep the lights on. One woman's jealousy could've destroyed us."

"But it didn't." Duncan blew out an exasperated sigh. "It's in the past." The resentment he detected in his father was why he had to let go. He didn't want to end up old, bitter, and full of regrets.

"Is that what you tell yourself now that that pretty girl is running around here showing you interest? Don't be blind. I raised you better than this. You're only good enough now because of the money." Bitterness dripped from his father's words.

Duncan went around his father and sat at his desk. His father was nothing like his mother. Where Pearl was sweet and encouraging, David was all about tough love. He credited it to

Duncan's excellence in academics and the success he'd found after college.

"Reese's interest in me started long before I had any of this. I seriously doubt she cares about my money. She has plenty of her own."

"Then it's Hill House."

"Dammit, Pop." Duncan banged his fist on his desk. He refused to believe those were her motivations after she'd danced with him at the rink, told him she'd missed him, and then kissed him. It was a bridge he was willing to cross if it meant they could have another chance. "It's not."

Duncan silently prayed it wasn't as he and his father engaged in a stare down. Most of their disagreements were related to the business of the restaurant. When his father doubted having a social media presence, Duncan sent a team in to illustrate what having one could do for business and his father came on board. After recommending the addition of gluten-free menu options, sales increased by 30 percent, and they permanently added the items to the menu. In this case, he couldn't show that the outcome of interacting with Reese had positive benefits. In fact, he had no clue.

"I'm not so sure, son." His father was finally the one to break the tense silence. "Besides, I thought you and uhh, what's her name…Rebekah were se—"

"Not for months." Duncan cut his father's question off while adjusting his tie. He was twenty-eight not fourteen. There was no need for chats about the birds and the bees. "By the way, *she's* the gold digger."

His dad nodded with understanding, then approached his desk. "Sometimes the things we think we want aren't meant for us to have." His father sighed and turned his attention out the window for a few minutes. "Please don't get mixed up with the

Devlin girl, Duncan. It's already bad enough that Destiny has to be around those folks. It's keeping your mama up at night, and now she's worried about finding her a new escort."

Duncan recoiled. "What's wrong with Andre?"

His father shrugged. "Nothing, and that's my point with all this foolishness. Just ask your mother. I regret all of you talking me into letting Destiny accept that invitation." His father turned and started toward the door. He opened then closed it. "Promise me you'll stay away from her."

A flash of contemplation passed over Duncan. He had yet to escape the hold Reese had had upon his heart since the moment they first kissed. This was his only chance to determine if what they had shared back then wanted to be found again or lost forever. "I can't."

Without another word, his father walked out the door. David McNeal was a humble man that didn't believe in arguing. To avoid further disagreement, his father would leave one to ponder the decision he disagreed with. However, this was an inconvenient time. Duncan had Hill House and more importantly, there was something that wouldn't let him walk away from Reese. Only, now his father had him second-guessing everything.

Was it wrong for him to want what he had once lost? Had the purchase of Hill House been a mistake? Why did his family have to be denied a seat at the table when they had so much to give the community?

He'd spent years cycling through meaningless flings, searching for a woman that could erase Reese from his dreams, and the same amount of time overcoming self-doubt. He was done believing he wasn't good enough. There was no going back.

Duncan stopped questioning his actions over the last few days. He deserved a chance to revitalize his community, uplift youth, and to hold Reese Devlin's heart.

Fifteen

"**FATHER-SON HUDDLE** gone wrong?"

Duncan peeked up from his laptop to see Rebekah standing in the doorway. Once upon a time she would have been a welcome sight. Today, there was nothing she could do for him. No matter how many times he'd lain with her, she wasn't the woman holding the key to his heart. She knew it and so did all the others who'd prayed he'd develop feelings for them. But never did.

It wasn't their fault someone had stolen his heart. Yet, it was the reason he had issues with commitment. Therefore, he wasn't in a headspace to rehash a conversation that happened half an hour ago. Not when the subject of his father's visit was the reason he'd never been able to give Rebekah what she wanted, in addition to her being after his money.

She stepped into his office. "I didn't mean to pry. I saw him on his way out and he didn't seem too happy. Plus, you totally forgot to come back to the conference room."

"Shit," he whispered as his head crashed back into his chair. "Are they still in there?"

"No." She sashayed into the office and claimed a seat in front of his desk. "You seem distracted. Anything I can do to help?"

The wicked gleam in her eyes told him she was offering more than he was willing to take. Even if he were to let his dick over-rule his mind, he no longer found mixing business with pleasure suitable. It was different when she owned her own firm and he was her client. He definitely wouldn't do it now that she was his actual employee—and they had agreed, so why was she trying?

"You can figure out a way to spin that false narrative the news aired this morning."

A sly smile curved her lips. "That's not what I meant." She pushed up from her chair, slid her hands along her curves, and began moving to the side of his desk.

"Eh-hem." The sound of someone clearing their throat halted Rebekah's pounce and forced his attention to the door. Tasha had an *I told you so* expression written all over her face. "You have a visitor, Duncan. It's Chareese Devlin."

"As in the woman who was at the Hill House project the day you were interviewed?" Rebekah snapped her attention to the door and then looked at Duncan with a wrinkled brow. "Maybe get legal in here in case—"

"Show her in, please, Tasha, thank you." His heart raced with anticipation.

He had not planned on seeing Reese until later after work like they had talked about earlier. A part of him feared his father's words could be true. Yet, it was better this way. He needed to face reality and see if the friendship and love they once shared resisted her father's coup and truly deserved another chance.

* * *

"Ms. Devlin, follow me, please." The short woman who had asked her to wait in the lobby reappeared. "Mr. McNeal can see you."

Reese followed the woman, hands fidgeting as she cataloged the space Duncan had made into his office. She silently envied the designer who had been given the chance to explore color and texture while planning the interior space. The design was carefully curated with a modern take on an old-fashion gentleman's office that celebrated accomplishment, imagination, and somehow brought about calm.

The dark walls were a bit moody, like Duncan. However, she loved the overall aesthetic, and adored the old, worn books perfectly housed within the stained shelves. There were hints of gold hardware that paired well with the rich furnishings and an eclectic art collection that expressed Duncan's taste for the finer things without being ostentatious. It reminded her of the way he dressed in the most sophisticated designer clothing without flashing the brands like some men did for clout.

The way she wanted to peel his luxury threads from his body until he stood before her in all his naked glory was something she had fantasized about since leaving him last night. Damn her father. She would probably never have the chance to make things right with Duncan. Not after watching how her father had publicly challenged Duncan's purchase of the property on the news.

Her father's actions would certainly have consequences. She said a silent prayer, hoping it wasn't another brick wall she'd have to tear down to find her way back to Duncan.

The woman in front of her abruptly stopped and gestured for Reese to enter the open door on the left. She stepped into the room, wishing she could stop her heart from beating out of control at the sight of Duncan behind his oversized desk. God, the way his eyes charmed her was a sin. She was tempted to do things with him that were absolutely unladylike.

"Duncan," she exhaled, preparing to apologize for all the

mud her father slung on TV. But something in her peripheral vision stopped her. A pair of long legs crossed in a chair in the back right corner of the room.

Her head turned and she recalled the woman's big hair from the day he'd been interviewed at Hill House. Reese remembered thinking that there may have been more to the pair based on the way Duncan ushered the woman from his car. However, that mind-numbing kiss she shared with him last night had erased all thoughts of any other woman being the center of his universe.

"What brings you by?" His deep voice reclaimed her focus as she watched him rise from his chair and come around his desk. Her eyes cut back to the corner. His followed. "I don't believe you two have been formally introduced. Rebekah, this is Chareese Devlin, an old friend. Chareese, Rebekah Wilson, my PR director."

Old friend...Reese ground her teeth. Friends held hands and ran around chasing each other in the park like they used to when they were young. They did not French kiss. The intimate exchange she and Duncan shared was something different. What, she had yet to understand.

However, she was determined to tread along the path that could free her from regrets of the past. She just hoped the way the woman sat sizing her up wasn't another obstacle to overcome.

"I uhh..." She did her best to ignore the woman at her back. "I saw the news this morning." Her gaze intentionally missed his as she glanced to the ground, sadly broadcasting her shame. "I had no idea my father planned to attack you so publicly."

She finally looked up, watching as Duncan leaned against the edge of his desk and folded his arms. His blank expression was less than she'd bargained for. Right now, she would have gladly taken rage over the disappointment beginning to etch onto his face.

"Duncan and I were just discussing this subject." Both Duncan and Reese whipped their heads over to Rebekah as she got to her feet. "There was supposed to be a feature with Duncan's acquisition in the paper today that would've counter-acted negative press. It was put on hold."

"Why?" Reese asked while noting the glower Duncan set on the other woman, who had gone to his side and started rubbing his shoulder.

Duncan pushed off his desk and made his way over to Reese. "I've seen your dad and Mr. Sampson play golf together at the country club. My guess is that your father called in a favor from his friend."

Reese huffed a cynical chuckle. "My godfather is protective."

"Your godfather?" Duncan guffawed. "I had no idea," he muttered.

"Yeah, well, I'm sure he thought he was acting in my father's best interests." The nonchalant nod given by Duncan equally matched her cynicism. "Good thing is, he doesn't run the day-to-day. Lockhart does. I can ask him to reconsider."

"I don't understand why you would do that if your family is hell-bent on preserving the house as an inn."

"Yea—"

The look Duncan gave Rebekah silenced her, shrinking what-ever status the woman thought she commanded in the room. He then turned his curiosity back to Reese, awaiting an answer. She was reluctant and not ready to show her entire hand. Nevertheless, she knew ground had been lost since breakfast this morning and she was desperate to recover it.

"Regardless of my stance, which you know, I do not agree with what my father did. He potentially subjected you and your firm to public ridicule and that wasn't right."

He analyzed her as if he were searching for holes, then said, "No," and pivoted back to his chair. "I don't need you calling in favors with Lockhart Sampson for me."

"What!" both Reese and Rebekah exclaimed at once.

Duncan was about to let his pride get in the way. That was the very reason old folks said it came before the fall. Reese couldn't let him fail. She owed him the chance he wasn't given all those years ago because she had caved to fear.

Reese sprang forward, grabbing his wrist. "Dunc, wait," she pleaded. By the way he searched her eyes as his chest rose and fell, she could tell that he was willing to listen. "PR is not my gig. However, in my line of work, when designers want consumers to view their brands as socially conscious, they attach to a cause. For example, do you recall GAP's RED campaign? The campaign sought to bring awareness and raise funds to help eliminate HIV/AIDS in Africa."

Duncan shook his head no. Rebekah nodded yes. "Of course! The youth village is exactly that. Duncan is creating a space for all youth to find achievement."

"Not everyone shares that opinion because they may see the youth village as too much change in this quaint town." She cut her eyes away from Rebekah. "Anyhow, you could become a sponsor for the Lakeside Debutante Ball."

"The ball," he responded deadpan, then pulled away and plopped down in his chair.

"Contrary to what you may believe, the debutante ball has done a lot for the community over the years. They have several scholarships for Rosewood and Ocoee survivors, in addition to funding twenty-first-century learning centers that operate in at-risk neighborhoods. Your sponsorship of the ball benefits the platform of achievement of youth from historically marginalized populations. The recognition you would receive from a contribution will resound across the South, bring awareness to what you are attempting to do here in the Shores, and display your character."

Duncan rested his chin between his forefinger and thumb. Reese saw the wheels turning in his head. The option she was presenting was one that people who came from her privileged circle used to enhance their businesses and image year after year. She hoped her family wouldn't outcast her for betrayal.

"I'd have to look into everything you've said to confirm, of course. If true, it sounds like a viable option, Duncan," Rebekah stated.

He nodded. "Rebekah, would you mind leaving us alone, please."

Shock swept over the woman's face. She stepped back from his desk and then turned and left the room. His gaze landed on Reese. "Why are you telling us all of this?"

Reese struggled to find words, debating how much of the truth she could confess. When her eyes met his, she was full of confusion around wanting to preserve Hill House, but also having love in her heart for the man who had stolen hers. "Because I can't see you get hurt again by my family."

She began fidgeting with her fingers, completely missing the fact that Duncan had come out of his chair and was now so close she could steal his breaths. His lips hovered over hers, seducing the desires she kept trapped inside.

"Is that why you kissed me last night? You think I'll be hurt?"

"No." She looked up into his face, wishing she could break his enchantments. "I kissed you because…because…"

"Looking out for me, huh?" His lips crashed down upon hers as he pulled her into his arms. She felt safe, cherished, and above all else, loved in the warmth of his masculine hold.

Sixteen

ONLY A DAY had passed since Reese last saw Duncan in his office, and she didn't know if she would ever stop craving him. Every word, kiss, and touch was on a constant loop in her mind. She found that she'd started comparing now to back then when their conversations were easy, the friendship was trusting, and her mind was always dreaming of him. She was never ready to leave at the end of summer, and most times hoped August would never come because that meant months might pass before seeing him again.

The emotion he had stirred up that summer when they finally realized they desired to be more than friends was exactly how she felt now. Unfortunately, the same fear she had experienced so many years ago over disappointing her parents still lingered. They had given her everything.

Most importantly, a life that had allowed her to defy societal stereotypes and achieve excellence. Every wish she had, from sewing lessons to meeting fashion icons like Patricia Cleveland, they made come true. Her parents had been instrumental in paving her vision for the future and she didn't ever want to be told she was ungrateful again.

Reese pushed the thought from her mind and refocused to the task at hand of getting ready for a night out with her friends. Her goal was to be gone before her parents arrived home. She had been able to avoid them, since everyone had been coming and going to remain active in their social circles. However, as she slipped into the little shift dress she'd plucked from the closet, she heard them in the house.

An interrogation was coming. They, or mainly her mother, since her father didn't exactly agree, would want to know if there had been any progress with Duncan. And she'd have to lie, because her reasons for engaging with Duncan contradicted those of her parents.

Her conscience never allowed her to do their bidding for the sake of preserving a family name. So, lie it was since they were not prepared for her to be true to her heart. They had not let go of their old ways and she couldn't handle being judged and condemned as the rebellious daughter once again.

Still, Reese needed to find a way for her family and Duncan to find balance. Her father was already itching to take matters into his own hands. The TV stunt was the beginning. A compromise over Hill House had to exist. It was the only way and she needed to find it fast.

"Chareese," her mother called.

With a final glance in the mirror and a spray of perfume, she dashed out of her room and down the stairs, where she heard her mother call her again. "I'm here," she replied as she rounded the staircase and found both parents in the kitchen unpacking takeout. "I'm leaving to meet Quinn, Peyton, and Carrah for dinner at some new spot called The Nix."

"Oh yes, I hear the food there is good." Her mother put down the food container she pulled from the bag, wiped her hands, and then came to stand in front of Reese. "White has always been such a pretty color on you." Her mother picked and prodded at her dress for a bit before she started doing the same with her hair.

"Heard you also tried the breakfast at Mama's Place earlier this week." Her father's tone bit sharply. "How was it?"

"Delicious," Reese snapped, as she took a step back from her mother.

"When were you going to tell us, Chareese? Did Duncan mention anything about Hill House?" Her mother reached for her hand, but she pulled away.

Reese knew this was coming. She just hadn't anticipated the double-team tactic. Then again, she hadn't expected her father to go on the news defaming Duncan's motives. All for the purpose of maintaining their status within the old guard.

She sighed long and heavy. "Didn't realize you needed a briefing of my coming and going."

"Save your snark for your friends. Your mother asked you a legitimate question."

"Please stop treating me like I'm twelve."

"Then start acting like an adult and do your part for this family." Her father had displayed this insolent behavior once, and it was here in the Shores when she was seventeen, and it was over the same boy.

Anger boiled inside of Reese. If she were a tea kettle, her whistle would've already blown. There was always an unrealistic expectation of her. Her earliest recollection was going on pointe shoes early, and then making first chair in the youth symphony. The pressure of being the perfect daughter, student, and becoming a renowned fashion editor was easier to bear than what they wanted from her when it came to Duncan.

Besides, this was her third week in town, and getting reacquainted with Duncan was a process that couldn't be rushed.

The chasm her father and grandmother put between them was far and wide.

"Why didn't either of you tell me his family opened a restaurant?" Both parents avoided eye contact and neither offered words. "I take it your opinions on his family have kept you away, but you're missing out. The morning I visited was like waking up and eating breakfast at Hill House."

Her father harrumphed. "Well, Pearl was my mother's cook."

Reese turned away from her father's cavalier remark and looked at her mother, who began busying herself with the bags on the counter. "Anyhow, Dad…just so you know, there was a write-up for the paper that you had my godfather stall. According to Lockhart, Duncan went on the record and stated that he'd considered other properties before Hill House became an option for the youth village. Duncan didn't say it, but I'm certain the exterior will go untouched. He admires the architecture too much."

"So is he just going to gut the inside?" Her father raised his voice a decibel. "That's even worse. All the people, the memories, the love that happened in that house are going to be wiped from existence. I need to make some calls." He dropped silverware on the counter and then headed toward the living room.

"Why do you care what Duncan does with the house?" Her question halted his stride. In slow motion he faced her. "Remember you prized your career above family legacy." She challenged her father's glare while ignoring her mother's gasp. Yes, she crossed the line. She didn't care. It had to be said because they were asking her to do what her father had been unwilling to. "Duncan may have been more willing to open up to me had you not run to the news and painted him as a villain in the Shores."

"Kent, Chareese, let's calm down. This has been a stressful situation for all of us."

He huffed and then glared over his shoulder at her mother.

"Apples never fall far from their trees do they, Genevieve?" Her father stormed out of the kitchen.

"What does that have to do with anything?" Reese asked her mother.

She shook her head. "Nothing." Her mother's golden skin darkened as she watched him leave. Moments passed in silence. "Have fun with the girls" was all she said before she went back to the counter and started plating their food.

Good lord. Her mother was using that voice she used when trying to hide her disappointment. If only she really knew. "The both of you asked me to talk to Duncan, and now I'm ridiculed for having breakfast with him. Did you really think I could waltz into his office and ask him to reconsider his purchase without first reestablishing a relationship?"

"No," she whispered. "Just don't lose sight of what you are doing. Sometimes the things we think we want aren't meant for us to have. Remember that, and go enjoy the night with your friends. It's been a long time since you've all been here like this. They've missed you."

A rare side of her mother was on display. Reese wasn't sure if she should stay or go…or confess her true motives for wanting to get close to Duncan. "Mom, are you okay?"

"I've been fine for over thirty years." She shrugged with a half smile. "Now go, you look pretty. Besides, I like when you go make good trouble. It makes the best gossip." She winked.

Reese went to her mother and kissed her cheek before darting from the house. In less than fifteen minutes she arrived on the outskirts of downtown and parked in the lot of a warehouse that clearly had been renovated. She entered the contemporary wine bar and felt as though she'd left the Shores and arrived back in Manhattan. A place she was in no rush to return to since she had to make a decision about her career at the magazine.

"Reese!"

Reese searched for Carrah. Once she found her friend waving from the other side of the floor, she made her way over and plopped in the booth beside Quinn, where a glass of wine awaited her.

"We took the liberty." Peyton gestured to the glass inches away from Reese's fingers before raising hers in the air. "Finally, an evening with just us. To summer in the Shores! May all good debutante dreams come true." They toasted, giggling at the old saying that had been passed down from mother to daughter, and then sipped the light-bodied white.

"Thank God for this night out." Carrah sipped from her glass. "The five to sevens have been such a drag."

"Ahh…the la cinq à septs," Reese chuckled. "They really do still love those."

Peyton threw her head back in laughter. "They do! At least we're all together again. It's been so long. I mean I know we keep in touch, but it's been ten years since we've all summered together in the town we explored as kids. We're still missing Ava, though." She sipped a little more wine.

"I told her that the other night." Carrah held the stem of her glass, sniffing its contents before draining it. "Not sure how you managed to get outta debutante alumni duty for so many years, Reesey Pie."

The four of them fell into a mess of laughs. "So, deb alumni duty. Is that what it's called now?"

They laughed harder and then began reminiscing about their own debuts. As Mrs. Russell had said to the latest group of girls, Chareese, Quinn, Carrah, Peyton, and Ava were part of the most celebrated debut in the history of the ball. Four of the five had all come from some of the most notable and influential Black families in the South and were representing generations of women from their families. Ava had been the exception, which elevated interest in the ball because she had been the first local to impress the ball committee enough to receive an invitation.

"Sooo…on the note of alumni duty thanks to Quinn assigning me as a mentor…" Reese playfully punched Quinn in the arm and then became serious. "My sister mentioned that Destiny McNeal's escort isn't exactly the right fit."

"No, he's not." Quinn shook her head. "The committee overlooked her choice since they know she is the first from her family to be invited."

"Ava was the first from her family and she debuted with your brother," Carrah threw back at Quinn.

"She did. However, her father is also a respected principal and the town historian. He was, and is still, well connected and knew of all the inner workings. Ava also benefited from our mothers being sorority sisters. Despite her being a local, she came from an educated family that had an understanding of how cotillions, debutantes, and the quote, unquote 'Black Bourgeoisie' worked. Destiny's parents are well-known, good people of the community. Unfortunately, they don't have many relationships that benefit her with the ball."

Oh, to have the world they grew up in explained in such a polite way. Quinn had always been the political one of the group. Perhaps it was because her father was Senator Roland Hightower, her brother was aspiring to be the next, and she'd learned at a young age that semantics mattered. Either way, she reminded Reese in a roundabout way that Destiny's family had no clout or affiliation with the people who seemed to matter.

This was the very reason she had chosen to give Duncan the idea of sponsorship. He had relationships with people in the Shores, and had even made a name for himself with his firm beyond the tiny town. However, he needed to reach into the minds of all the people in the South that came from near and far to summer in the lakeside village, to elevate who he and his family had become. Destiny's debut would also help. Reese just had to get her the right escort.

"Speaking of the McNeals." Peyton tilted her chin up, and Reese looked over her shoulder to see Duncan with many of the boys, now men, he'd been with at the rink.

She watched Duncan stroll in. He oozed sex appeal with an arrogance that commanded the room and sent a shiver up her spine. "What are they doing here?" Reese snapped her head back to the table, hoping she didn't appear as desperate as she really was for Duncan.

Carrah snorted. "Are you kidding? God, you really have stayed away too long. They own this place. The three musketeers: Duncan, Gavin, and Chris." Disdain dripped off her friend's tongue at the mention of Chris Chennault. Everyone knew the Chennault and Andrews families were the modern-day Montagues and Capulets. "Duncan's genius in urban planning and architectural design addressed the need of creating sociable spaces for the younger crowds. The other two became equal investors."

"Yeah," Quinn chimed in, staring across at the group. "Duncan has done a lot to keep the Shores a desirable summer destination for all ages while drawing people to live here year-round, like he does."

Reese sipped from her glass. "I've seen what he has been doing for some of the small businesses. I didn't realize he resided here permanently or invested so much."

"I guess your father doesn't either." Quinn cut her eyes at Reese before throwing back the rest of her wine. "Not all of us have the luxury of staying away. Politics keeps Daddy visiting the Shores year-round. Our little enclave isn't just for Black elites anymore. Well, it never was only Black people. There are more white families choosing the Shores for their summer residences, and many of them are equally influential.

"The work Duncan is doing has to be done. With all the people and business industry he's brought here, a youth village is simply brilliant. Daddy supports him and he wishes yours would too, considering how your family's bed and breakfast hasn't operated in the same manner since your grandmother passed. I mean it's been closed what, the last five or six months? Don't worry, he won't say anything publicly. His relationship with your father means too much."

"Quinn!" Peyton's and Carrah's perplexed expressions were everything Reese felt inside.

Carrah scoffed, "Must you be so blunt?"

A tense quiet fell over the quartet. Quinn had never been one to mince words, and it was clear Quinn had issues with a few Devlins. Her friend had already expressed concerns with Alex, frowned upon Reese negating alumni service, and now called out her father's news spectacle.

"All I'm trying to say is we can't be like the old guard. I scratch my head every day at how our parents turn their noses up at progress and upward mobility in the name of tradition. That can't be us."

Reese didn't want it to be them either. They had all accomplished so much so young. True, they were given a few more opportunities to roll the dice and collect two hundred dollars before most of their peers. Therefore, it was time for them to use those advantages to do some good.

They began formulating a game plan to get Destiny a more suitable escort, which included a future chat with Gavin. His younger brother could elevate Destiny's presentation to society and create contacts that would be long-lasting for her future goals of working within the justice system. Afterward they sat reflecting on how much the Shores had changed since they'd first arrived for the summer years ago.

"I hear you and Dunc never kept in touch," Peyton blurted out of nowhere as her attention returned from the table across the way. "It seemed odd given how close you two were during the summers, and that so many of us remained connected even if it was only through posts and comments on social media."

What else had she heard? Reese didn't ask aloud for fear of what might be said. She had never gotten over being forced to debut with a boy she loathed after being snatched away from Duncan and thrown into the back seat of her parents' car. Most of all, she had found it difficult to outrun the humiliation of betraying Duncan's heart. Ten years hadn't been long enough. So, she simply answered, "No, we didn't."

"Why would they?" Carrah rolled her eyes at Peyton.

"Because everyone knew Dunc had a thing for you"—Quinn pointed at Reese—"and you had one for him too."

"It was summer days and puppy love, as our parents say. Besides, Reese chose to debut with Drexel Collins that last summer she was here. Stop trying to make something out of nothing."

The simple reference of Drex put bile in Reese's throat. Still, she would thank Carrah later for saving her. Carrah was the only one who stood by her when she refused the boy her mother and grandmother had matched her with. She knew all the ugly behind-the-scenes drama, and like a true friend, she had never told a soul. Even when she thought Reese was batshit crazy for standing up to her mother and requesting Duncan as her escort, she remained at her side in support of free will. Carrah had been the only one that didn't want to see Reese throw away something special.

"Bet you wish you had chosen differently," Quinn taunted. "Duncan is one of the South's most eligible bachelors, while your old escort is some wannabe producer spending all of his parents' money in Atlanta."

Reese's hands formed into tight fists. She had to fight against the irritation Quinn incited within her. "Wh—"

"Ladies." A server popped up at the end of the table holding a bottle of wine. "This is from the gentlemen." He pointed to the large table where Duncan sat along with his friends.

* * *

Duncan watched, waiting for Reese to look over and acknowledge that he'd sent the bottle of wine to her table. Her tawny skin glowed, calling to him like the sirens luring drunken sailors to the shore. Only, he wasn't drunk. He wanted to go and fall over the cliff if it meant he could hold her heart again.

The second her head whipped in his direction, he raised his glass of whiskey and winked. He didn't think she could get more beautiful than she had been when she barged into his office to help him overcome the roadblocks her own father had set. But she was and it wasn't solely physical. The concerned spirit she had displayed, along with that brilliant mind that helped him plot a path to success, outshined any physical attraction.

The remorse she had for the actions of her father was evident. However, it was the desire she had to help him instead of succumbing to familial duty that struck the deep layers of his heart and made it beat hard for her. She had also kept her word and visited his sister on multiple days to prepare for the ball. It was possible she was atoning for the hurt inflicted that summer...because what else would it be?

Regardless of their obvious attraction and the nostalgic pull to find what was once between them, significant damage had been done. His dad's concerns had prompted his mother to question Destiny's participation in the ball. It was all proof that their families might never mend bridges together.

"Damn, Dunc." Gavin nudged him, then recast his gaze to the table where all the prettiest girls in the Shores sat. "Feeling generous tonight?"

"I'd say so," Chris chimed.

Duncan shrugged. "Y'all believe in second chances?"

Gavin set his drink down and gave him a pointed look. "If they all looked like Chareese Devlin, maybe. You do know her father hates your guts, right, man."

"I knew this shit was going to happen. She's been in town what, like three weeks?" Chris reclined back in his chair and glanced over to where Duncan couldn't stop staring.

"Almost three." Duncan smiled at the sight of Peyton, Quinn, and Carrah waving their thanks as the waiter poured fresh glasses of wine.

His breath hitched when Reese slid from her seat and began making her way to their table. Beauty was truly her name. The white dress she wore clung to her body, exposing her hourglass figure. Erotic thoughts rolled through his mind as he cataloged every curve he wanted to explore.

"Gav, Chris, Dunc." Her sultry voice seduced him as her eyes met his for a second. She then nudged Gavin and plopped down beside him at their table. "Thanks for the bottle."

"That was all Dunc, Reesey Pie." Chris teased her with the nickname Duncan had heard the other night at the skating rink.

Duncan frowned. "Not sure how much I like this Reesey Pie business." Reese and his friends chuckled at the comment. "Where did it come from anyway?"

"One day at a regional Jack and Jill group activity, we

must've been what…five, six years old." Chris looked to Reese for confirmation, and she nodded. "We were making a Thanksgiving dessert, a pie to be exact, and it called for Reese's Pieces. Somebody said it was Chareese's name on the package, and from then on we always called her that."

A tinge of jealousy tormented Duncan, reminding him that he was the outsider. While Chris and Gavin had been a part of that world where their parents attended each other's summer parties and spent time together outside of the Shores, his playtime with Reese as a child had been more accidental than intentional.

"Well, enough about me. I hear the three of you own this spot?"

They nodded in unison. Gavin then said, "That's correct, and we have another location opening in Atlanta next month."

"Still so braggy, Gav." She playfully punched his shoulder, eliciting laughter from Duncan, because it was true. "Well, I just came over to say thank you and congratulate the three musketeers on this venture." She gestured to the space around them as she got back to her feet. "I had no idea this spot existed until tonight."

Maybe if you visited more frequently you could have seen how much things have changed. Duncan wanted to say it. However, he didn't, because he was thinking more about him than the town. Had she come back sooner, maybe they wouldn't have missed ten whole years from each other's lives.

"What kept you away for so long?" Chris asked.

Reese's bright smile faded. Once more her eyes locked with Duncan's. Gavin and Chris didn't know, regardless of how close they were. Reese wasn't allowed to date, and Miss Constance had already warned his mama of roaming eyes where her granddaughter was concerned. Besides, no one broadcasts being ridiculed for not having enough. The pain Reese had strummed over his heart wasn't for spectators.

Duncan could tell she wasn't ready to answer that question. However, she owed him some form of an explanation beyond what he already knew, because not only did she stay away, she'd pulled away. They were friends before discovering they wanted to be more.

"I'd like to know too." Duncan doubled down, hardening his gaze upon her.

He should've questioned her when they were alone at breakfast or his office. He didn't, because those warm and fuzzy feelings had taken over. At some point they had to discuss that summer and her lack of an apology or explanation. If she thought showing up this year and acting like that time never happened would erase that incident, she was wrong.

Gavin jumped to his feet and wrapped an arm around her shoulders. "Tell them it ain't none of their damn business."

Duncan slumped back into his seat, experiencing a bit of chagrin from Gavin running interference. Reese giggled. The panic he'd seen in her eyes seconds ago had evaporated. He would thank his friend later for not letting him make an ass out of himself.

"He's right, my bad," Duncan conceded. "You and the girls busy this weekend? We're going out on the boat tomorrow or Sunday. May end up at Dorian's Cove."

"You know we ain't missing church for the cove," Chris heckled while Gavin gave a long slow shake of the head. "It has to be tomorrow."

"That sounds fun!" Her face lit up. "Haven't been in ages. I'll let them know. Not sure about Carrah because…" Her eyes darted to Chris.

Chris shrugged. "We'll have fun without her. Always have."

"Okay, well, I'll message you later to confirm."

Duncan nodded, then struggled to contain himself as she walked back to her table. No other woman had ever made him feel like he was losing his damn mind. At least he finally understood the confusion between his mind and his heart. He and Reese should've never been apart.

Seventeen

REESE RANG THE bell at the oversized front door, then took a step back to inventory the Mediterranean-styled home. Duncan had set out to conquer the world, and he got it. In the time she'd been back in the Shores, she'd learned that he made sound business decisions and that many of the people admired his efforts to keep their town relevant. However, nothing could've prepared her for the reality that Duncan had amassed a fortune large enough to own a home only five minutes from her parents' lake house.

There was no disrespect or snootiness intended in her thoughts. She, and everyone in the South, simply knew Lakeshore Drive in the Shores as millionaire row. A part of her wondered if this was where he chose to live because he liked it or because he wanted to be recognized in a world that had once excluded him. The hurt from that exclusion had clearly made him determined to accomplish so much. Reese feared that his gaining ranks within a world that cared more about the congregation a person worshipped in or a debutante's escort might corrupt his kind spirit.

Reese inhaled once more, after hearing his deep voice on the other side of the door. Her nerves had been on edge ever since he invited her here last night. She entwined her fingers and attempted to subdue her excitement at seeing him again, as well as the shock of realizing what he had become. She dared not think about the desire corrupting her thoughts, begging for another chance to be alone with him.

"Reese." The door swung open. She gulped hard. His smooth, dark skin was exposed by the tank top he had on, and she had never seen such well-defined arms. She imagined him holding her, saying that they could start over again. If he only gave her the chance, she would chase all the pain away. "Come on in." He stepped aside as she stutter-stepped inside the well-appointed home. He caught her gaze and grinned. "See something you like?"

Definitely, she wanted to say but didn't. Lust interrupted her wholesome thoughts of their reunion. Dear God, she could almost imagine the man picking her up with those strong arms and pinning her against the wall as she kissed his full lips.

Reese wanted to wipe the smirk clean off Duncan's face. However, there was something sexy in his not-so-subtle acknowledgement of her physical attraction to him. So, she shrugged, trying to play it cool.

"Perhaps." Her bold and brazen gaze made him turn away.

A small smile curved his lips. "You're the last one. Everyone is waiting out back by the dock. You ready?"

Reese nodded and began following him as they moved through his house and down a few halls. The man was a damn dream with those broad shoulders, strong legs, and big hands. There was no second-guessing her physical attraction to him. However, she wondered if he felt the same. One minute she thought he did and that he was warming up to her, the next she didn't know.

"So are we going to pretend like the last few days never happened?" Mind games were not her forte. She was tired of trying to figure him out.

He abruptly stopped and faced her. His hands slid into the pockets of his swim trunks. "What do you mean?"

For a second, Reese avoided his intense brown stare. Finally, brown met brown, and she hoped to God she wasn't setting herself up for heartbreak. "I told you I missed you...we kissed—"

"You kissed me first." He walked up to her, closing the distance between them. "I've wanted to kiss you again. I'm just too afraid of becoming addicted." His lips hovered above hers.

"Why would you be afraid," she whispered, closing her eyes and erasing the small space that was left between them.

"As hard as I've tried, I haven't been able to forget the last ten years. You threw everything we had away. If that happens again, I may not recover."

"Then let's live today as if that night never happened." She brushed her lips above his. "I can't be near you and act like you don't do something to me."

His arm wrapped at her waist. He pulled her tighter and she tingled all over with anticipation.

"Yo, Dunc!" The boom of Gavin's voice made them jerk apart. They turned and saw him waiting in the opening of the sliding glass doors leading to the outside. A wide grin slid onto Gavin's face. "Oh, sorry, did I interrupt something?"

The hormones raging within Reese went still. She had a good idea of what Gavin was thinking. The exact same thing her father had thought when he'd found out they spent time alone as teenagers. At least this time there was no shame. She wouldn't be made to feel sorry for having enjoyed every second of the feel of his rock-hard body against hers.

"You're good." Duncan cleared his throat before bending

over to collect Reese's beach bag. "Reese just got here. We were on our way out back."

"Actually, since you're here, there's something I've been meaning to ask you, Gav."

"You can ask on the boat, Reese. We want to get to the cove before it gets crowded." Duncan placed his hand in the middle of her back and guided her to the sliding glass doors.

"I'd rather ask here." She stepped to the side, forcing Duncan's hand to drop down, and then turned her attention to Gavin. "Your brother, Xavier, is he in town this summer?"

"Not yet, he will be in a few days. Why, what's up?"

"Do you think he would be willing to be an escort for one of the debutantes? Would your parents support it?"

He shrugged. "You know it depends on who it is."

Reese nodded. Of course Gavin knew the rules. He'd been one of the most sought-after escorts along the East Coast. The only reason she hadn't made her debut with him holding her arm was because there was someone better in her parents' eyes at the time. Irony was not lost in the fact that her mother attempted to connect them at the skate party.

Only, Reese knew Gavin and he knew her. They kept in touch via social media like many of them did, and she saw him as the older brother that couldn't keep his dick in his pants. So, no thank you. But she needed him now. And she knew how discerning Gavin was with favors.

Which was why she refused Duncan's request to ask on the boat. Gavin would be put on the spot and Duncan's pride might not be able to take a punch.

"It's for Destiny."

Gavin's eyes widened in surprise as he looked back and forth between Reese and Duncan. "Why didn't you ask me, Dunc? You know I would do anything to help Destiny."

Duncan ignored his friend's question. "I'm trying to figure out why Chareese is asking you this for my sister."

Shit, he used her full name. "Because I'm your sister's mentor. My goal is to ensure her debut is successful and exceeds all expectations. Gavin, you know the importance associated with a girl's escort selection. You were asked what, three or four times? Don't you remember going to Atlanta for the Links ball to escort Summer Bradshaw?"

"Stop." Duncan exhaled a deep breath. His pensive stare went from Reese to outside the glass doors where everyone was calling for them to go. "This all sounds so silly. Why does it matter who dresses up and walks beside my sister?"

"Tradition, Dunc. I'll ask Xavier. He'll do it." Gavin pulled out his phone and began texting.

"No." He took Gavin's phone from his hands. "Destiny's person is fine. She isn't changing."

"This is not about what you want. We have to make sure she's ready. Having a Lancaster at her side as she is presented to society will have a huge impact. His family's connections and favor are extended to her, and with the way she aspires to be a federal judge, this gives her many more opportunities."

"So no one cares about the potential through self-achievement? My sister just graduated at the top of her class and was accepted into every school she applied to. Her opportunities shouldn't be linked to a nineteen-year-old boy that walks her—" Duncan went still. An expression of understanding flashed across his face. "This was why, isn't it?"

Reese's line of sight went to her feet. She knew where this inquisition was leading and was sad they had to rehash it; mad because it might set them back again.

"Dunc...we don't make the rules." The remorse Gavin possessed was unlike anything she'd ever seen from him.

"Maybe you don't, but you both still live by them. This conversation is proof."

Reese choked and she wasn't even the one speaking. She'd had her own misgivings about how families like hers and the Lancasters viewed tradition. She had tried once to rebel against it. That battle had left her with a grandmother she never had the chance to say bye to, mommy issues, and a weak sibling bond. However, it was also the reason she felt compelled to help give Duncan a fighting chance at saving his reputation after her father tried to drag it through the mud, all the while prepping Destiny for a spectacular debut.

Maybe it was her way of making amends.

"We've been friends our whole lives, Dunc. You should know where I stand. I'm going back to the boat." Gavin frowned at Reese, then proceeded to walk down the path leading to the dock where everyone else waited.

"Can you answer me? Was it the escort selection that created the chain of events back then?"

She finally looked back up into his eyes and said, "Yes."

"Remind me again why I should forget." Duncan walked through the sliding glass doors. "If you're still coming, we're leaving now."

Eighteen

DUNCAN GRIPPED THE handle on Reese's beach bag and kept walking until he got to the dock. He didn't dare look over his shoulder and show how much he still wanted her to come despite the latest revelation. Confusing, but that had been his emotional state since she'd arrived in town. Today was yet another example. They had literally gone from almost burning up the sheets to being doused in a cold shower.

When would they be able to take one step forward without moving two back? Simple, he just had to keep his feet in front of him.

He reached the edge of the boat and turned to see that she was not far behind him. The way her breasts bounced in the bright, yellow bikini top as her hips swayed in the colorful sarong gave his dick sweet dreams—and right now he couldn't afford to think with that head.

Not if he wanted a chance to find what they'd been missing. After struggling through years of heartache that he'd concealed through meaningless relationships or hiding behind work, something about a second chance with Reese felt right. More importantly, he wanted to find peace with the Devlins. Their family had history and influence in the town, and he wouldn't let it destroy the legacy he intended to leave behind.

"Watch your step," he said, waiting at the end of the dock as he extended his hand to Reese. She accepted his help, unable to mask her shock over his gesture as he brought her close to him. "I can't pretend that it didn't happen. However, I'd like to see what we find if we let go of the past."

"I'd like that." Her smile was cautious, eyes sincere as she searched his face for understanding before she stepped down into the boat. "No more whiplash?" His face contorted as he came down behind her. Before he could ask what she meant, she said, "One minute you seem cool, the next not so much."

He nodded, knowing he couldn't help it. Nonetheless, he had to try if he wanted to let go and move forward.

"Nice of y'all to finally join us," Quinn teased before Duncan turned his evil eye on her.

Dammit, he wasn't in the mood for Quinn's jokes. However, he had to turn the lemons he'd received into lemonade or his day off would be ruined. "Reese was running on CP time." He chuckled, moving away as Reese swatted at him.

"That makes no sense, Chareese Antoinette Devlin. You live like two minutes away." Carrah plopped down in a seat and began drinking from a bottle of water. They were all still shocked she'd decided to come, given she often stayed away when Chris was present. "We really need to leave before the swimming hole gets crowded. Everybody and their mama's been talking about Dorian's. It's about to be a reunion. Peyton's going to be mad she missed it."

"Did you really just use my whole government name to make your point?" Reese sat next to Carrah, using her butt to push her from the seat she occupied, while everyone else roared in laughter. "Thought we were friends." She chortled.

"Stop, Reese!" Carrah laughed, pushing her back with her bottom. "You know I'm right. Dunc's just being nice and not calling you out for being late."

"Wonder why that is." The boat went quiet as Quinn side-eyed both Duncan and Reese.

Duncan disregarded Quinn's innuendo for the second time and gave everyone orders to prep for launch. The six scrambled to get situated, and then Duncan sat behind the wheel. Minutes later he eased off of the dock. The water was calm, the sky was clear, and the afternoon breeze helped to set his mind at ease.

He coasted the waterways, enjoying his time in the open air observing the wildlife of the place he called home. Originally, he'd planned to go fishing to clear his mind. Except, the need to see Reese again made him quickly come up with alternate plans. She would've easily declined a fishing trip since she never got past the bait or possessed the patience.

And as he caught a glimpse of her legs hanging out over the edge of the boat while she was laughing with Quinn and Carrah, he knew the change of plans had been worth it. The banter, laughter, and time with people he'd known all his life was the perfect remedy to life since purchasing Hill House.

A sense of rightness entered him the second he stopped resisting the way he felt about Reese. He'd made plenty of decisions in his life. None had been harder than deciding to no longer dwell in the past. It didn't mean he was forgoing his plans to convert Hill House into a youth village. He simply would not allow the anger he'd held over the actions of Reese's family to hold him prisoner anymore. Besides, he could no longer deny that fate had brought them together again.

"Y'all see that?" Chris shouted over the motor.

Duncan dropped the speed as they approached the narrow stretch of water that led to the heart of Dorian's Cove. There was a line of boats, music echoed all around them, and he could already smell the booze. Carrah had been right. Not sure what was going on this summer, but everyone was back.

"Blame it on Reese." Duncan gazed over his shoulder at her and winked. The way she winked back at him before dropping the sarong from around her waist made him slam on the brakes.

"She gonna be the reason you crash." Gavin slapped him across the back, releasing a deep chuckle.

For a second Duncan thought the same, and truthfully it had very little to do with the boat, and everything to do with his heart. Not wanting to linger on what-ifs, he refocused steering at what was in front of him. Once they cleared the narrow waterway, the iridescent blue waters of the cove came into view.

Their entrance was met with more excitement and energy than usual. Duncan, along with everyone on the boat, began cheering their arrival, yelling across the way to old friends, and celebrating the tradition they had all come to know as the salacious salute to summer in the Shores.

After a series of maneuvers he rafted up on the outskirts where some of their mutual friends had anchored. The space on his boat instantly turned into an official party, with Chris and Gavin breaking out the drinks while the girls turned up the music and began dancing.

The day passed with everyone enjoying the water, fun, and friendship. The cove lived up to its party-like atmosphere with boat hopping to racing on Jet Skis. By the time the sun was starting to set, summer madness had completely taken over, and they still had hours to go if tradition held and someone brought fireworks.

Duncan stepped back onto the platform of the boat. To his surprise he saw Reese sitting alone looking out at the water. All day he had wondered if they would find some alone time and now he had it. He toweled off and went to where she sat at the front of the boat.

"Surprised you didn't go tubing with the girls." Duncan studied the sunset before claiming the seat beside her.

"You know I'm not that adventurous. Jet Skiing is pushing it." She laughed, forcing one from him. "Thanks for inviting me. Today has been fun. Sad to say, I forgot what this place was like."

"I doubt you forgot. Maybe you didn't want to remember." Their eyes met for a second. "I know because for the past ten years, I've tried to forget our last summer together. I didn't want to be reminded of how you left." An awkward moment of silence sat between them. "Do you reme—"

"Vividly," she gasped, cutting him off. She turned away, her mind attempting to claw out of the memory of her father barging into the McNeals' front door, dragging her inside with his mother behind. She wouldn't dare look at Duncan now with the shame of that night holding her hostage.

"Your father addressed me as 'son of the help' before he accused me of taking advantage and defiling you. His threat to ruin my college career with a simple phone call was scary. I was a kid who had finally broken through barriers to be the first one in my family with a shot at changing my life by getting a college degree."

Reese faced Duncan. She wanted to reach out to him, but he seemed so far away as his gaze remained fixed on the water.

"Miss Constance finished off your dad's insults by telling me I would never be good enough for you because I was a have-not. A word I had not heard until then as she expressed that I had *overstepped* my station in life. Guess I was only good enough to be her errand boy and keep you entertained when she was busy…Do you know what hearing stuff like that does to a person?" His question was laced with pain. She shook her head no. "And you never stopped them or claimed otherwise."

He looked her dead in the face. "You threw us away and left me out there alone. I wouldn't have ever left you like that. Hell, I had just finished defending you against Drexel Collins at the lighthouse."

"I'm so sorry, Dunc." Tears welled in her eyes. "I was mentally battered and bruised from defending our relationship after they'd found us at the lighthouse. By the time we arrived at your place the fight was stolen from me. I'd suffered allegations of giving myself to you and being pregnant because they believed that was the only reason I would jet out on a boy like Drexel and throw away my future." She sniffed, wiping at her nose, and then took a step closer to him. Her fingers reached out and tangled with his. "There are no words that can express how sorry I am for how things went down. I loved you, Dunc…never wanted to hurt you," she whispered.

He'd never stopped loving her, which was why the slashes she cut into his heart had taken so long to heal. Finally hearing her say sorry out loud touched him in a way he never expected. A long, loud exhalation passed his lips.

"You don't know how long I've waited to hear you say that." The shackles fell away from his heart.

"That I loved you?" she asked, and he shook his head. "That I'm sorry." He nodded. "I didn't know. I once thought that by saying sorry, it meant I was the reason we were pulled apart…and I didn't want to accept that responsibility. However, I've come to realize that by not saying anything, I hurt us so much more. I guess it's the reason I've been so determined to find a way back to you."

He squeezed Reese's hand and pulled her until she was sitting on his lap. He kept the head on his shoulders focused because the one below was stirring, rising to meet her warm, luscious body atop his. Had they never lived in this world without each other they may have never known how much they seemed to need each other now. His hands framed her face as his thumbs wiped her tears, and he stared deep into the eyes of the only woman he had, and probably would ever, love.

Their lips collided. Passion and desire flowed from one to the other as his tongue slipped between her lips demanding all of her affection. His fingers threaded the fine strings of her hair, holding her the way he had dreamed of for so many nights.

"Dunc," she whispered, catching her breath. "I missed you so much."

He claimed her lips again, loving the feel of her hips rolling into his lap. Where this would end, he had no idea. For the moment his heart was in her hands, and he prayed she wouldn't break it this time.

Nineteen

DUNCAN TURNED HIS face up to the shower spray. Two days had passed since he kissed Reese until her lips were plump and bruised. He wanted more of her, but that moment couldn't be rushed.

His hand reached down between his legs, grabbing the heavy hardness that would never forget the way Reese had straddled him on the boat before she ground her hips against him. Their kiss had set his body ablaze, and all he'd fantasized about since then was her beautiful brown legs being spread wide in his bed.

He gripped his manhood, stroking it as his mind flashed back to her sexy body in that yellow bikini. His hand froze. He let go of himself and reached for the shower handle and then flipped it to cold water. His body tightened as the chill tempered his lust. Reese was so much more than a warm body he desired between his sheets. She was the one he had promised sunshine, the moon, and stars. It seemed as though he'd waited a lifetime for her, and he'd do it all over again because he only wanted her—mind, body, and soul.

Once he'd reset his priorities, he moved through his morning routine with an efficiency that allowed him time to review project updates before he left home for a site visit. His mind began pondering new ideas for the properties in queue when his phone rang, displaying Rebekah's number. After seeing Gavin's social media post of them prepping for the cove, she'd called and texted him more than what was required for a PR director.

It was Tuesday, though, and he'd spontaneously taken a three-day weekend, so he needed her to share the progress she'd made with Hill House. Besides, he had time since he was on his way to visit a project south of the Shores. He also wanted to avoid making things awkward once he arrived at the office later. Although, if he was honest, she'd already done that.

"Morning, Rebekah." His corporate tone was a must lately since it seemed she needed a reminder that they would never be a couple again.

"Duncan," she whimpered. He could almost see her pouting. "I've tried reaching you all weekend, and then you took Monday off."

"I had to unplug. Needed some personal time," he clipped. "Do you have an update on the public relations for the youth village project?"

"Yes." She perked up. "Turns out your friend was being honest."

"Was there a doubt?"

"Uhh...well, no, I guess not." Her breath was audible through his car speakers. "At any rate, the fifty-thousand-dollar donation in honor of continuing to educate and uplift youth across the South made local and regional news. The *Gazette* combined it with the interview they did of you for the front page. The story is trending, and a few national outlets have reached out for a comment.

"Overall buzz is positive. It did what she said it would. However, there's one catch. The Lakeside debutante committee would like you to attend a breakfast. I'm sending the date to your calendar. If you can't make it, I'll represent the firm."

"No need. I'll make the time. Thanks for your efforts. You know what this project means to me."

A loud sigh filled his ears. "When can we talk about us? I moved here to be near you."

One, he never asked her to move to Florida. Two, there was no more us. If he'd been the kind of man to string Rebekah along, promising to eventually patch things up, then he might have empathy. However, he had been honest about their status before she packed her bags and came to the Shores. And it was clear she couldn't maintain her professionalism within their boundaries. He needed to consider having her removed.

"Rebekah, this is not the time." A beep from his phone prompted him to look at the screen. Reese was calling. "I have an incoming call. We can chat when I get to the office later." He disconnected and accepted the call. A smile took over his face before he spoke. "Good morning, beautiful."

"Morning." He could hear her smile even as she yawned.

"Still in bed?"

"No," she sighed. "Just still a bit sleepy."

"But I didn't keep you up last night." The line went dead silent. Dammit, he was getting ahead of himself. "I—"

"That's if you can," she purred into the line.

"Is that a challenge?"

"It can be." She paused and then cleared her throat. "I was actually calling to congratulate you on making the front page of the *Gazette* and the *Sentinel*. The phones have been buzzing off the hook here. You've caused quite the stir, Mr. McNeal."

He chuckled. "I owe it all to you. Thank you."

"You deserve it, Dunc." Her voice was serious, solemn almost, and it humbled him. Like it used to when they were young after he became frustrated with his sketches of the antebellum columns or ornate gables from historic buildings downtown—and she'd encouraged him not to give up.

Making the decision to let her back in had been a risk that consumed him. In the back of his mind he still held his uncertainties. Moments like this were why he'd dived into the deep end not wanting to be rescued. "Will I see you this evening?"

"I'm not missing Miss Pearl's cooking. She promised me a smothered pork chop, and I plan to claim that." He laughed hard. "Plus, Destiny and I have a few things to do so, yes."

"Well, all right then. I'll see you later."

"Okay."

* * *

Reese hung up the phone. Her mind could've easily traveled along the naughty highway Duncan's silky, deep voice tempted her down. Instead, she chose to focus on the excitement of seeing him this evening and darted from her room to downstairs.

Her mother and sister were waiting in the hearth room for her so they could leave for the debutante's community service project together. A chill went up her spine as she entered the space where neither of them offered or returned her greeting. Clearly something had happened to make them ignore her.

"Is everything okay?" she asked glancing from her mother's pursed lips to her sister's folded arms.

"Marvelous," her mother replied in her haughty tone before cutting her eyes at Alex as she got up from her chair.

For a second, Reese was caught off guard, seeing her mother dressed down in blue jeans and a T-shirt. Once she regained her bearings, Reese scrambled behind her mother and sister as they moved to the garage and entered the car, where she again asked if they were okay. Only it seemed as though she were talking to brick walls. The silent treatment remained as her mother drove. Not in the mood for mind games, she decided to try once more.

"Did something happen? Why are you both acting so strange?" Reese glanced away from her mother's profile to look at her sister in the back seat.

For a while she didn't think they would answer her. Finally, Alex said, "Xavier Lancaster."

"What about him?" Reese asked, now that she was alerted to Alex's jealousy and became unconcerned with the tantrum her sister was having.

"Jolie called and told me her son was coming into town to escort Destiny McNeal." Her mother huffed as her hand slapped the wheel. "Of course, she's excited. All of those accomplished boys and no girls to doll up. She also mentioned that you had asked Gavin if Xavier was available. How could you, Chareese? This is Alexandria's time to shine."

Breathe, count to three. Was her mother serious? "You wanted me to volunteer my time as a past debutante, and I did. The committee assigned me as Destiny's mentor. The girl's escort did not meet committee standards, and so I did for her what I would've done for any young lady I was assigned to help. How is that taking away from Alex's shine? My God, she's being escorted by Carter Chennault." Her voice had raised a decibel.

"Lower your voice, Chareese. I am still your mother."

"I never said you weren't."

"You do realize Xavier Lancaster was the national teen president and an All-America and Gatorade Baseball player of the year who turned down Division One athletic scholarships to study medicine at Johns Hopkins." Alex lashed at Reese with her anger. "And he's super hot."

"This is ridiculous. So, the two of you are giving me the cold shoulder over a freaking escort. If there were ever a definition for shallow"—she turned and gestured at the both of them—"you two are it."

"I did the same for you, Chareese." Her mom turned into a parking lot, pulled into a space, and slammed on the brakes.

"What?"

"You heard me. I was the one who arranged for Drexel to escort you while you begged for a boy that would have dimmed your shine as you were presented to society. Your debut is one that people still talk about. It's the reason why Alexandria has such an image to uphold."

Reese stared at her mother. She had no idea of the ripples she had created in her quest to preserve a stupid image.

"Don't look at me like that. You did the very same thing for Destiny. You're more like me than you'll ever care to know or admit." Her mother snatched the keys from the ignition and exited the car with Alexandria in tow.

About fifteen minutes passed before Reese finally gathered herself from their blowout. She had never been so close to calling her mom out. One of the tenets of the ball was to help young ladies establish friendships and lasting relations with other like-minded girls. Together they would gain confidence and have the support of each other as they entered a world that might sometimes require support beyond the familial unit. If Alex and her mom wanted a competition, they should have participated in a pageant.

Rather than see them again, Reese called for an Uber. She was done wasting time on people who were afraid to evolve and uplift each other.

Twenty

"ONE, TWO, THREE, one, two, three, one, two, three...make sure your hand is rested firmly at her waist, Andre."

Duncan heard Reese call out before he shrugged off his coat and stepped into the archway of the small studio. From afar, he watched as Reese adjusted Destiny's posture before she repositioned the duo, explaining the rules of the waltz. His curiosity, however, was piqued, and he wondered why Reese had gone through all that trouble of asking Gavin for his brother to escort Destiny if his cousin was here practicing with his sister now. He didn't want to jump to conclusions. However, it was rare for Destiny to mention boys, so he wondered if it was a comfort thing.

"No, that's not right. You have to be close while still giving Destiny space so you're not stepping on her feet." The boy began asking her a question, seemingly frustrated by the process. "Duncan," Reese called from across the room. "Come, help me show them."

He pointed to himself, needing to make sure she was talking to him. "It's been years. I doubt I remember." They had only danced a few times when the world wasn't watching, when they'd mimicked the people who danced in the inn's music room at formals her grandmother hosted.

"And just like I told you back then"—she motioned for him to come inside the small studio—"it's like learning to walk. Once you learn, you don't forget." She took his jacket from his hands and draped it over a chair.

Reese sashayed back to him, heels clicking against the wood floor as she flaunted her curvaceous body, which was bound in a tight purple top and leggings. He pulled his mind back from debauchery and accepted her in his arms as she came to him. She coached his hand placement and reminded him of the dance's movement. The two practiced a few minutes before she told Destiny to cue the music.

When the music started, they began to move. "One, two, three, one, two, three…" she whispered to him before gently placing his hand slightly below her waist. "You're doing good." She smiled up at him.

He smiled back. "I had a good teacher." He whirled her around and gave her a turn, then brought her back into him and continued the traditional step.

"I didn't teach you that." Her lips became stiff and humorless while maintaining her rhythm. "Must've been someone else."

"Even if it was…Who am I here with now?" Her eyes met his again. "I missed you too."

Her abrupt stop caught him off guard. He fumbled to make sure he didn't step on her, then saw she had gone slack-jawed. "Why didn't you tell me when I first told you?"

His shoulders shrugged. "You didn't deserve to know." He nudged her to continue moving. "Why is Xavier not here?"

"Because Destiny deserves the choice I wasn't given. My mother reminded me of that this morning." She gripped his hand tighter. "And, you were right the other day. It shouldn't matter. The focus is on Destiny and her accomplishments. She has a decision to make after she meets Xavier. Honestly, I doubt it will be hard since your cousin isn't all that interested in escorting her. He's merely keeping the peace with his big cousin." Reese looked over to the teenagers, who had begun their waltz again, and barked a few commands. "At least if she chooses Xavier, then she may not have aching feet after her dance." They both laughed and broke apart so Reese could provide further instruction to Destiny and Andre.

Duncan tried not to, but he couldn't help wishing Reese was still in his arms. Years ago, when he first came to this very studio to learn the waltz, he thought she was crazy. His uncultured mind had believed it to be something only white people did at their functions.

Reese had explained otherwise, sharing the origins of the dance and why they did it for the debutante ball. She had opened his eyes, like she always did. Every summer for as long as he could remember, she'd helped him to understand that there was a world beyond the one he lived in in Mount Dora, and he deserved the chance to be in it.

"Dunc," his sister called. "Snap out of it. I've called you like three times. Come dance with me."

He started toward his sister. "Sorry." He paused, looking around, then gave a quick goodbye wave to their cousin as he walked out. Reese was already gone. "Where's Reese?"

"She went to the bathroom while you were in la-la land. You like her, don't you?" Destiny met her brother in the middle of the floor and then positioned herself to be his dance partner. "Don't lie to me, big brother. I can tell you do. I also heard Mom and Dad saying this was like some summer from a long time ago."

Duncan chuckled, "Why are you all up in my bidness?" He

smiled down on his sister to soften the blow of giving her nothing. He loved her and gave her the answers to most of the questions she asked, but not this.

"So you can be all up in mine, but I can't be in yours?" She smacked her teeth.

"That's how it works. I'm the oldest and—"

"It's okay to like someone, Dunc."

* * *

Reese returned to the studio to find Duncan and Destiny practicing the waltz. She turned her head up to the ceiling still unbelieving that God had given them a second chance. She had finally done the right thing instead of blindly choosing familial ambitions that were only rooted in self-gain.

His kind and caring spirit shone bright as he twirled his sister around. It was sweet, and obvious that their bond was close. She let them continue until the music faded.

"We need to hurry and get to the ice cream shop." She gathered her belongings swiftly.

"Ice cream shop? I thought we were going to my mom's for dinner."

"When's the last time you checked your messages, Dunc?" Destiny asked as she sat on the floor and began changing out of her heels into tennis shoes. "Mom had to cancel because her meeting at church is running long, and Reese has to introduce me to Xavier Lancaster."

A myriad of expressions ran over his face. Finally he said, "Wait a minute. I honestly don't understand why Andre was just here if you're about to go meet Xavier, and vice versa. I get you're trying to figure all of this out. However, both of those boys have lives. You can't string people along, Destiny."

"She's not." Reese jumped in. "I will introduce her to Xavier. She's going to politely thank him for being willing to escort her and then make small talk about the first year of college. If she chooses him, they can start to build chemistry. If not, then she's made a friend. A debutante must build a network, and he would be a great addition."

Reese stood quiet while Duncan processed her words. She had been one hundred percent honest. Ever since earlier today when her mother compared how she had arranged her escort to what Reese had done for Destiny to get Xavier, Reese refused to rip Destiny's choice from her.

"Just don't put my sister in the middle of any drama, Reese. I know how things get when certain families feel slighted."

She worried about it too, but wouldn't say it aloud. The saving grace was that Duncan and Gavin's friendship was rock solid. They would prevent a rift. "You have my word. I'll speak to Mrs. Lancaster myself." She nodded, still trying to get a read on him as Destiny stood fidgeting her fingers.

"Well, ice cream it is." He clapped his hands and started to the door. He quickly did an about-face when Destiny reminded him of his coat. "Dessert before dinner, you girls are going to get me in trouble." He pushed the main door open and held it as they exited to the sidewalk.

"Nothing wrong with good trouble, Dunc. It'll be like old times." She winked and kept walking.

No less than five minutes later they were entering the parlor. Unlike the candy shop, Miss Mabel's had changed. The sweet smell of fresh waffle cones didn't greet her, nor did a little, old, white-haired lady. In fact, it didn't even seem that fresh-churned ice cream was their signature anymore.

The carousel-themed decorations that used to adorn the walls and ceiling had also vanished. They had been replaced with images of milkshakes with toppings that included brownies, cupcakes, and donuts. Hopes of indulging in the best praline pecan ice cream she'd ever had in her life quickly diminished.

"Duncan, my friend!" A young, blond woman came from around the corner and hugged him, then Destiny. When she pulled away, she scanned Reese quizzically. "Why do you look so familiar?" The woman's chubby cheeks deflated as she looked to Duncan for help.

He smiled, then folded his arms. "You two really don't remember each other?"

Reese studied the woman's face. Her bright blue eyes sparkled with mischief as a smile stretched back onto her face. Reese then recalled a girl a few pounds lighter with a pageboy haircut helping around the parlor. As if Duncan had read her mind, he nodded at her.

"LaVonda Harrison," Reese said, though not a hundred percent sure she had guessed right.

The woman giggled, "Yeah, it's Vonnie! Oh my God, no one has called me by my real name since Mama passed away." A wave of sadness rolled over the woman before she reached over and wrapped her arms around Reese. "It's good to see you, Chareese, been a long time."

"I know. I've promised everyone to be better about visiting." She paused, remembering Miss Mabel. She had been a huge ally for the Black community in the Shores, and even supplied fresh vanilla ice cream to her grandmother at Hill House for fancy dessert nights when they served peach cobbler. Her mouth watered recalling those fond times. "I'm sorry to hear about your mother."

"Thank you. It's been a rough couple of years." She headed to go behind the counter. "Mama loved to make ice cream. That's why she opened this shop and ran it as a one-woman show.

Sadly, that's also why everything fell apart. She never taught me anything. Luckily Mrs. McNeal knew a thing or two from when she had worked here and was able to teach me enough to get by for a while. Y'all having the usual?" she asked Destiny and Duncan, who both nodded yes.

"Your mom worked here too?" Reese asked Duncan while trying hard to contain her shock.

"She had to make ends meet." His lips pressed together while Destiny's eyes went to the ground. "A maid's salary doesn't always put enough food on the table."

He wrapped an arm around Destiny and stepped past Reese to move to the counter. She listened as they made chitchat with Vonnie while pretending to study the menu. Not once in her youth had she viewed Duncan and his family as people that struggled to make ends meet. The relationship she had witnessed between him and his family was so whole, loving, and rich.

After Reese wrapped her privileged mind around the divide of their socioeconomic status as youth, she focused back to the menu. Her sweet tooth ached seeing ice cream layered with crushed cone and caramel mixed into a shake and topped with a Belgian waffle. She had never sampled anything like what was displayed, and she licked her lips at the whipped cream piled high on top of an oversized pecan sandie with pecans and drizzled fudge. Once they finished ordering, the three of them sat down while Vonnie and her team prepared their shakes.

"Wow, I never imagined ice cream…or a shake in this way," Reese admitted.

"It was Dunc's idea." Destiny gave her brother a pageant girl smile. He frowned at her. "Well sorta," she corrected with a sigh.

"Do tell," Reese said, staring at the two, excited to hear more about how ice cream turned into shakes with toppings. Only Duncan shook his head in protest. "Oookay, never mind then."

Their table went quiet for a few minutes. Duncan wasn't ready to let her all the way in. His refusal reminded her of the connection that had been lost. She thought the day on the boat had helped to mend those fences, but it was apparent he needed more time.

The tension floated away, and the trio became lively again once their order arrived. Reese marveled at how different and delicious each dessert was, presented in old-fashioned mason jars. There would be no room for dinner.

About halfway through, Duncan glanced at his watch. "I thought Xavier was meeting you here."

Destiny's shrug prompted both Reese and him to pull their phones out.

Before Reese could hit send on her text message to Gavin, Xavier walked in with her sister on his arm. Had it not been for the loud door chime, none of them would've noticed the way Alex pranced at his side, giggling like a wannabe trophy. It made Reese see red. There was an unwritten rule among debutantes that said a girl's escort was off-limits until after the ball. So even though Destiny still had a choice to make, Alex wasn't aware of that fact. Reese knew that Alex was fully complicit in schemes that reeked of Genevieve. But why?

She couldn't recall animosity like this between her and the girls she debuted with. A little friendly competition, yes. They all had long lists of community service, high grade point averages, multiple college acceptances, boys from the most wealthy families as their escorts, and, of course, designer gowns that made most brides jealous. However, this mean-girl business she witnessed with her sister had no place in the Lakeside Debutante. Her sister's attitude toward the event was in direct conflict with the mission of empowering girls to form bonds and make an impact in society.

Reese gripped the handle of her spoon. The frustration she'd held for her sister had reached its boiling point. She ignored the giddy wave from Alex as she led Xavier over to where they sat, and didn't miss the vacant expression that settled over Destiny's face.

"Dunc." Xavier rushed over, extending his hand to Duncan. "Didn't know you would be here. Good seeing you." They shook hands and then he moved to Reese. "Hey, Reese, been a long time." Reese stood and hugged the once little boy that now eclipsed her in height, before he moved to the other side of the table. "You must be Destiny." He offered her his hand. She took it and stood. "It's nice to finally meet you. I've heard a lot about you."

Destiny blushed while returning pleasantries. Duncan's patience seemed to be wearing thin. He looked as though he forgot Xavier was his best friend's brother and not some random guy giving his baby sister attention.

"We should hurry up if we plan to catch the movie, Xavier." Alex went around to where he was and tugged his hand.

Reese shot daggers at her sister. Once the ball was over, she wouldn't hold back her words of ridicule over Alex's thirsty actions. For now, she'd play her sister's game and hijack the planned movie. After all, they had the same teacher. "Movies?" She then turned back to Destiny. "Didn't you mention a new release you wanted to see earlier today? Maybe you could all go together."

"Yeah, it's okay though. I don't want to intrude."

"You're not." Xavier smiled back at Destiny, and Duncan released a long, audible breath. "Besides, I never said I was going to the movies. Alex found me on my way in to meet you and asked if I wanted to go. I'd much rather sit here. Kinda hard to get to know someone while a movie is playing."

Once Reese sensed Xavier had a genuine interest in meeting Destiny and that he couldn't be manipulated by her sister, she tuned their conversation out and started small talk with Duncan. By the time the three teenagers moved to another table, she held very few reservations about their ability to gel.

"Thank you," Duncan whispered before he glanced in the direction of his sister. Alex's attempt at launching a wrecking ball had been that obvious. And Reese couldn't stand by and be complicit. She'd already done that to a McNeal. Shame on her if she allowed it again.

"Why are you thanking me?" Reese picked up her spoon and began messing over the treat she no longer had an appetite for.

The whole time she avoided eye contact with him. There was no doubt in her mind that her sister's efforts to sabotage the meeting between Destiny and Xavier had been orchestrated. She planned to confront her mother when she got home, since Alex could've only found out about their plans from Xavier's mother spilling the beans to theirs.

"Because I said no drama," he chuckled before his face became serious. "I think I was like eleven when your grandmother swore up and down that I pocketed cookies." Her brows creased together. "Of course, now we know it was the maintenance guy. But I'll always remember how you defended me, and you just did the same for my sister."

"I don't know why I stopped…standing up for you." She sighed. "Now that I think about it, my grandmother did like to accuse you of things."

"She did." His entire body tightened. "Miss Constance blamed me for you never returning home to see her when she was sick. She also said it was my fault that you would never fulfill your duty to Hill House."

Fulfill my duty? Everyone in town knew Reese had a sweet spot for the inn. She shadowed her grandmother, learned the day-to-day operations, how to host, and how to change the house over for the seasons. At no point in her childhood or teenage years did she desire to be anything like Constance Devlin...until recently. Her imagination ran wild thinking of ways to beautify a space. Reese would unpack it all later. For now, she needed Duncan to understand that none of where they were now was his fault.

"Duncan." Reese reached over and grabbed his hands. "That woman disowned me after accusing me of doing things with you that I didn't know much about at seventeen. You were never the reason."

"Then what was?"

"If I tell you the answer, will you tell me why you are so determined to turn Hill House into a youth village?"

He nodded.

"Can we talk and walk? There's a lot of ears here."

He slid from the booth, extended his hand, and helped her from the seat. After saying bye to Alex, Destiny, and Xavier, they began down the path that would lead them back to the old lighthouse. It was the starting point of that night ten years ago. Maybe confessing truths where they met a bitter end could help them begin again.

Twenty-One

THE EVENING BREEZE swung through the branches of the ancient oaks, filling her lungs with courage as they walked through downtown. The last time she visited the lighthouse she had been with Duncan. It was the night chaos erupted. Her father had found her with Duncan as he stood ready to fight Drexel Collins for touching Reese inappropriately. Duncan's act of chivalry exposed what they really meant to each other, and her father wasn't having it. So he carted her away like a criminal because she had feelings for a boy that was from a different side of the Shores.

Status had been the root of her parents' evil. She'd run away from it and everything that confined her to being someone she didn't want to be. To learn her grandmother blamed Duncan for her absence from summer over the years again proved that her people maintained privilege instead of accepting responsibility for their mistakes.

It was similar to the situation with Hill House. Her father had not acknowledged the business was doing poorly, even though there had to be signs of mismanagement. Yet, he didn't care about those particulars. He couldn't take accountability for the failure that gave Duncan the opportunity to purchase. He simply wanted the house back because it was his mom's.

"I didn't know how much I missed it here until I got back." She looked around at the lakeside shops as they got closer to where the buildings ended and the marina began. "I never thought I'd admit that."

Duncan's fingers tickled her wrist before his hand took hers and held it the way he used to. "Before I left for college, I thought the same. Philadelphia quickly reminded me of why I love the Florida sun." He upturned his face to the sky. "I couldn't wait to get out of there."

Reese laughed, and they continued exchanging stories of their time away from the Shores…their time away from each other. Not for the first time did she ponder what life would've been like had that night ten years ago never happened.

"Over here." She guided them as their feet went from the cement to the grass.

"Can't believe I'm out here in my good shoes," Duncan said as he carefully walked through the grass.

"Yes, you do pay a lot of money for your shoes. Is it your fetish?" She peeked over her shoulder at him and smirked.

They stepped onto the base of the lighthouse and were captivated by the view of Lake Dora. A thousand stars hung in the sky, casting a glow on the water. She had forgotten that some of the most beautiful sites she'd seen in this world were in the Shores.

"Did you say *fetish?*" He leaned in, whispering in her ear. "Wouldn't you like to know." He winked at her and then straightened at her side and looked out at the water.

Her knees got weak and she struggled to find her breath. There was no denying the physical attraction begging for attention. Except, now was not the time to be consumed by lust. This was a moment she had rehearsed in her head too many times to count. She had to get this right; had to unlock everything she was holding inside because of stupid pride.

"The last time we were here"—she clutched at the tightness settling into her chest—"I thought the world was about to end." He turned to her, pain etched across his face.

Reese closed her eyes and blocked out the images of her father, his mother, Drex, her grandmother, and everyone else who had altered the landscape of her life that night ten years ago.

"Before we met that night, I was told you weren't allowed to be my escort then forced to attend a mixer for debutantes and their escorts at Hill House."

"I remember. Unfortunately, I now have an understanding of the escort selection process," he sighed.

"The part you don't know is that I couldn't accept my parents' judgment. I was downright determined to have you in my life in a special way, and since I couldn't debut with you, I decided to give myself to you." His brows furrowed and she caught another steadying breath. "I was a virgin without much knowledge of how it…sex…worked.

"So, I found your mom, who was serving at the party, and asked her, since she had been like a second mom to me through-out the years. She asked if I was having sexual thoughts about you, and I confessed that I was. She watched me sneak out of Hill House after messaging you to come here. Drex followed me, but she was the only one who knew I was leaving to meet you here. Not long after, my father showed up."

"What!" Duncan shouted, jerking back. He paced in a circle for a few minutes before clasping his hands around her arms and squeezing her tight. Disbelief was written all over his face.

It was the very reason she never told him. She had not

wanted to taint the way Duncan viewed his mother. And while she would suffer remorse over revealing these facts, she would get it all out tonight. A tear slid down her face. "You know the rest. We showed up at your house for my grandmother to ensure our paths would never cross again. You asked why I stayed away. The shame of that night, upsetting my family, and losing you were all reasons. But the one that hurt the most was being let down by a woman who was like a mother to me. Your mother's betrayal stole away a true friend and the boy I loved while leaving me shunned by my family. How could I come back?"

"You don't think I could have stayed away? There was always an internship, job, trip… But dammit I came back, every summer, hoping to see you." He took her face between his hands and kissed her to the depths of her soul. Her heart rattled against the chains of the cage her parents had trapped it in, then burst free. How long had she waited to feel like this? "I'd come back a thousand times if it meant I'd always hold you like this."

* * *

Nathaniel Hawthorne had once written that the passage of time leaves shadows behind. Their shadow was love, and Duncan didn't mind that it had followed them for ten long years. His heart exploded as she wrapped her arms around him, accepting his affectionate demands.

He broke the kiss. "I always thought your family owed me an apology." He nosed her before pressing his lips to hers once more. "I believe my mom owes you one as well."

"No." She shook her head. "Everyone did what they thought they had to back then."

"At our expense." He backed away from her, his jaw twitching before he turned and started heading over to the lake. He lumbered along the shoreline, picked up a handful of rocks, and threw them into the water. "They robbed us," he shouted out into the night.

She moved quickly to comfort him. "I know," she whispered and slid her hand into his. His anger idled as he relished the rightness of her hand in his. Why did everyone else think they were wrong? "I still try to understand why. I mean, is where we come from really such a big deal?" She sighed, "I thought your mom liked me."

He huffed, "So did I. I'm still trying to wrap my head around it."

He had a sinking feeling that his mother's betrayal was rooted in the fears she harbored about seeing what happened when someone crossed one of the Shores' most influential families. As someone who witnessed the reach of Constance and her sons, he wanted to believe his mom had acted out of desperation to protect him. He would one day forgive her, but he needed Reese to understand why it had been a struggle to bestow the same courtesy to her family.

He braced himself for what could come after he shared his thoughts. However, he'd promised to be open.

"My fondest memories of Hill House are only the times you were there." He avoided eye contact, afraid of what he might see. On the other hand, he was determined to go on. "Your grandmother was not always nice, and she intentionally belittled my mom and ignored my grandma. When she found out they were selling hot plates from our home to raise money so they could start their own restaurant, she threatened their jobs, then attempted to blacklist them in the community. She ultimately fired them and then hired new people to cook the meals they created at Hill House and compete against them. Thankfully, people could taste the difference. But your grandmother never wanted them to have a restaurant."

"My grandmother wasn't the type that set out to ruin people. She spent a lot of time giving back, Duncan."

"Even after she came to my parents' home with you and your father and told me I was a *have-not* and therefore unworthy of holding your affections? You would still believe she was incapable of doing what she did to my family? Your grandmother was a spiteful old woman that couldn't stand to see us do better."

A tense silence sat between them. He couldn't get a read on Reese. She was shielding her thoughts and probably had instincts to run and never look back. Meanwhile, he began contemplating why he'd chosen to jump off the deep end again. The last time it didn't end well, and right now it felt like history could be repeating itself. No one had learned.

"This is why you bought the inn, isn't it? You're exacting revenge on my family."

He put his hand up to stop her and the schemes he had no doubt were being conjured in her head. "After the night you were ripped from my life, I was determined to prove to everyone in this town that your grandmother's declaration of me being nothing was a lie. I may not have had money, but I had enough smarts to go into the world and make something of myself, and so I did. I returned home often and saw that while other places were evolving, the Shores remained the same. I then set out to make it better here." His hands slid into his pockets.

"Part of improving the Shores is helping old businesses remain relevant while creating opportunities for new ones. When we decided to open a restaurant for my family, my parents had a trying time with the city. They got so much red tape, and it made me curious as to why there was so much resistance. I bided my time, studied the land acquisitions, properties, and families in the Shores to better understand how all of you had accumulated so much wealth and influence here while only residing three months out of the year. In the process I uncovered a little secret council that influences much of what happens here, including the opening of my parents' business.

"I wanted a seat at that table. However, my lineage wouldn't grant me one. But then I discovered your uncle had an illegitimate child with a woman on my side of town and that he liked to gamble. Didn't take long for the rumors to start about him not paying the staff, vendors, or his taxes. It was also clear that he hadn't been keeping the property up to your grandmother's standards. Eager to claim a seat at that table, I paid off all your uncle's debts and acquired a lien on the property. I had planned to remove the liens and give him back the property free and clear for his seat on the council. Except, my firm found an investor snooping around town trying to purchase land and properties with hopes of creating a touristy resort town.

"A man like your uncle with a gambling addiction would sell to anyone. So, my desperation to be a part of that little group was put on hold because I cared more about doing right by this community.

"When he tried to sell to that investor, he couldn't, so he came to me like I knew he would because I held all the liens and we struck a deal.

"Now that Hill House is a part of my portfolio, I approached it like all other projects. My firm conducted a PEST analysis, which is a review of the political, educational, social, and technological forces impacting an area, and determined that there weren't any nearby youth programs. There also aren't any centers providing core skills training or college readiness to help close educational gaps. Members of my team knew that I had always dreamed of having a place to help kids who came from similar backgrounds as me. We expanded my original vision a bit and imagined a youth village. I know what receiving an education did for me and I believe other kids need a chance too. The community needs this. It also allows us to preserve structures like the old inn while keeping commercial investors out. So, to answer your question, no this isn't about revenge."

Duncan released a breath he didn't realize he was holding. "And yet, I've been wrestling with myself over converting the inn to the youth village because I can see how you feel about the old house. I'm just curious why only you?"

"What do you mean?" She finally turned toward him again and began scanning his face.

"No one else from your family has reached out to me, unless you count them villainizing me on TV." He sneered. "You're the only one who seems to really care."

A small smile curved her lips and then she became serious again. "Can we go to Hill House? I think I can better answer your question there."

Reese extended her hand to him. Duncan took it, waiting for her to say more. She didn't and he had no clue of what she thought about his explanation. But she hadn't left, and she still wanted him by her side. Her actions said more to him than any words could right now.

Twenty-Two

"REMEMBER WHEN WE used to try coming in this way and your mom would shoo us away and send us to the side door?" Reese giggled as they took the steps up to the back door.

Duncan remained silent as he reached into his pocket for the key and then unlocked the back door. They entered inside the kitchen. "That was only because of you. In the months when you were gone it was the only way I was allowed to come in."

He brushed past her, cut on the kitchen light, and then pushed through the swing door. The same shame she'd experienced less than twenty minutes ago as they stood at the bank of Lake Dora had returned. She hadn't known how to respond then and she still was uncertain of what to say now.

Light filtered through the door prompting her to follow. The house was too still…dead like her grandmother. Perhaps it really was time to say goodbye. After everything Duncan had told her, why should she care if the house remained? "Dunc," she called.

"In the parlor," his voice carried from the other side of the downstairs area.

Reese took her time moving through the house. Every step was a transfer back in time. She remembered learning to set the buffet table, arranging fresh roses in the vase atop the piano, and fetching hot towels from the laundry room and carrying them to guests. Not once had she thought of the things she did around the inn as chores. Her grandmother had always assigned tasks that she believed prepared Reese to understand and learn the family business.

To fulfill her duty… Duncan's words from earlier hit her like a Mack truck, and she stopped dead in her tracks. What exactly did they mean? She closed her eyes and, for the first time in over ten years, wished to hear her grandmother's voice. Had the old woman foreseen the future, knowing that one son was too busy coddling hurt feelings over being left out while the other blew his inheritance at the gambling table?

In either case, Reese was the only one who had inherited her grandmother's creative nature that lent well to restoring and preserving the bed and breakfast. Suddenly, the thought of tinkering within the walls of Hill House with color, textures, and furniture, to transform it into a modern lakeside retreat, bloomed. The life she once thought she wanted as the art director for a magazine no longer seemed to make sense. Contemplation set in and questions began to mount in her head. And yet, Duncan's reality made her question the urges she felt to tap into the interior side of design and be the savior Hill House needed. She finally came to the archway of the parlor. Duncan had taken the chair nearest to the fireplace and was feverishly typing at his phone.

"Why did you never tell me?" Reese asked him the first of many unanswered questions running circles in her brain. This one was important. She had to know if she could bear the answer because if she couldn't, Hill House might not deserve a second chance.

His brows rose and his thumbs went still. "Tell you what, Reese? That your grandmother was an elitist that enforced the crabs-in-a-bucket mentality."

"That's not fair," she snapped.

"Maybe not. However, it is true."

She sighed, unable to resist fidgeting with her hands. It was hard to look into his handsome face after learning of all the not-so-nice things her grandmother had done to him and his family. "I'm sorry. I had no idea."

"I don't blame you for how Miss Constance was to me or my family."

"But, and you can be honest, it was a factor in your purchase."

He shot to his feet. "Even if I flirted with those notions, my mama raised me better than that." He huffed, throwing his hands in the air. "Reese, you wanted to come here to answer my question. So, I'll ask again. Why does it seem like you're the only one from your family who cares about this place?"

Reese dropped her eyes and began tugging her bottom lip between her teeth. She was afraid to disclose her epiphany, but holding it in could bring ruin. Before she could answer he started speaking again.

"I know you and Miss Constance remained at odds regardless of how much you both still loved each other." Their eyes met and he took a step to close the distance. "Being here can't be easy. The two of you used to be all over the place greeting high-profile guests, changing Maypole decorations to Juneteenth, hosting picnics, and so much more. I guess knowing those things makes me wonder if you are okay, and if it is why you seem to care more than your family."

God, he still had that sixth sense about her. She choked down a sob. No, she wasn't okay. And it shouldn't have taken them coming inside for her to realize. Still, he wasn't allowed to see her cry. She had teared up enough tonight, and right now he needed to see her strong and determined for the sake of this place.

Reese turned away from his gaze. She didn't have the courage to tell him her family did care. After all, her mom's plan was to send in the perfect Trojan horse for the purposes of wearing down Duncan's defenses. Except…she cared about him too. Her hope was that she could have both him and Hill House. So she would show him, like she planned to when she asked that they come here, why she cared so much.

"Did you know that during the Jazz Age, my great-grandmother Josephine let rooms to Black entertainers visiting the South on tour?" She took his hand, walked to the mantel, and scanned the photographs that were displayed. She picked up a picture. "This is Noble Sissle and Eubie Blake at the piano down the hall in the music room. Grandma Connie would often tell me how she felt like the vaudeville theater had come to Mount Dora when she was a little girl. Sissle was also a member of your fraternity."

"Your dad is too, and that doesn't stop how he treats me." Duncan shrugged halfheartedly and then refocused on the picture she was holding.

Reese put the picture down and walked out of the room. She motioned for him to follow and he did. She couldn't give up. There was too much at stake.

They stopped at the library that still held the antique secretary's desk. She rubbed her fingers across the carvings in the burnished walnut before pulling on a brass knob that opened a hidden drawer on the side. She pulled out an old fountain pen and pencil set then turned and placed it in his hand.

"Before Thurgood Marshall became a Supreme Court justice, he traveled here to help the local NAACP in the case of the Groveland Four. Grandma said it was a scary time. She witnessed her father and other men providing safety to Mr. Marshall. His dedication to fighting for what was right gave my great-grandparents and this community strength. They were able to protect Mr. Marshall. Of course, you know the men he was defending weren't so lucky."

Reese gestured to the old pen. "Before he returned home, he gifted those old pens to my grands for providing a safe haven."

"I knew the story of the Groveland Four. Never realized Thurgood Marshall stayed here, in Hill House." Duncan looked around the library and then closed the pen case before inserting it back into the hidden drawer. "He was also a member of my fraternity."

"Humph"—a grin curved her lips—"I know."

Reese continued taking him around the house, hesitant to reminisce on their memories for fear that it might uncover more misdeeds, so she focused on exposing him to unique moments and events that made Hill House special. It was apparent that he was learning a few things he never knew about the inn. However, she didn't know if they would be enough to convince him to preserve it as a bed and breakfast.

As they walked down the last hall that led up to the third story, an audible sigh escaped him. She glanced down to her watch, noting how late it was, but ignored it because she had one more thing to show him. To Reese, it was the most important.

"Reese." His hand came atop hers, stopping her from turning the doorknob. "It's late and I have an early meeting tomorrow. We don't have to climb those stairs. I get it, Hill House is special. Only, the reasons that made it special no longer apply. We don't live in a time that refuses lodging to people because they are Black. I am grateful that Hill House was here to meet a need for people who looked like you and me. Now, it must deliver on a new need, and that is to better prepare kids who look like you and me to become leaders in society."

She didn't disagree with fostering leadership development for the youth in the area. She'd met the girl in the boutique and saw the excitement upon her face at the chance to make something of her life. Duncan and Destiny were proof of what the right resources could do for those confined to the small town. However, it didn't have to be done in this space. There was still so much potential to bestow the hospitality of the South to clientele from all walks of life.

Black and white people could enjoy the history of Hill House while recharging their batteries in the lakeside town. It was always her grandmother's vision to make the bed and breakfast a respite for all people. And there was still something she needed him to see so that he could ponder if tearing down walls and renovating the space was the right thing to do.

"There's one more thing I want to show you. Will you let me?" His hand fell away from hers. She turned the knob and began up the short flight of stairs. "In this house we discovered our friendship. We played on the stairs, chased each other in the backyard, and hid in closets. When we got older, this was the one place my mind was free to think about you in ways that extended beyond friendship."

They entered the oversized room, which, just like her bedroom at her parents' home, had also become a time capsule.

Reese went to the iron-framed bed and got down on her knees. For a second she played with the ruffled French tulle bed skirt that her grandmother had custom-made for her after she'd fallen in love with one from the JCPenney catalog. She reached underneath the bed, pulled an extra-large screwdriver from an iron slat, and went to the small desk.

The second she started moving the desk, Duncan came over with a curious twinkle in his eyes and helped her. He watched while she took the screwdriver and wedged it between two wood planks and popped one up. She pulled a small box out and sat back on her heels.

"I hid things here because Grandma Connie wasn't a snoop like my mother. She actually encouraged me to have a special place to keep my secrets." Reese giggled, opening the box, and pulled out a cassette tape. "She said that everyone had one. This was mine." She held up the tape. "You gave this to me when I was sixteen."

She stared at the tape, recalling old-school and new-school R&B songs that had filled her head with giddy notions of teen love and made her wonder if he liked her as much as she liked him.

He cleared his throat. She lowered the tape from her line of sight and focused on him. "I was seventeen. That was my love letter to you." His hands went inside his pockets. "I didn't know how to say what I felt, nor did I want to ruin our friendship, so I made that tape, and hoped to God you wouldn't think I was weird."

He took the tape from her hands and began thinking of how he sat listening to songs that were at the top of the Billboard chart when they were teenagers, and even went all the way back to Motown hits. He'd played hundreds of songs in order to find the perfect ones that expressed all that she made him feel whenever they were around each other. Instead of burning a CD, he'd taken the time to make a cassette. They both had a thing for music and enjoyed playing old records and tapes. Plus, this way, she couldn't simply press a button and skip to the next song. She had to listen to the entire symphony that his heart had conducted for hers.

The moment was surreal, and it had completely caught him off guard. He remembered the day like it was yesterday. He had rushed over on his bike after hearing she had arrived in town. They went out back to the gazebo, and for the longest time he didn't offer any words as she lamented over him going away to college and meeting someone else that was older and on campus with him full-time. Finally he built up the nerve and gave her the tape. If he thought he was uncertain before her little historical tour, then he was standing at a brick wall now. He'd never been more torn on what to do with a property.

"Humor me." Her voice recaptured his attention. "Let's play a game. I give you a song that was on that tape and you tell me why you chose it. No holding back either. I want the truth."

He nodded, accepting that their night of truths was being given a second chance. "Think you can handle the truth?" His question was sincere. He was not interested in rediscovering a path of regrets when the future held possibilities for this reunion.

She nodded. "So... Troop, 'All I Do Is Think of You'?"

"Legit, was me all day every day even when you were here or away."

"'The Way You Make Me Feel' by MJ." She got up to her feet and began mimicking MJ's iconic moonwalk.

"I imagined us in that video." He chuckled. "Me chasing you until you realized you were the one for me."

Her feet went still and then she whispered, "'Ebony Eyes.'"

He couldn't help staring into her pretty brown eyes. They had always spoken to his soul, which was why he had chosen the song all those years ago. "All you had to do was imagine me singing those lyrics to you. Even now, the song wouldn't change."

She opened then closed her mouth. Whatever she wanted to say never came out. He could practically see the invisible wheels turning inside of her head, trying to catch his thoughts. This was the open book she asked for and he was giving it to her. She would never be able to say she didn't know. She fired away a few more songs and each time he confessed his heart.

Finally she swallowed hard and reclaimed the tape from his hands. "Trey Songz—"

"Made me want to do every naughty thing my seventeen-year-old self had ever heard of back then to you."

"And now?" Her teeth clipped her bottom lip.

He was the one to take a step to close the space between them. He cupped her neck before he leaned in and pushed his lips against hers. "If you let me, I'd do every naughty thing I know how to do to you."

"Please," she exhaled, dropping the tape, and then yanked off his coat.

Their kiss went from sweet to passionate as he pushed her against the wall. He caged her in and then pressed his lips into her neck before continuing down to her full breasts. She moaned, begging for more, and he planned to give her every rock-hard inch of him.

"Are you sure you want this, because when we get in that bed, I'm not holding back." He pressed his forehead to hers, waiting to make sure this was truly what she wanted. He refused to let them get carried away in the moment and then have regrets they couldn't forget in the morning.

Her fingers began making quick work of unhooking the buttons on his shirt. "I want this." She kissed him until they were both breathless. "I want you, but most of all I want us."

Their lips met again. His shirt fell to the ground and in a matter of seconds he'd stripped her down. He stood mesmerized. Her beautiful brown skin held every curve he ever wanted to explore.

He melted the minute her nipples pressed into his bare chest. She was soft and warm, and he couldn't wait to be inside her. "You feel so good." The feel of her skin against his was everything he could've ever imagined.

Duncan's palms filled with her breasts before they traveled down her flat belly, traced the hourglass of her waist, then grabbed her ass. He lifted her up and carried her to the bed, where he gently deposited her to the center.

Her hungry eyes had his manhood begging to break free of its confines. He took a step back unzipping his pants, never breaking eye contact. The way she watched him was hotter than hell. He had to calm down or it would be over before they could even start.

"Protection," she gulped with her eyes trained on his manhood.

He smirked and then retrieved a condom from his wallet before tossing it and his pants to the floor.

Reese came up on her knees, moved to the edge of the bed, and took the condom from him. She tore the wrapper with her teeth, removed it from the package, and rolled it down with an efficiency not even he could beat. Later he might ask where she picked up that skill.

She collapsed back into the pillows on the bed and spread her legs. He climbed atop her, his heart racing. His tongue parted her lips, and she greedily took over the kiss, wrapping her arms around his neck. Duncan pulled back, breathing hard, and began working her up for entry.

Her moans were the sweetest thing he'd ever heard. "Ready to take all of me, baby?" He gently pushed inside. A euphoric rush drowned his body and made him go still. She was incredibly tight, yet willing to receive him.

"Don't stop, Dunc," she moaned. "I can take it." She raised her pelvis, helping him to slide deeper inside of her.

He growled and leaned in, kissing her as he stroked in and out of her. This was his first taste of heaven, and he didn't think he could ever leave.

Twenty-Three

DUNCAN LAY LOOKING up at the ceiling while his fingers traced over Reese's soft skin. Tonight had been his wildest dreams come true, and he didn't know how he would ever go back to a life without her. He wanted this to be much more than a summer fling.

Perhaps if he found another location for the youth village, Reese would reconsider how frequently she visited the Shores. He got the sense that there was more than her guilt over not making amends with her grandmother that made her challenge the conversion of the inn.

Only, she had never said that. For all he knew she had only come to town to support her sister in the ball and…and…her family might still cling to notions of their relationship being forbidden. The acquisition of Hill House had done him no favors with the Devlins.

"Mmmm," she moaned, stretching beside him before her lips brushed against his nipple.

Round three, he was ready. Not sure if she was, but he ached to be inside her again. "You should stop. I'm not in control of him tonight." He glanced down to the tent that was pitched under the covers, and she giggled before her hand slid down his waist and wrapped around his thick rod.

"Maybe I don't want you to be." Reese stroked him, whispering dirty thoughts in his ear of how she wanted to feel him inside of her again. And then she straddled him.

There was nothing he could do to make his body not respond to her. The heat of her sex made him desperate to become one with her again.

She looked down into his eyes and said, "I have a question?"

Ah, damn, he prayed this was not one of those well-intentioned inquiries that would lead them down endless black holes. Although, he did harbor questions about her condom handling skills— He would never ask because it wasn't important. His ego was in charge, and based on the way she had responded to him, he knew no one had ever given it to her like he had. Last night was more than physical; he'd caressed her emotionally and there was so much more between them.

"I'm only answering if I can't be judged," he finally responded.

She nodded. "It's not like that."

"Then ask." He gripped her tight by the thighs, repositioning himself as her wetness spread across his manhood, making him want to table her Q&A.

A deep breath escaped her. "You said the tape was your love letter to me. How long had you loved me before you made it?"

They stared into each other's eyes. The question once again confirmed that this was a night of chance and unexpected revelations. His internal battle systems were going crazy. If he told her the answer, she'd know how long he'd agonized over her not being in his life. If he lied, he could maybe still protect a sliver of his heart. He refused to allow pride to stand in their way. After all, it was why they had lost so much time.

"I had loved you since we were old enough to ride bikes, Reese. You never looked at me or treated me like I was different because my mother cleaned this house or we lived on the other side of town. You were always so nice. Your beauty was both inside and out. Then one day I went from just thinking of you as my friend to daydreaming about holding your hand, kissing your lips, and whispering sweet nothings in your ear."

Reese gulped, then turned away from the intensity of his lingering gaze and dismounted him. He pushed up to his elbows, ready to defend the declaration he never thought he'd make, then paused, watching her go to where she'd retrieved the cassette tape.

She picked up the floorboard she'd removed and then returned to the bed and sat at his side on the edge. A second, maybe two passed before she offered him the wooden plank. "Turn it over," she requested softly.

He flipped the board. After a few minutes he glanced up at her. "You felt like this about me and never said a word?" His attention went back to where she had written their initials in a heart every summer since she was thirteen and he was fourteen.

"I didn't know how. We had been friends for so long, and then all of a sudden you became the hot, older boy that made my heart race. Every girl in the Shores wanted you...even those who I called my friends thought you were cute. They always asked me about you because of how close we were. I didn't think I could compete with them, especially the girls your age. Besides, I wasn't allowed to date, and I didn't want to lose you as a friend."

She fiddled with her thumbs.

"I never wanted any of those other girls, Chareese." His hands caressed her shoulder. "I always only wanted you. Exactly like right now, you're all I want."

* * *

Her eyes closed and she exhaled. She wanted him too, and not just for the summer. However, she knew Duncan would never leave his business or the life he'd built in the Shores for New York. On the contrary, she now understood why she lacked job satisfaction. Learning of her grandmother's last wishes from Mrs. Willingham helped her realize that her talents could be used to reimagine Hill House into something spectacular for travelers seeking a one-of-a-kind, small Southern town experience. She now considered what it would mean to pick up the mantle and fulfill the duty she had unknowingly been groomed for.

Still, her parents would probably never approve. They would remain upset about the inn, and while her father might get over Duncan not coming from an old-guard family, her mother would not. Genevieve had proven time and time again that bloodlines mattered.

Did it really matter what they thought? For so long her happiness had been rooted in pleasing their pride for appearances. Not for the first time, she wished to be bold enough to live life unafraid of her parents' influence. She deserved happiness too.

"Same," she said as she turned and crawled back into the bed. "I've never wanted anyone as much as I want you. Do you still love me?"

"*Love* is a strong word, Reese. I know I have feelings that never went away. To say I am in love with you would be lying."

"Sumthin' is still in my heart for you, Duncan."

"We've only been back around each other for a few weeks. Maybe it's just because we're here for the summer in the Shores. The nostalgia of it all."

She shook her head. Nostalgia wouldn't make her contemplate leaving a life she'd worked hard for behind. This thing with Duncan meant something more to her, and so did Hill House.

"I don't know…maybe. I did think of you often over the years. I was just so caught up in wondering what people would think and—I never forgot the way you looked at me before I left with my father that night."

"Can we finally talk about that?" He sat up against the headboard of the bed when she nodded. "I understand that my mother may have had a hand in how that night unraveled. Yet, I still have a hard time understanding why you allowed them to ruin what we had."

"I was seventeen." Her exasperation echoed within the room. "Every time I tried to stand up to my parents, I was knocked down. The gravity of what happened that night altered my life because you were no longer in it. I even had to decline my admission to UPenn beca—"

"You were admitted to UPenn?" His question made her look the other way. He slid closer to her. "Answer me."

"Why does it matter? We can't undo the past."

"You were really going to give up the fashion program at Cornell to come be with me?" She didn't answer his question. The taste of the bitter fight with her parents still lingered in her mouth. "You don't have to answer. Your body language says it all. Nobody should have that kind of power over someone else's future."

"They are my parents, and they were the ones paying tuition…And I wasn't giving up fashion. I would've studied retail merchandising. Between the school and my parents, I had internships at Saks Fifth Avenue, Macy's, and *Ebony* magaz—" She stopped before resentment consumed her.

"Your mom and dad manipulated both of our lives, and for what? You're not laid up with Drexel Collins. You're here with me."

Reese pushed the covers back and sprang from the bed. She

grabbed her clothes from the floor and made a beeline to the door. Before she could get out of the room, his arm reached in front of her and pushed the door closed. She was trapped.

They were caught in that space where they only had two choices. One choice never left the past behind. The other focused on the future. Sadly, it was still possible that their past might be too much for them to overcome.

"Is running your default for when shit gets hard?" The heat of his naked body almost made her crumble. "That's privilege, Reese. To be able to leave something...or someone behind without worrying what will happen is not how ordinary people operate."

"Stop saying that to me," she hissed, still unwilling to turn and face him. "If my privilege meant anything, it would've let me choose you." She wished the ache in her heart would heal too. "The years I spent without you have haunted me, so forgive me if I'm unable to grasp your current concept of privilege."

His arm dropped from the door, and he must've taken a step back, because the heat of his body no longer danced around hers. "Turn around." The solemn request allowed her to take a deep breath and get herself back under control before she turned to face him. "I'm sorry. We were both kids. I shouldn't have—"

She pressed a finger against his lips. "You don't owe me an apology, Duncan. I believe I owe you one. I'm sorry for not being brave enough to stand up for our love and friendship."

His forehead rested against hers before their breaths became one. She went on her tippy-toes and covered his lips with her kiss. The feel of his well-endowed cock made them come apart and her eyes dropped down to that erotic zone as it pulsed hard with need. Their mouths fused together again, and then his tongue pushed inside her mouth, sending her up in flames. Her clothes dropped from her hands, and she became putty in his.

His fingers trailed down her chest and went to her apex. She moaned against his lips as he slid a finger inside. "Ten years...I've been so deprived."

"Then let's not waste any more time."

Twenty-Four

"I'VE GOT A meeting to get to. Lock up before you leave and I'll see you later." Duncan kissed Reese, then dashed out of the room.

He flew down the stairs and through the house until he was in his car. He tapped his brakes while backing out of the driveway. He had never been more torn on what to do with a property. Last night did him no favors.

Now wasn't the time. He had to get his head right for his meeting with the Debutante Ball Committee. They had invited him to a breakfast after his contribution, and it was important that people recognize what he was doing and why. He hated knowing there was press circulating that called his character into question.

Once the house was out of sight, he zoomed through town at unsafe speeds and only stopped when he pulled into his garage. He felt like Clark Kent making a Superman change with how fast he showered. However, he slowed down to perfect his three-piece ensemble.

The Italian charcoal suit he selected was bold yet conservative as it highlighted his taste for the finer things. He accented it with a blue tie, another power color that was associated with focus. His days at UPenn had trained him well in the art of appearances. Today, he would use that knowledge to ensure he made a lasting impression on a group of people who often judged books by their covers.

Beyond appeasing shallow minds and his desire for positive PR, Duncan wanted to ensure the goodwill he gave to the ball committee would be distributed to youth residing in the Shores. More than that, he knew Reese's mother would be present. He hoped that she was ready to see the man he had become and not the boy she believed was not worthy of her daughter. Content with the confidence he exuded both in and out, he ducked back out of the house and raced against the clock to be on time for the breakfast at the Lakeside Inn.

Duncan arrived at the old hotel with a few minutes left to spare. He strolled down the halls prepping himself for every possible question over his acquisition of Hill House and the proposed youth village. He slowed when he spotted Rebekah waving to him from a set of closed double doors.

"Morning! Power play today," she said with a bright smile, staring him up and down as he approached her.

"Nah," he chuckled, adjusting his suit coat. "I'm just here to let these folks know that McNeal Urban Planning and Design Firm means business."

"Well, that's good because this isn't a typical morning meeting with a committee." She rubbed the back of her neck before crossing her arms. "Their brief simply stated breakfast with the ball committee. However, it's not only the committee members inside. I checked some credentials and there's a ton of high-profile Southerners roaming the space. Many have come to town for the ball. A lot of lunch and dinner dates are being set since most are here for the remainder of the summer. I nabbed a few for you."

She winked at him. "Glad I got here early, and that you're dressed for the part." He could tell she resisted saying more and was happy that all of his hints were finally paying off. "Now, our table is at the front to the right. We're sitting with Mayor Fleming, a city councilman, and another donor that is being recognized. His contribution isn't as significant as yours, but it was large."

Duncan nodded, summoning his charm as he turned the handle and opened the door. Rebekah told no lies. The room was full of politicians, businessmen, physicians, and socialites. Many faces he remembered from his childhood, the rest from the paper or other forms of media. Either way, they were all members of the wealthiest Southern families that annually summered in the Shores.

Before UPenn and joining the oldest Black fraternity, he would've been out of his element. Today, he was forever grateful for the experiences and mentorships that had placed him in the midst of the upper crust. It was where he had learned the art of tooting his own horn, building networks, and performing social niceties. He mingled, knowing that while everyone pretended to be easygoing, they were probably wondering what his lineage and social circles were. He didn't give a damn. He'd climbed to the top and no one would push him back down because of an acquisition or last name.

"Good morning, everyone," the familiar feminine voice piped through the microphone, signaling everyone to find their seats.

Duncan glanced up to the podium and saw Genevieve Devlin. He admired the woman for a second. He'd always marveled at how Reese bore an uncanny resemblance to her mom. Genevieve cleared her throat after everyone claimed their seats, and the room became pin-drop silent.

"Thank you all for joining us today. This is a long-lived tradition, and it is so nice to see so many old and new friends." She gazed out from her vantage point flaunting a smile that was Miss America worthy. "As some may know, in 1924, my grandmother, Essie Austin, along with Frances McNeal, led the charge for the Progressive Women's Club to establish the Lakeside Debutante Ball as a social event to benefit the Milner-Rosenwald Academy in Mount Dora, Florida.

"Our ball has occurred every year since its inception. We owe its preservation to the strong allyship and generosity of the Fleming, Pierre, and Morgan families during those dark times that plagued the South with racial injustice."

Duncan almost choked on his water. He sat the glass down as a round of applause filled the room, prompting Mayor Fleming, along with four others that represented the Pierre and Morgan families mentioned, to stand. Duncan had always known and respected the white families now standing for how much they'd supported the Black community. What he'd never known was that his great-grandmother was a founder of such a prestigious event that none of her offspring had participated in up until now. He had to learn why.

"This year we are thrilled to have Alexandria Devlin and Destiny McNeal, who are descendants of the original founders, make their debut into society. The committee is even more honored that Frances McNeal's great-grandson, Duncan McNeal, has chosen to bestow a charitable gift that allows us to continue our support of educational and community outreach programs that benefit children all over the South."

The sheer volume of applause became deafening. Rebekah's nudge against his arm got Duncan to his feet. For so long he'd wanted to prove he belonged, when now it seemed as though his family had all along. He suppressed the shock, hurt, and anger rolling over his body at the intentional exclusion of his family and managed to school a face that was front-page worthy. He grudgingly acknowledged the crowd's recognition before reclaiming his seat.

He sat listening to but not hearing the remainder of the program. He wondered if Reese had known or if she thought he already knew and never cared. Above all else, he wanted to understand why his parents had allowed the erasure of his great-grandmother and her impact in the community. He never even knew a Progressive Women's Club had existed.

"Hello, Duncan." Mrs. Lancaster gained his attention as he stood up and began pushing in his chair. He turned around and embraced her like he always had whenever they saw each other. "Thank you for your generosity. I see why Gavin is forever bragging about you. You're doing amazing things here. We're all so proud of everything you've done. Beyond it all, I can't wait to see our Xavier escort Destiny."

The woman clapped her hands together with unquestionable delight. Even without him knowing the rules and traditions of this uppity world, he got the feeling that Xavier participating in the ball as Destiny's escort had given the Lancasters a little more shine.

"Thank you, Mrs. Lancaster." He knew she wasn't putting it on like the rest. Jolie Lancaster had always encouraged him to do his best. She was one of the few who openly welcomed him into her home and sent care packages to him while he was away at college, and she had approved of Xavier escorting his sister before the news broke.

The woman had never allowed her social status to interfere with how she or her children interacted with people. Her attitude was the very reason why he and Gavin had become best friends.

They chatted for a while, long enough for Duncan to plot his escape. He didn't have it in him to pretend that the news of his great-grandmother's contribution to society hadn't impacted him. And not in a good way. The confidence he'd held on the way in had evaporated and now he wondered what other strings the people around him could pull. Just as he pushed the door to leave, he heard Genevieve Devlin calling out to him. He ignored her, acting as if the noise from the room had drowned her voice, and kept going until he was out the door. He took a deep breath and began down the hall.

He was no one's token. There were questions his father had to give him answers to before he could embrace the history of his lineage.

"Duncan," her elegant voice called again. He couldn't pretend he didn't hear her this time. He stopped and turned around, watching as she walked to him. "My God, you look so much like your father."

He took a step back. "I could say the same of you and Reese."

Her smile faded as her light brown eyes scanned over him like she was reading the morning paper. "You and my daughter are so much like me and David that it's scary. We too played together when we were young"—her face went blank, truly vacant for a second—"but sometimes we leave things behind for a reason."

"In the same way my great-grandmother was erased from the ball history up until now?"

"You should ask your father about that. Your great-grandmother not being included in our public history was not the committee's decision. In fact, the majority disregarded an old request to ensure you and Destiny received proper acknowledgement." Genevieve pushed her chin in the air, reveling in an unnatural haughtiness.

"The significance of the founders' lineage making a debut together should not be underestimated. Nor should we ignore that Frances's great-grandson possesses her spirit to enhance this community even if it embarrasses my family in the process." She winced, then somehow found a smile. "Thank you for your donation, Duncan. I meant what I said in there. Many youths will benefit from your generosity."

When she turned to leave, Duncan regained the confidence he had when he first kissed Reese this morning and left to start his day. "Mrs. Devlin"—he reached for her, and she stopped— "I thought you didn't like me."

"I did not like your circumstance." Her head turned up to the ceiling for a second before she faced him again. "Do you really think societal class is no longer an issue? While it's true that we are not living in Jane Austen's time, who a person marries is important in maintaining our legacies. You could say thank you. I just gave you yours back."

His face scrunched at her harsh yet revealing words. "After all this time. Why now?"

"Because my daughter is more like me than she cares to admit…and you look just like the boy I used to love. Unlike him, you chose a different path. Talk to your father. It is his story to tell."

Twenty-Five

"WHAT ARE YOU doing in my office, Chareese?" Her father's stern voice gave her butterfingers, and the photograph she held of her grandmother slipped from her hands down to the floor.

She quickly kneeled to pick up the picture frame and then placed it back in its space on his shelf.

"I forgave you, but I didn't forgive her." Reese continued studying the picture of her grandmother standing on the front lawn of Hill House with the magnolias in bloom. "I've searched myself for the reason why, and still can't find it. Why did I only remain angry at her when you both came that night and ripped my heart from Duncan's?"

He cleared his throat. "Only you know the answer to that question."

She turned to her father and watched him make his way across the room to where she stood. He began rubbing her back. "I never said goodbye." Tears welled in her eyes then rolled down her cheeks. "And now it's like she's whispering to me to become the lady of Hill House. But I don't know if her memory or the house deserves me to give so much. Duncan enlightened me on the treatment his mother and grandmother endured under Grandma Connie."

"The what!" He snatched his arm from around her. "I'm sure that boy has no idea what he is talking about, Chareese."

"Then why don't you tell me," she challenged, lifting her chin in defiance. "Then I can stop envisioning my grandmother as a cantankerous snob with shady business practices that shunned me for liking someone who lived on the other side of town."

Her father whipped around. His eyes threw daggers that punctured her. "You have no idea what you are talking about, and you should know better since you spent more time with her than anyone." She had, but now she knew Duncan's side and it wasn't pretty. "Your grandmother did what she did to protect us. Although it seems karma has a different view of things."

He sighed, "We probably won't win the appeal. Duncan has made news all over the South, and now I have friends telling me how his youth village is genius and a rebirth of Black excellence."

"It is, Dad." Reese had to take a stand and defend Duncan this time. "While I disagree that Hill House should be converted, I support the idea of a place that helps youth from around here prepare for college and careers. At least Duncan won't stand by and let the house rot. He'll create jobs that will pay the staff, which is more than you or Uncle Quincy were doing."

"How dare you," he snapped. "I told your mother her bright idea was a mistake. Instead of you working to get close to him, he got to you. I guess I shouldn't be surprised you stabbed us in the back."

She scoffed, "I would never."

"Rebekah Wilson tells a different story. I heard her PR strategy was birthed by you." Reese went numb. "Disgruntled lovers sting hard."

From the minute Reese saw Rebekah, she knew something was off. Intuition rarely led her astray. While in Duncan's office, Rebekah had been hungry for ideas on how to withdraw him from the limelight, where he was painted a villain. Reese gave her the perfect plan, it had worked, and now she was blabbing it to her dad. She had several bones to pick with that woman.

"I—"

He threw his hand up as a somber expression etched across his face. "Again, I'm not surprised. Like mother like daughter. I can't even look at you right now." Her father strode off.

"What does that mean!" she yelled.

An answer never came. Reese balked at the notion of being defeated and reset back at square one. The side effects of living under a roof with Kent and Genevieve Devlin began to suffocate her. She grabbed her purse and keys, then burst out of the side door.

Reese drove around town for a while not knowing where to go. Things were different now and she couldn't just pull up at Quinn's or Carrah's house. This was not the venting spell of a sixteen-year-old complaining to her friends about having to go to a dinner party instead of the roller rink. No, she was a grown twenty-seven-year-old woman who was falling for the one person her parents had forbidden her to love years ago. And while she was learning that her grandmother may have been a scrupulous businesswoman who was more judgmental than anyone had a right to be, Hill House still deserved a second chance.

She gripped the steering wheel harder as she rounded the bend in the hill and came up the backside of Lakeshore Drive. She noted the Andrewses' home, elegant and ornate just like them. The Lancasters' was next, large and full of simplicity, yet wealth was apparent. She continued along the two-lane road, passing the Hightowers', Pierres', and so many others before the Italianate-style mansion with its Mediterranean roof came into view.

It stood out just like Duncan and communicated the very same as all the other homes: money, power, and prestige. To her, it didn't matter that he had asserted his influence later in life. Honestly, she probably would've never cared if he hadn't become a millionaire. She liked him for who he had been to her all those years ago, and their intimacy last night had not faded from her mind.

Her impulse highjacked logic and she cut the wheel into his driveway. A fit of surprise washed over her at seeing his garage door up with his car parked inside. He was the only one she could talk to that would understand.

Maybe not. Duncan had been firm in communicating that Hill House was destined to become something new. He had also dashed out of the bed this morning and had not called or texted her once in the hours they'd spent apart. It was possible he might not at all empathize with her current feelings and that she was overthinking last night. After all, it was just sex. There were no commitments, and he didn't know if he loved her again. Thank God she hadn't spilled her secret desire to remain in the Shores and transform Hill House, for it could end up a casualty of heartbreak.

Reese sat in the car for a second hoping that she was overanalyzing things. She then realized that her frustration had levels. She could not pretend that she didn't care about Hill House, even after she'd learned what her grandmother had done. She actually did want her parents to accept Duncan. And last, she would never forget the way his lips pressed against the secret parts of her body. It couldn't just be sex. At least she hoped it wasn't.

Knocks struck against her driver's-side window causing her to leap out of deep thought. Her heart skipped several beats seeing Duncan decked out in a three-piece suit that fit his athletic build perfectly. She cut the car, stepped outside, and wrapped her arms around him.

"What's wrong?" His deep voice mixed with his delicious, masculine scent steadied her out-of-control heart as she buried her head in his chest.

"So much," she admitted, not yet ready to dive into detail. Now wasn't the time to ask if he was reconsidering his stance on Hill House or confess her aborted mission to convince him to return it back to the Devlin family. "I thought I would've heard from you by now. How was your meeting?"

* * *

That was a loaded question. He had a few to ask her himself. Like, *Did you know about my great-grandmother or that your mom loved my dad?* Afraid and mentally unprepared for the answers he might get forced him to table his questions.

"Intriguing," he sighed, dropping his arms from around her and then leaning against her car. "Your mom played nice today."

Duncan chuckled as her brows arched in response to his comment. "Of course she did. She's the consummate socialite in a room full of status-conscious individuals."

"Reese," he snickered. "Give your mom a little credit. It actually reminded me of the way she used to be before I secretly wished for you to be mine." He pulled her back into him. His hands roamed over her body until they cupped her ass. "I'm serious."

Their lips met, and he deepened the kiss. He wanted her again, this time in his bed, and he wouldn't stop until she screamed his name. Losing himself in her delectable body would help him forget everything that had happened, for now.

"Duncan."

Duncan broke the kiss to see Rebekah standing a few feet away from Reese's car. He gathered himself. "Rebekah, what—"

She held up his phone. He'd been in search of it since arriving home. "You left too fast." They met halfway and he took the phone from her hand. Before he could offer a thank-you, she began sizing Reese up. "Your mom was the one that spoke at the breakfast?"

Duncan hesitated. Reese piped in, "I…think so." She glanced at Duncan, who nodded confirmation. "Yes, Genevieve Devlin is my mother."

"You look just like her," Rebekah said in a way that made the hairs stand up on his arm.

"Is that why you told my father I created Duncan's PR strategy?"

Rebekah shook her head fast. "No. It didn't happen like that. He actually complimented me on the strategy one evening while I was out…and lonely"—she made eye contact with Duncan—"…and almost drunk. I simply mentioned that I had you to thank for the idea."

Duncan's jaw went tight. "You didn't think telling that to a man who has attacked me in the media was a problem?"

"You don't see how me moving down here to be with you, but we're no longer together, is a problem." She shrugged. "I gave it all up to be here with you, Duncan."

Shit, he could've screamed. At least she finally said it. Now they could get that elephant out of the room without him breaking any employment laws. This morning he thought the hints were taking effect. Clearly they were being missed, and that was a problem.

This was not the drama he needed right now. He had a legacy to uncover and didn't need any distractions while he and Reese were trying to find their way back to each other. Just this morning on his way home, he had determined he would take a chance and convince her to spend more time here. He knew it was a long shot since she had a whole life to go back to. But now, Rebekah may have made it harder. How would he ever get Reese to move back to the Shores if she thought he would bring her back only to end up apart?

"I never made any promises, Rebekah. You did, however, break your NDA when you told Mr. Devlin elements of our strategy."

"So that's it. You're going to fire me over her?"

Duncan never made rash decisions. Rebekah was one of the best in her industry. She had done phenomenal work up until now. Perhaps their arrangement wasn't the best. However, he was learning that everyone deserved a second chance.

"I'm taking the rest of the day off. We'll talk tomorrow when I get in the office."

"I'll see you then, thanks." She faced Reese. "I really am sorry. If it's worth anything I think it's pretty cool how your sister and Duncan's are debuting as descendants of the founders. This little town has so much going on, it's hard to keep up."

"Wait, what happened?" Reese turned to Duncan, nose scrunched and eyes full of curiosity.

"Is there anything else, Rebekah?"

"Uhh, no, I guess not. Just wanted to get your phone to you. See you tomorrow."

They said their goodbyes and then he took Reese by the hand and brought her into his house. He shrugged out of his jacket and vest, then loosened his tie before he turned to see she was still standing by the door.

Reese folded her arms and stared him down. "Context helps. Why didn't you tell me you dated her?"

Duncan pulled the tie from around his neck and dropped it on a chair. He moved until he was standing face-to-face with her. "I don't kiss and tell."

"That's why she told my dad." She sidestepped him and plopped onto his couch.

"Does it matter?"

"It does. The woman thinks she's going to be fired because of me. She's not over you either. That's what made it so awkward outside."

"Ha! Awkward, I think you're imagining things." His sarcasm was thicker than molasses. He shouldn't have tried it. Regardless of what Reese heard outside, he had no plans to explain his relationship with Rebekah to her. They had bigger things to discuss than a woman who simply wanted him for his money.

She pursed her lips, shaking her head. "The lies you tell, Duncan McNeal. No woman stares another woman down unless competition is present. I didn't imagine that." She sat back in the couch and sighed out loud. "What did Rebekah mean by our sisters making their debut as descendants of founders?"

He fiddled with the button at his neck, attempting to keep his calm over being kept in the dark for so long. "You really don't know?"

"Don't know what?"

Duncan sat beside Reese and repeated what her mother had stood in front of everyone at the breakfast and said about their great-grandmothers, the Progressive Women's group, and the debutante ball. They both began recalling oral and written histories they knew as it pertained to the events in the Shores. The only record of community engagement of a McNeal started with Duncan's high school community service. It was as if information on Frances had been scrubbed away.

"You could ask Ava's dad. He's still the town historian. I'm sure he'd know."

"I'll ask him only if I need to after speaking with my dad. Your mom gave me the impression that all the answers I needed were with him." He paused, again contemplating if he should tell her what he suspected of his dad and her mom.

Not because he didn't want to. He was afraid of the way his heart sank every time he recalled her mom's words. Could what happened to their parents become their fate? It was the very reason he hadn't wanted to define what they were or the one night they shared together.

"What are you thinking?" She fingered his chin until their eyes met.

He lied. "Actually, I was wondering if you were free Saturday evening. The mayor invited me to a reception and I'm not interested in flying solo."

"I can't. There's a dinner with the debutantes and their escorts. It's a chance for all the alumni to meet the new girls prior to the big shebang. Sorry." Her eyes searched his before she reached over and grabbed his hand.

"No need to apologize." A niggling thought entered his head. Maybe she wasn't ready to be with him in public in a more-than-friends kind of way.

And then his mind flashed to the vacant expression on her mother's face when she referenced his father. He had not forgotten his father's strange words during their last conversation at his office. About wanting things that aren't always meant for people to have. Duncan now wondered if his father meant Genevieve Devlin was the thing he wanted but couldn't have.

"Reese…" Duncan didn't want that to be them ten or twenty

years from now, wondering, wishing, thinking about the love they'd shared and lost. "There's something else."

Duncan slid from the couch and kneeled so that he could see her entire face. He had her undivided attention and he wanted to make sure he read her response correctly. He needed to know if she was as in the dark as he was or if she was flirting with the fate that had doomed their parents.

"My great-grandmother's role in this community wasn't all I learned about today." He took a deep breath. "I believe our parents, your mom and my dad, were in love with each other at some point when they were younger."

She sat up in the couch. "How's that possible? I mean, my mother didn't spend a lot of time here when she was young. They moved for her father's career."

"I'm not sure, Reese. Maybe it's exactly like it was with you. She may have only returned during the summers." A silence rested between them that began sucking Duncan into a void.

"How did you find this out? Who told you?" She stood from the couch and began pacing. He wished for mind-reading capabilities. He wanted to know why she seemed so worked up.

"Your mother stopped me today on my way out."

"My mother says a lot, and is extremely manipulative, Duncan. What exactly did she say?"

He went to where Reese stood and quoted her mother's final words. That same distant yet haunting expression that had run across her mom's face earlier was now upon hers. Her eyes met his, as he continued giving the full detail of the conversation that made him question his father's integrity.

"Why is this the first time I'm hearing this?" She asked the question aloud, but he could tell it wasn't for him.

"Why do you act like it was a crime?" He jammed his hands into his pockets and took a few steps back. "Is it always this way with you uptown girls? Boy toy for fun until you meet the one. Isn't that what your mothers tell you? I heard your grandmother say it once. Perhaps it's the reason she let me stay around—"

"Like mother like daughter," Reese mumbled. She closed her eyes and took a deep breath before she reclaimed the space between them.

"What?"

"Today, after you left me, I went home full of anger and questions…thoughts of never saying goodbye to my grandmother. I waited for my father in his office and confronted him about the way things happened. We sort of got into it, which is how I found out about Rebekah. At any rate he said those words to me." She stroked his jaw, subduing his doubts. "If you were simply a boy toy, Duncan, my parents wouldn't have worked so hard to tear us apart. They saw what we were because maybe they had seen it before with my mom and your dad." She exhaled as if it were her last. "Now here I am wondering if all of this is a coincidence. I don't want to end up like them, Duncan."

"Neither do I."

"There has to be a way to help our families escape generations of bias, because whatever this is between us doesn't want to be forgotten. We can't deny it."

He nodded his head in agreement. "I won't even try."

She went up on her tippy-toes and pressed her lips against his. What began as sweet and innocent quickly turned into raw lust. There was no secret that he desired her again. He'd hated leaving this morning without having the chance to properly say goodbye to her.

He stripped her down then circled her, admiring every delicious inch of her sexy body. He stopped in front of her, tracing his finger between her breasts, down to her belly button and then to the dripping heat of her... He bit her neck before he pushed one, then two fingers inside.

"Duncan," she cried, moaning as he worked his fingers in and out of her.

"Mmm... That's right, call my name, baby." His lips grazed her ear. "Now, you know my fetish."

She gasped before whispering his name, taunting the passion he was ready to unleash. He hauled her to the couch and nudged her into the cushions headfirst then spanked her pretty brown ass. She panted, rolling her hips as she begged for more.

He obliged by taking off his clothes, sheathing his cock that was harder than hell, and sinking inside of her.

Twenty-Six

THE DOORBELL CHIMED. Reese slowly untangled her body from Duncan's and allowed him to roll out of the bed. She admired his smooth, dark skin, and how it covered those washboard abs and inverted V. She felt the blush staining her cheeks as her sex ached at the sight of the way his manhood hung between his legs. She still couldn't believe it all fit inside of her, but it had, and she had enjoyed every thick inch.

"Perve," he teased as he pulled on a pair of shorts. "Be right back. I wasn't expecting visitors and I'm definitely not done enjoying you."

Reese giggled watching him leave and then slid back under the covers knowing she would never get enough of mister tall, dark, and handsome. She hoped her mother would forgive her for not being able to use Duncan's attraction to her as a means to change his mind on Hill House. Beyond all, she wanted both of her parents to accept Duncan. However, after this morning her father may prove to be a rock not primed to climb.

She strangely held on to hope for her mother since she'd dug up buried history and reestablished Duncan's family legacy.

Reese knew Genevieve well enough to know that she operated on ulterior motives. The woman hadn't been blind to their teen love, and she doubted she was now. Genevieve was preparing for something she couldn't control. The stage for acceptance of them in social circles was set during her speech at the breakfast.

Raised voices halted the many scenarios attempting to play out in her head. Her attention flew to the open bedroom door before her phone buzzed beside her. More than a few calls from her parents and sister had been missed. Dread poured over her. Did the voices from downstairs belong to them? She kicked the covers away, found a shirt, and sprinted out of the room.

"Son, you insisted and then somehow got your mother to agree. I never wanted Destiny in that ball. Why must you feel the need to fit in? Ever since you were little, you wanted to be like them, but they don't want people like us around them, Duncan."

Reese slowed on the stairs. It wasn't her father. It was Duncan's.

"I'm glad you brought that up. What exactly do you mean by people like us? From my understanding, the McNeal name was once influential in this community. Why and when did that change?"

A whistling breath escaped Mr. McNeal. "Son, there's a lot you don't understand."

"I got all night, Pop."

"Sure about that? Isn't that the Devlin girl's rental car in your driveway? I saved you from that mistake once."

"Yes, Chareese is here, and what do you mean?"

Reese came off the stairs and walked to where they stood in the foyer. "I'd like to know as well."

David McNeal drew back, then turned and reached for the

doorknob. He opened then closed the door, clearly debating whether to stay or go. Finally he released the knob and faced them. "Do your parents even know where you are right now?"

She and Duncan glanced at each other before turning their attention back to his father. "I'm an adult, Mr. McNeal. I don't always tell them where I come and go."

"You don't have to. They keep tabs." He scrubbed his face, removing all expressions. "They called my house looking for you. It reminds me of how they showed up all those years ago to make sure we all understood that whatever was between you and my son was forbidden."

Reese tried but couldn't swallow the thickness in her throat as she noted the pain and frustration upon the man's face. She reached for Duncan's hand and found it. His father watched as their fingers laced. The man's obvious apprehension blocked the confidence she normally felt when standing at Duncan's side.

"Would you do that out in the open?" He gestured to their linked hands. "Are you ready to walk beside my son in public or do you first have to prep Gena and Kent so they can maintain their personas at the next town event and blame your infatuation with Duncan on the summertime?"

Reese squeezed Duncan's hand even though his words were somewhat true. It was one thing for her parents to think she was working to change his mind. It was another if she showed up somewhere as Duncan's date.

"I have not heard anyone call my mom that in a long time," Reese said, because it was true. And she wasn't ready to answer his question even though she knew she would never forsake Duncan again.

Mr. McNeal snorted loudly. "No, she's too high class for that now."

* * *

"Pop, you can stop taking digs at Reese and her mom and answer my question. When and why was Great-Grandma Frances stripped from the town history? Destiny and I should've known about her being part of the Progressive Women's Club and founding the ball."

"I beg to differ. I've already saved you from all this once. I won't be able to this time."

"Save us from our legacy?" Duncan's voice raised a decibel. "I need to know what you're hiding, Pop, and why."

He met his father's gaze. Both were upset and determined to have the other see their way. Finally, his dad walked past him and sat down at the dining table. His line of sight went to Reese. "When Pearl told me you'd asked your parents' permission for Duncan to be your escort and they denied it, I knew then they still turned their noses up and harbored a grudge against my family. Despite my son going off to an Ivy League, pledging that fraternity, and gaining acceptance into a world we couldn't give him.

"That's why I called Gena and told her that you had ditched your little escort and sneaked out of your grandmother's to go meet my son at Grantham Point by the old lighthouse." His focus went to Duncan. "I'm not sorry, Duncan. I did what I thought was best, because neither Gena nor I wanted our kids to tread the same path as our ill-fated romance. She and I learned a long time ago that people were unforgiving of legacy preservation."

"So, it's true." Reese sat across the table from his dad. "You and my mother were in love with each other?"

He harrumphed. "It goes deeper than that, young lady. Your mother and I were promised to each other."

"Then, what happened?" Duncan questioned as he claimed the chair beside Reese. He wanted to look his father in the eye while he told his tale of woe because maybe it would help him understand why he grew up believing his family was beneath others.

"My mother and Constance Devlin are what happened." He got up from the chair, went to the bar, and poured himself a scotch. He took a sip, grunting from the burn, and then reclaimed his seat.

Duncan's dad started by explaining the rich friendship between their great-grandmothers, Frances McNeal and Essie Austin. The women had both attended college together and came to teach at the Milner-Rosenwald Academy. They used their influence as educators to cofound the Progressive Women's Club to cater to the needs of the community. Eventually they created the debutante ball to aid children graduating from the school with financial assistance for college.

Both women planted roots in the community and eventually married and had sons. Since their sons were only children, they raised them as brothers. The women their sons married became best friends and the children they had included Duncan's father and Reese's mom, who also became friends. Through Reese's mom and Duncan's father the families finally saw a path to unite beyond friendship.

"And it was simple. I only had eyes for Gena and she had chosen me as her beau." His dad smiled in a way Duncan hadn't seen in a long time. "Remember though, I told y'all legacy preservation was important. The old guard, as we called it, were and still are caught up in matching their offspring to form power couples and all that weird shit. Lineage often dictates how previous generations can impact the future. So, when my parents separated, it was a big deal."

"Let me guess." Reese cleared her throat. "You and your siblings were damaged goods, no longer suitable matches. People worried about financial stability, and no one wanted to hitch their daughter to a boy whose parents had abandoned their sacred union for fear you may repeat the same."

"Those were some aspects." He fiddled with his thumbs for a few minutes, seemingly searching for words as he sat looking around the room. Finally, he went still and stared them in their faces. "The reality was that no one wanted their daughter to be courted by a boy whose mama was rumored to prefer women over her own husband." Both Duncan's and Reese's jaws dropped. Before they could ask questions, his father put his hand up. "Let me finish and then you can ask all the questions you want."

They nodded and he continued. "Constance had lost her husband in the war and my mama, Suzette, was single...actually divorced after coming out to my father. Both of them were raising kids on their own, and so they had more in common than Mama's other friends that still had husbands. Mama and Miss Connie were quite fond of each other until the rumors started. Mama had no issue with the townsfolk gossiping about her. On the contrary, Miss Connie did.

"Back then being queer got doors closed in your face. It coulda put Hill House out of business, and Miss Connie had big plans for that place. She also had two boys to put through school. She chose to elevate her status and that of her boys, so she denied whatever feelings she had for Mama, ignored the fact that Gena and I had been promised to each other, and orchestrated a match between Gena with Kent. Uniting families and building legacies happened through marriage...of course Kent didn't mind. He had wanted Gena from the first time he saw her.

"I thought things might get better the night Kent and I found our mothers kissing in the old shed, but it got worse. The Devlins treated us bad and tarnished our reputation beyond repair. My guess was it was to make sure no one would believe me or Mama if we told anyone about Miss Connie, and it worked. Afterward everything soured. Daddy stopped sending money for us.

"My grandparents refused to help. They disassociated from the town and made my father do the same after he disowned us. We were forgotten. Then one day, I guess out of pity from seeing us hungry, Miss Connie offered my mama a job cooking and cleaning at Hill House. By then, the original scandal had died down, and the townspeople thought the Devlins were being charitable.

"The anger I experienced from the way my grandmother, the benevolent Frances McNeal, had abandoned us, coupled with the shame of Mama's lifestyle, is why I prohibited any public recognition of her community service. My grandmother had let down the one community that should've meant the most: her family."

"Dad, there was nothing for you to be embarrassed about. You could've told me all of this." Duncan looked across the table at his father. "I still don't understand why everyone had such a problem with me and Reese, considering the history of you and her mom."

"That is exactly the reason. It's why Kent moved as far from the Shores as he could and only came home during the summers and the occasional holiday. You reminded him of me, and Reese is just like Gena. Never mind that he claimed the McNeal family was cursed."

Reese and Duncan looked at each other and then back to his father.

"So I'll ask you again…based on what you now know and the way your family has historically treated ours, are you ready to be public with my son? Duncan has done a lot for this community and plans to do more, and right now he doesn't need distractions from a woman who plans to leave after the ball and never come back again."

Duncan didn't agree with his father's views. Yet, after hearing his family's past in the Shores, he understood why he was asking. Now that Frances McNeal's involvement was made public, people would do their own research and discover a son who abandoned his kids and a daughter-in-law that embraced her lesbianism during a time in society where people who were not mainstream were outcast.

He looked over at Reese. She stared at his father, obviously contemplating his words. She had said that she didn't want to end up like her mom and his dad. Did she mean it?

"Duncan." Their gazes locked. A small smile curved her lips and made his heart stir chaotically before she reached over and took his hand in hers. "Will you do me the honor of escorting me to the debutante ball?"

Twenty-Seven

REESE WOKE UP in Duncan's arms but couldn't stay. She had never responded to the many messages and calls from her family last night and felt it would be best to arrive home before they rose. She tiptoed in through the side door of her parents' home. The scent of bacon and maple syrup wafted down the hall, raising red flags at her attempt to sneak in under the radar. Somehow she maintained her steps to the stairs that led up to her room, despite the way her stomach rumbled.

"Glad you finally made it home." Her mother stood in the archway, purse-lipped with her bonnet still on, twirling a metal spatula in her hand. Those famous from-scratch hotcakes she smelled on the griddle came at a price. When she was younger, her mother used them to lure her to the breakfast table and bargain for details on the event she had attended the night before. It was how Genevieve learned everything that happened at teen parties.

Sensing that old trick, Reese opened her mouth to ask her to save some for later, but then her stomach growled. She wrapped an arm around it as if to make it stop. "You should eat. You sound hungry." Their eyes met before her mother turned on her heels and went back to the kitchen. "Your father went fishing for the day and Alexandria is asleep," she called over her shoulder, issuing code for *we can talk*.

Reese dropped her arm from around her waist, took a deep breath, and followed at a snail's pace. She didn't feel like participating in whatever inquisition her mother was queued up for, yet. She hadn't had enough time to process the bombshells her mother and Duncan's father had dropped yesterday. The secrets she learned featuring the McNeal family were capable of scandalizing her own. How could she protect them both?

The more she thought about those revelations, the more she realized she was ready to ask her mom the questions that burdened her mind. She dropped her purse on the counter and took a seat at the nook table. Her mother leaned over her and set a plate down with a hotcake, bacon, and eggs.

"You smell like him," her mother said withstanding her usual disdain. "Is that where you've been?"

Reese pushed the plate away and came out of her chair. She'd gladly go hungry before enduring an interrogation like she was seventeen again and being accused of losing her virginity. "Why are you asking me a question you already know the answer to?"

"I don't know, that's why I'm asking. Your dad told me that the two of you had words and that it seemed as though your efforts to have Duncan reconsider his stance on the property were going nowhere. Whenever you used to get upset with us, you would go to your grandmother's or one of your friends' so…"

"Yes, I was with Duncan." Reese finally turned away from the table and faced her mother. Her mother displayed no shock in her confession. "You aren't surprised, are you? I mean, wasn't it you who said we were more alike than I cared to know?"

Her mother flinched at the way Reese mocked her words. "I am curious about one thing. Were you referring to the fact that we have both loved McNeal men?"

This time Genevieve gave Reese her back and went to the kitchen sink. For once in her life, she had managed to disarm her mother. It didn't feel as good as she imagined it would.

"That was a long time ago for me, Chareese." Her mother sighed long and hard. "David and I were much like you and Duncan. That young man looks so much like his daddy…but David and I were doomed the second his parents separated. I was told to think about my future and refocus my affections to your father, especially after some not-so-nice rumors of David's mother, Suzette McNeal, greeted us when we returned for the summer.

"It took me ages to get over David. So, you're right, I'm not surprised that your supposed quest to convince Duncan to reconsider his purchase of Hill House led to you spending the night with him. In the back of my mind, I guess I knew something like this could happen. Unfortunately, it can't go any further."

Genevieve went back to washing dishes as though she hadn't delivered a life sentence. Reese couldn't help how her hands tightened into fists and that she wanted to scream that *she didn't give a fuck what everyone else thought.* She took shallow breaths until the red she saw was gone and then joined her mom at the sink. She began helping her dry the dishes. "Why do you still allow society to dictate who we love?"

Her mother shrugged, shaking her head. "This is the world in which we live. You know the rules and would be wise to honor them. Your father and his family will never accept Duncan regardless of whether he agrees to a deal over Hill House."

"Why?"

"Your father has never forgiven me for loving another man more than him. Duncan reminds your father of David and the McNeal charm he claims seduced his mother to becoming affectionate with another woman." Her mom covered her mouth with her hand and backed away from Reese.

"I already know." Reese's words froze her mom's steps. "Mr. McNeal told us yesterday. Your little lesson in town history at the breakfast created a chain reaction, Mother."

Slowly Genevieve lowered her trembling hand. She began pacing the kitchen. "There's something I need to tell you. Sit down."

Reese lowered into a chair at the table and listened as her mother told the same story Mr. McNeal had the day before. Only she didn't pity her mother because unlike Reese, Genevieve was given a choice and she selected what meant the most to her: money, power, and prestige, not love.

"Do you understand now?" her mother asked pointedly, and Reese shook her head no. "To this day, your father believes his mother was corrupted by Suzette McNeal. He hated that your grandmother allowed her to work at Hill House, and has long been paranoid that if ever the truth of her sexuality was exposed, it would dim the Devlin legacy. When Duncan purchased Hill House, he believed it was the start of revenge."

"The purchase of the inn was never about revenge, Mother." Reese gestured for her mother to take the seat beside her at the table. "Originally, Duncan wanted to leverage it for a chance to sit on that little secret council Dad and his cronies control. However, he discovered an investor was secretly trying to purchase properties to transition the Shores into one of those commercial touristy destinations, and he's against that. His knowledge of Uncle Quincy's gambling and the financial woes with Hill House made him acquire the B and B to prevent the house from falling into someone else's hands who would've more than likely torn it down and built something in its place."

Her mother's perfect posture slumped in the chair as she clutched at her chest. Her mouth opened and closed twice, and still nothing came out. Reese understood without her mother offering words that she was stunned. After all, they never expected good things from him because of where he came from.

"I guess it is shocking." A smirk danced across Reese's lips. "Despite how much Duncan hated the way Grandma Connie treated his mother and grandmother, he still found enough compassion to save the old place."

"Ha!" Genevieve's sarcasm was thick as she came out of her haze. "Is that what he told you? Your grandmother played the charitable citizen and gave Suzette and Pearl work since everyone else had blacklisted them for Suzette being open about her sexuality. It wasn't Grandma Connie's fault that Suzette ruined her family's standing in the community.

"Still, she cared about her and couldn't watch her struggle making ends meet. In my opinion, the arrangement allowed them to love each other from a distance. Suzette may have been upset that Connie didn't come out like she had, but she never told a soul. She wanted better for her. Maybe you young people see things differently."

Reese smacked her teeth. "Dad and Grandma burst into his family's home and declared them have-nots. They made him think he wasn't good enough for me. I think Duncan has spent his whole life trying to prove them wrong."

"That night tested us all." Genevieve released a long, hard breath. "David and I were seeing an unfortunate history repeat itself. Your grandmother was acting to preserve our legacy while still mourning the loss of the one she'd shared affections with. However, she knew that it was the only way for us to continue holding our prominence in society. No one ever imagined Duncan would do so well for himself.

"And to be frank, your father does not care. He simply wants the bed and breakfast back and for you to find someone who doesn't have McNeal as his last name." Her mother rose from the table at the sound of footsteps on the stairs. "Only…" She paused, and for the first time in a long while there was a contrite expression upon her face that no one outside of their house would ever see. "I wonder if he knew what Duncan did…would he still feel as he does now?" She shrugged, then started back to the sink. "I gave Duncan back his family legacy yesterday. He's more than capable of rebuilding it when you leave."

"I came here at a crossroads in my career. Last night it finally hit me, the reason why I've been unfulfilled at work. I love Hill House, and I don't want to see it changed. Heck, I want to fix it."

"You do," she exclaimed or asked, a mixture of both that made her voice high-pitched. Reese nodded. "That's admirable, but…"

"But what, Mom? Even after everything I've told you, you still harbor doubts about me being here because of him." Reese snatched her purse from the table and stormed from the kitchen, brushing past her sleepy-eyed sister, and shot up the stairs to her room.

She sat on her bed replaying her mother's words over and over again. At twenty-seven, she still struggled to understand why her family maintained buckets of "us" and "them." Their class distinctions made it impossible for them to accept Duncan, no matter his accomplishments, because her father believed his family's pedigree was tainted.

How would she make them understand that Black society had evolved from brown paper bag tests, summers in the Shores or Oak Bluffs, or networks that were tied to sororities and fraternities? Michelle Obama, David Steward, Oprah Winfrey, and many more were prime examples of how there were avenues to success beyond the hallmarks of the Black elite's status quo. And yet, she didn't know if she could choose how she felt for Duncan over the grip of family.

The cowardice she'd experienced ten summers ago returned like a witch flying in on a broomstick and became suffocating. She ignored calls from Duncan, avoided her parents, and sank into the deepest, darkest hole she had ever found and wasn't sure if she would escape.

Twenty-Eight

"WHY DO YOU always have to piss them off?" Alex hissed at Reese as she slammed the rear passenger door of their mom's car.

"Is everything okay?" Genevieve peeked over the roof of the car, her eyes jumping from Alex to Reese.

"Fine." Reese closed her door and cocked her head at Alex, displaying a fake smile.

She knew her sister was referencing the ice-cold silence that hung between them as they drove over. If her mother could pretend that their morning conversation had never happened, then she could too. She proceeded to her mother's side while Alex lurked behind.

After ten years, the splendor of Lake Dora, anchored by stately oak trees flowing with Spanish moss, still welcomed guests to the Beauclaire. The restaurant was one of the most exclusive fine dining venues in the Shores, and the first to allow Black citizens a chance to dine in elegance. Which is the very reason the ball committee selected it year after year for their dinner reception.

Once they entered, the hostess greeted her mother and immediately led them to a private dining room. The tension that had coiled around them during the car ride like a rattler waiting to strike disappeared the second the double doors opened. Right away, Reese was smothered in a hug from her old friend Ava Hamilton, who had finally made it into town, before they were joined by Quinn, Carrah, Peyton, and other girls they had summered with in the Shores.

Their reunion was interrupted by the commotion Alex created as she bragged about the dress Reese had brought her straight from the runway in Milan. There was no doubt that her sister was stunning in the lively, strapless sea foam–green cocktail dress. The minute Reese had spotted it, she planned for Alex to wear it tonight. This was the evening when past debutantes returned to welcome those promising young women into their exclusive sisterhood before being presented. Much of the enthusiasm for the debut started here, since many would leave and share with family and friends what girl they were eager to see come out at the ball.

Reese remembered the importance of this dinner and had wanted her sister to have something unique. However, her sister was undeserving. Reese turned her attention away from how Alex was being fawned over, slightly disgusted that she'd been an enabler of her sister's behavior, and then continued catching up with her friends as the new debutantes were arriving.

Surprise took over the room when Destiny came through the door with Xavier Lancaster. Destiny floated in like a supreme queen and possibly challenged ideals of what it meant to be a celebrated debutante, since she had not been entitled to generations of preparation. Reese was beyond impressed with the young lady's dazzling smile and perfect posture that captivated all in attendance. The etiquette of a debutante took some girls years to grasp. Destiny had made it look flawless within weeks. It was a reminder that hard work could overcome privilege.

Destiny waved to Reese before they began making their way to each other. They met somewhere in the middle of the room and exchanged the *I'm too cute with my makeup and hair done* hug that Reese had taught her. The girl's cheery disposition was contagious, and it formed a shield against the daggers her mother and sister tossed her way.

"You are so beautiful," Reese finally managed to get out.

"Thank you!" Destiny then cleared her throat, straightened up, and extended her hand. "It is a pleasure to meet you, Chareese. I am Destiny McNeal." They shook hands as Reese rolled her eyes at the protocol her mentee had not hesitated to exercise. It was a good way to ease the nervous tensions Destiny must've had about meeting many of the other women. Reese also admired how Destiny did not ask for her approval, she commanded it. The mentorship had been successful. She would be well talked about after tonight. "This is my escort, Xavier Lancaster."

"Of course, pleasure seeing you again, Xavier." Reese shook his hand for show before leaning into Destiny and teasing, "You two look wonderful together."

The girl's eyes went big as she nervously slid a little away from Xavier. He chuckled and quickly pulled her back to his side. He rubbed Destiny's shoulder and whispered something in her ear before she relaxed into a smile.

"Thank you," she said, fiddling with the clutch purse in her hands. "Mrs. Lancaster poked and prodded at me all day." They all laughed and then Destiny finally looked at Reese. "I tried calling earlier to tell you but didn't get an answer."

Reese ignored the reference to the time she'd spent in her black hole earlier today. "No worries. The waltz is a big deal, and you want to be comfortable in front of everyone when you do it. I'm glad you two were able to connect."

"Me too!" Destiny gushed then smiled at Xavier, and it became clear that he only had eyes for her. Alex would throw a tantrum later at home. "Anyhow, Dunc asked me to give this to you." Destiny offered Reese a small, square envelope. "Guess I wasn't the only one that couldn't reach you today."

"He said don't be late," Xavier added.

Reese nodded. "You two should go mingle. And great job introducing yourself! I'm proud of you. You will make an impression."

Reese retreated to a private corner in the room. She flipped the envelope over a few times before using her fingers to try and determine the contents inside. She finally gave up on guessing games and opened the envelope. An old Hill House key slipped into the palm of her hand, while a small square fell to the floor. She picked it up and read *Meet Me After*, in Duncan's scribble. She fisted the key and set to making rounds in the room before she would go to him.

* * *

Duncan tuned out the conversation with Senator Hightower and Councilman Trout and glanced down at his phone. He couldn't suppress the urge to smile as he read Destiny's text message that confirmed she'd delivered his note to Reese.

He might not have gone for an old-fashioned approach had Reese answered her phone earlier. Then again, he was no longer certain of what he would or wouldn't do when it came to her. One day she was in town and the next she was lodged so deep in his heart he had no idea what he would do if she left again.

"What say you, Duncan?" The senator patted his back. "What

do you think about this outdoor mall that the developer has proposed?"

"It's an abomination. I'm disgusted that Mayor Fleming would even entertain such foolery." Kent Devlin's deep, refined voice joined their private conversation and forced Duncan to perk up.

Duncan scanned the man, fully aware of the resentment he harbored. He had unapologetically displayed it with his little media attack. A voice inside encouraged him to speak up. After all, the senator had asked him the question. "I'm in agreement with Mr. Devlin, Senator."

Councilman Trout's face became pale as snow. He was one of the few men that openly sided with Duncan's strategy for revitalization and knew that Duncan and the Devlins were like oil and water. Regardless of the lingering hostilities, Kent made himself more comfortable and set his glass down on the high-top they were standing around.

"For once…" Mr. Devlin remarked. "Why do you oppose the development?"

A challenge? Or was it a test to see if all the rumors about him being the best at what he did were true? Didn't matter, he had an answer. "It infringes on nature and the natural beauty of the Shores. Runoff from the development would contaminate the ecosystem. I care not to explain how the proposed architecture significantly deviates from the aesthetic of the existing buildings near the site and diminishes the town's preservation efforts."

At first the man seemed satisfied. He even nodded along with the senator and councilman. Suddenly, his face became tight and his eyes dark. Duncan's memory was transported back to that night when they took Reese from him. "Then why do you want to turn my mother's dream into some new age Boys and Girls Club?"

"Kent," the senator cautioned his friend. "You asked Duncan a question and he answered."

"It's fine, Senator." Duncan's focus went to Mr. Devlin. He maintained his cool, unwilling to give anyone a reason to suggest he was less than a gentleman. "I never planned to alter any of the external architecture of Hill House."

Mr. Devlin's chest puffed up like a rooster on an early morning stroll. He motioned for the senator and councilman to leave. With some hesitation, the other men drifted away to another circle made up of more stuffy elites. They were all vying to court the mayor's ear and ensure their self-interests for a town they called home almost four months out of the year. Why had Duncan ever wanted a seat beside these people?

Kent Devlin came so close to Duncan that the scent of the man's expensive aftershave tickled his nose. "I'd like to make you an offer," he spoke low. "I'll give you double what you paid my brother for Hill House to be returned to my family."

Time stood still for a second. Ever since the day Reese confronted him on the lawn of Hill House, he'd started having second thoughts on the acquisition. She had reminded him that people weren't the only ones who deserved second chances. Maybe Hill House truly deserved one too.

"Curious, Mr. Devlin, how was your brother able to sell the property without your knowledge in the first place?"

The man ran his hand across his face, scrubbing it clean of emotion, then stared down at his feet for more than a few seconds. "I used the portion I would have inherited to start my practice. I was never able to buy back in...or maybe Quincy didn't want me to since it seems he wasn't managing things properly." He shrugged. "I know you think you mean well. However, a town like the Shores needs a place like Hill House. The history, culture, and tastes of my family's bed and breakfast changed the lives of many…Black and white. I'd like to see that it remains relevant."

"Interesting you bring that up, Mr. Devlin." Duncan took a no-bullshit stance. He had an understanding of why the McNeals had been treated so poorly by the Devlins. Though, he didn't yet grasp why his grandmother and mother were kicked to the curb for wanting a restaurant, then made to watch on as Constance used the meals they created in the kitchen to compete with their hot plate sales. "One could argue that the food and culture of Hill House were influenced by my late grandmother, Suzette McNeal."

"Are those the lies your father tells you?" He bared his teeth. "If you knew how much my mother loved and cared for Miss Suzette, then you would know she could never intentionally hurt her, but she did have a business to run. Hell, my mother put our family's entire reputation on the line when she gave your grandmother and mother work so you wouldn't starve, boy." The man spat, then collected himself as he peered around the room.

Duncan's phone vibrated. He pulled it from his pocket to see Reese had texted him that she was on her way to Hill House, and it was right on time because he needed to escape. The past was rushing into the future, and it felt like they wouldn't be able to withstand the tests of time.

He looked back at her father. There were a million things he could and should say to him, except it wouldn't change anything. It was obvious he thought Duncan was still beneath him by how he casually referred to him as a boy and then called his father a liar. He would never do business with someone who failed to acknowledge and respect who he was because of who he had been born to.

"It's not for sale." He disregarded the obvious surprise on Mr. Devlin's face, then walked away. Reese was waiting for him.

Twenty-Nine

REESE ARRIVED AT Hill House before Duncan. She cut the ignition of her car and sat gazing upon the old, dark house. She couldn't ever recall a time where she saw it so vacant. A light or two used to illuminate from somewhere inside, while the coach lights lit up the front porch. Times had changed. This might really be her last time at the house before it was changed into the youth village, and she hated seeing it like this.

She scrambled out of the car and up the front steps. A gentle exhale calmed her stuttering hands long enough to unlock the door and push inside. The second she flipped the lights on, memories came crashing down. Her eyes closed, and she counted to ten, then opened them once more. Her blurred vision wouldn't allow her to escape how much of her life had been spent devoted to helping her grandmother make Hill House special—the Devlin family's pride and joy.

Once the overwhelming feelings settled, Reese began making her way through the house. Each room brought her a different memory of the many people who had once roamed within the halls. Fond recollections of her grandmother sprang to life.

There was the May Day social where everyone came for a glass of Hill House's signature front porch tea. She would never forget the Fourth of July, where her grandmother's famous potato salad and fried chicken were served.

Reese then went to the sunroom and recalled afternoon tea. In the dining room she huffed a laugh thinking of how her grandmother would often tell her that children were seen and not heard during grown folks' dinner parties. She lingered there for a bit and noted that the tablescape was still spring. By now it should be May Day with preparations to change over to Juneteenth.

The transition would never happen, and it was clear it hadn't in a while. How long, she didn't know. She was too afraid to find out for fear that if she hadn't been so stubborn, things might be different. Perhaps she would have realized sooner where she should've been using her gifts to make magic happen.

She needed to share her thoughts with Duncan on ushering the old place into a new era, and outright ask him to reconsider changing Hill House into the youth village for her. Not because her parents put her up to it, but because it was special and worthy of being preserved. But how could she make him give up his dream?

Reese palmed the tears of remorse from her cheek. She accepted the fate of Hill House. And yet, coming to terms with reality did nothing to quell her imagination. She continued through the house, imagining new wall colors, furniture that could be more transitional while complementing the current trove of antiques, and curtains she could...sew.

She paused and then took off down the hall and up the stairs to the west wing of the house. The door to the sewing room was closed. Maybe that was good, because there was so much going on inside of Reese that she needed a buffer to help prepare her for entering that once sacred space.

She turned the knob, hit the light switch, and the room came to life. An undeserved sweetness filled her heart as she stood staring at two sewing machines, hundreds of spools of thread, a cutting table, and a collection of fabric. There was still the bin of unfinished projects that appeared full, which was odd considering her grandmother had been gone for five years.

Reese moved deeper into the room. Her index finger traced along the cutting table and gathered a clump of dust. She did it again at the sewing machine and got the same result. It seemed as if no one had touched the room in a long while. She pulled the chair out from her grandmother's main sewing desk and sat down. Her mind began to rewind, and she relived being eight years old and sitting down for the first time to learn how to thread the bobbin.

From there she learned about patterns, straight lines, and double stitches. Her love of fabrics and their various textures and prints often kept her at her grandmother's side when she chose room themes to pair with them. A hearty chuckle escaped her while assessing the cutting board, remembering how she'd always collected the fabric scraps to make her dolls' clothes before imagining them on a runway.

All those years ago had placed her on this path and it took her a long time to find her way back. Though, she had to ask herself if she could stay on it. She wondered if it was what her grandmother always intended.

* * *

"Reese," Duncan called as he pushed through the back door and entered the kitchen. Every light in the house seemed to be on. "Chareese," he said again, this time a little louder from the base of the stairs.

"Up here," she finally responded.

Duncan climbed the steps one by one, taking his time. He

had so many things to say to Reese and needed time to prepare his words. At one point in his life he thought the heartache of losing her would never end. Like magic, it had faded away one day...or so he thought. The hurt in his heart had only truly healed the night they had lain together in this house and she told him that there was still something in her heart for him.

He hadn't been ready to do the same. Not then, because he wanted to make sure the nostalgia of them being together coupled with excellent sex wasn't clouding his mind. Now that he realized that the closeness between them was as pure as it had been every summer since she was nine and he was ten, it was time for him to share what he had been too afraid to say.

"Where?" he asked when he made it to the landing. He peeked in the rooms closest to him, but they held no traces of her. He then paused to listen for her movement. The silence was so still that he was unable to determine where she might be.

A loud crash sent him sprinting in the opposite direction. The sound of heavy furniture being dragged across wood floors pulled him down another hall until he heard shallow breaths and mumblings. He popped inside the open door and saw Reese tugging so hard on a handle that it caused the desk to move.

"I can't get it to open," she breathed heavily, releasing the handle of the drawer. She then reached up and kissed his lips.

Desire overtook his senses. He wrapped his arm around her waist, pulled her into him, and kissed her back. A euphoric high seized his heart. He felt like a teenage boy chasing his first kiss when he was with her. There was nothing he wouldn't do to keep this feeling.

"Looks like it needs a key." He brushed his nose against hers, then pressed their lips together once more. "What are you doing in here?" He scanned the room, noting that drawers had been gone through and stuff was everywhere. It honestly surprised him that the room wasn't empty, since Miss Constance had passed years ago. Maybe it was how her sons coped with losing her. "Are you looking for something?"

"The key to her sewing desk." She heaved while pulling at the other bank of drawers on the desk. They opened and revealed sewing accessories that looked as if they were purchased in the ice age. Not what she was looking for. "I'm honestly not sure if my uncle ever planned to properly clean or run this inn. It seems as though everything is as my grandmother left it when she died. This room appears untouched, as do many of the other rooms. It's all very odd."

"Your dad offered to buy Hill House back. I told him no." He rushed, needing to get the words out before they devoured him whole. He knew it was probably the last thing she wanted to hear considering the way she seemed to have moved about the house before he arrived. He just wanted to be honest so she could be too.

"After he insulted you in some way, I bet."

Not the answer he was expecting. "Yes."

Duncan peered down and saw that the contents inside the drawers she pulled out had been tossed around. Much like his life had been for the last month. He watched her shoulders slump as she sat on the small desk chair. He wasn't sure if his words were weighing her down or her father's jackass machinations.

He grabbed the chair at the other sewing machine and eased down next to her. For a minute he was distracted by the dainty floral scent emanating from her glowing brown skin. He had a lot to say, and still wasn't sure where to start. He knew how she felt about the house. It would be hard for anyone, let alone Reese, to escape the memories within these walls. It had already proven difficult for him.

"I'm sorry, Dunc." Her words were sweet, kind, and they

stirred his spirit. "I'd like to apologize to you for how my father continues to act as though he doesn't have good damn sense. Hill House is yours now, and you can do with it what you wish, no matter how any of us feels about it."

The sigh that ended her words stabbed him in the chest. It hurt to see her unhappy over a choice he had made. "How do you feel about it? You told me you understood the purpose of the youth village."

"I do," she huffed before she pulled at the locked drawer again. He watched her for a while before she mumbled, "I thought I had a chance."

"A chance for what?" he asked, placing his hand atop hers.

She went still and pulled her hand away before standing. Duncan came to his feet. Panic swept over him and settled within the depths of his soul. He couldn't lose her again.

A distant expression overtook her face as she cataloged the room. She then started toward the door but stopped. "To revamp this house," she whispered, avoiding his lingering stare. "And to be with you without disappointing the people we care about."

He had no words. They were lost in her confession. Silence hung between them like the sound of darkness. Questions started to formulate in his head, but they weren't about them. She became his focus.

He recalled the comments she'd made about her career and the somber demeanor she'd possessed during breakfast in his family's restaurant. He now wondered if the diversity promotion she'd mentioned was her only reason for job disenchantment.

"Revamp the house?" His head tilted to look her in the face. "You want to change this place?"

Reese's eyes cut to him. A stuttering breath escaped her and then she went to the small couch in the room. A tear rolled down her cheek before she closed her eyes. He kneeled at her feet and took both her hands. He opened his mouth to offer his sincerest apology, but then her finger rested upon his lips and she shook her head no.

"When I was little, Grandma Connie would tease that I would one day become the lady of Hill House." Reese snorted with disdain. "Gawd, I used to hate when she did that. I was not interested in catering to people. My love was dressing them. She realized the desires of my heart and gave me fabric, a sewing machine, and lessons." Reese gestured to the room, unable to hold her faltering smile.

"Naturally while learning to make clothes, she taught me how to do bedding, window treatments, and other knickknack décor things that had helped make this place beautiful. Never did I understand that my journey in fashion was a side road along a greater path until I returned here this summer. I knew something had changed in me late last year when I fleetingly wondered how different aesthetics from my visits to hotels could be done in my apartment, at my parents' home, or even at Hill House, after my father mentioned making it more current. From time to time, I even envisioned patterned fabrics on models as a wingback chair or accent pillows…heck, I did it again not long before you came in the room."

She sniffled, regaining her composure. "My point is, I have wondered if my career in fashion was where I wanted to be. This summer I came here for Alex, not really thinking I wanted to dabble within this space, but here I am, desperate to explore that other side of me that revels in my grandmother's memory. Except, it's too late…and I miss her." Tears choked her words. "I regret waiting as long as I did to return, because just maybe you wouldn't own this place. Maybe I would've had time to save it from my uncle and father's ruin."

Reese took a deep breath. "She knew…Grandma Connie

knew, and she had told Mrs. Willingham that I was the only one capable. I let her down, Dunc."

He replayed her words once more and then said, "You have a father and an uncle. They let her, you, and this inn down. You can't blame yourself for this, Reese, and I feel bad that you do because some of this is my fault."

"Actually it isn't." She stroked his jawline, and he closed his eyes, relishing her touch. "Hill House may have suffered a worse fate had you not stepped in."

He knew that, but now wasn't the time. He had to make sure he wasn't losing her. "What about us? I don't know if I can let you go after you've just come back into my life. If we are worried about disappointing everyone else, then we should first look in the mirror and make sure we aren't embarking on another tragic mistake rooted in the past."

"I refuse to repeat our parents' and grandparents' mistakes," she whispered. "This may be a second chance for us, but it's also about embracing the love that has always been between our families. So, you're right. We can't worry about who we will disappoint because…because I'm still in love with you."

The unsteady rhythm of his heart stole his breath. Once he reclaimed it, he pushed off of the ground and stood. He scanned her before cupping her face. "What if I told you that I feel the same?"

Her eyes got big. "You do? I thought you said it was just the nostalgia of us being around each other again?"

"That was denial. I wasn't ready to believe my heart after it had betrayed me once when it came to you." He took both her hands, helped her to stand, then wrapped her arms around him. He held her tight, as if he would never let her go, then looked down into her eyes. "I love you, Chareese."

* * *

A smile filled her cheeks, making them hurt. "Remember who said it first."

Their lips met and were claimed by raw passion as his tongue entered her mouth, dancing with hers in pure hedonistic lust. She kissed him back to the depths of his soul, hoping that he could feel all the love she had for him.

Despite her urge to be trapped underneath him, Reese pulled away. Her gaze lingered on a set of hooks on the back wall. She saw the pink and cream floral sewing apron her grandmother used to wear. Her mind flew back in time, and she could see her grandmother tying the apron around her waist and then sliding her ring of keys into one of the front pockets. Those keys never left her grandmother's possession.

"Soo…I know this may interrupt our prelude to a love hangover, but did your firm find a ring full of keys? I'm searching for my grandmother's journal." She exhaled, looking around the room. "You had mentioned my grandmother telling you I had to fulfill my duty. Mrs. Willingham claims my grandmother told her I was the only one capable of running the family business. I need proof that I'm not on some wild goose chase because of guilt."

"My firm hasn't touched the inside. Hill House remains as it was on the day I acquired it from your uncle. The only keys I received were from him at closing."

Reese sidestepped Duncan and went to the back wall where she took her grandmother's old apron off the hook. Hope was a living, breathing thing when she heard keys jingle inside the pocket. She pulled out a medium-sized ring full of keys.

"I see that key is more important than my 'I love you,'" Duncan chuckled. "You look like a kid that found the treasure at the end of the rainbow." He reached up and tucked a fly hair behind her ear.

Reese pecked his lips. "Not more important…closure." She held the ring of keys out for him to see while she studied it. "I think this is it." She singled out an old skeleton key before moving back to the desk. "It's possible I may find a clue of something she wrote about me and this house. She journaled every day." With a steady hand she inserted the key, turned it, and heard the clicking sound of the lock opening.

She reached forward and tugged at the top drawer. The wood tongue and groove caught, forcing her to jiggle the drawer a bit. Finally, it was open wide enough for her to see her grandmother's old journal and a stack of envelopes bound together. Reese and Duncan studied each other for a second before removing the contents.

"Coco," Duncan read aloud as he glanced over her shoulder at the faded cursive writing on the top of the stack.

"Who is Coco?" Reese set the journal on the desk, while Duncan began unknotting the twine holding the envelopes together. He passed the first envelope to her and she opened it. A picture of Suzette and Constance fell out along with a piece of paper that bore the signs of aging.

"Look at them!" Reese passed Duncan the photo. It showed their grandmothers standing at the bank of an unfamiliar watering hole in their bathing suits sharing a laugh.

He took a quick glimpse. However, his focus was on what had fallen out with the photo. He reached for the paper and unfolded it. He lowered it so that Reese could see too. She squinted a bit to read the perfect cursive penmanship. It was a letter from his grandmother to hers.

Heartache was the overwhelming emotion Reese suffered in reading Suzette's words to Constance. They were both only happy when they were together, and full of regrets for pretending they didn't like each other in public. Reese skipped ahead to a part of the letter where Suzette apologized for the pain and scrutiny. She expressed how she had enjoyed the time they had together at Hill House, cooking dishes from the heart that were inspired by their friendship. Her last line was that despite the circumstances, they knew what they meant to each other and their love would forever remain within the walls of the inn.

A sense of relief washed over Reese. Her grandmother wasn't the spiteful, uncaring woman who had intentionally crippled the McNeal women's business venture. And now she understood why the rumors persisted. Her grandmother would have never told her father, uncle, or anyone else that she and Suzette crafted the meals that were sold in Hill House and as hot plates together because it would expose the true nature of their relationship. Sadly, not much had changed with people attempting to keep appearances to fit in.

"Talk about forbidden. I can't imagine what it must've been like for them." Reese glanced over at Duncan, who had stopped reading the letter and was thumbing through the journal as if he were preserving it for the Smithsonian.

He closed the journal he held. "I can't," he mumbled as he turned away from their discovery. His palms pressed into his face. "How do I turn this place into a youth village with everything that has happened here? You should read your grandmother's last entry."

Reese picked up the journal. She glanced down and saw her name written in her grandmother's cursive. Did she truly want whispers from beyond the grave to confirm she hadn't done enough to live up to her duty to the Devlin family?

Duncan cleared his throat, grabbing her attention as he gestured to the book she held. "I would never tell you to do something that would bring you harm."

She took a deep breath. "'*Chareese was my girl. She was the little one that remained joined at my hip even when her mother offered her fancy parties over duty to this house. I pushed her away like I did Suzette, after caving to fears of not being accepted. I am a caged bird with clipped wings. I believe the time nears when I will be set free. My health is failing me and my sons, I fear, are unable to fulfill our legacy. I can no longer pretend the past does not haunt me. Perhaps mine and Suzette's offspring will one day be bold enough to accept the love that has always been between our families. Sins of the mother have proven to be harder than those of the father.'"*

Reese fisted the tears from her eyes. Duncan pulled her into his arms. There was a peace in knowing her grandmother didn't blame her. However, it didn't erase the guilt she suffered over never restoring their relationship.

"Thank you for making me read that. It helps knowing that she didn't have any anger toward me in the end." Reese sighed and stepped out of his hold. She looked him in the face. "I think you already know I never wanted to see Hill House become a youth village. I agree that a place like the Shores should have programs that can help kids become something in this world. However, there have to be other sites. I wanted to ask you again to reconsider but…" She stopped. She might put herself inside a hole she couldn't get out.

"I'm not cruel, Chareese." He sighed long and hard. "I heard you when we came here the last time. Honestly, moving forward with the project for the youth village has weighed on me since you returned home."

"What are you saying?"

"I think—" The ringing of his phone cut his words. He pulled it from his pocket and answered immediately. "Destiny." He pushed the phone closer to his ear. "What? I can't understand you. Calm down. Where are you? I'm on my way." He hurriedly left the room.

"What's going on?" Reese followed him.

"Not sure, she just kept saying your sister's name." He stopped and she almost ran into him. "She said your name too. Is there something you need to tell me?"

"No." Panic rolled over her stomach. What had Alex done? "The last time I saw Destiny was when she gave me your note, and everything seemed fine."

His eyes scanned her with an apprehension she hadn't seen since the day she first returned home. "She's at my house."

In a matter of seconds they shut off the lights, locked up the inn, and were on their way to Destiny.

Thirty

DUNCAN SLAMMED ON the brakes behind Destiny's car. He hopped out and darted up his driveway. Never mind that Reese had pulled up behind him. He was glad she'd driven her own car because he had yet to grasp the context of his sister telling him not to trust Reese. The words had chilled him to the bone as a series of possible regrets launched in his head.

There was no time to ponder what-ifs. Destiny needed him. He couldn't remember a time when his sister was so worked up. In fact, it was rare to see her cry. She always strove to be as tough as nails since she'd chosen to enter a career field dominated by men.

He entered his house and found her waiting in the living room. She immediately rushed into his bear hug. He wouldn't shed his protective big brother mode anytime soon.

"What's she doing here?" Destiny's words were venom.

He whipped around and saw Reese standing not far from them. He looked back at his sister, needing to understand her animosity while hoping he hadn't been wrong about Reese this time. "Why don't you tell me what's going on?" He glanced over at Reese. "She was with me when you called and is worried too."

"About what?" Destiny snapped. "Let me guess...My brother never giving you and your family back Miss Connie's bed and breakfast."

"No, why would you say that?" Reese moved closer. Destiny pulled away and took Duncan with her.

"Oh my God! You're worse than your sister. At least Alex kept it one hundred with the way she felt about me. I knew she was plastic, but to think that you only helped me so you could get close to my brother and change his mind on Hill House—that is really freaking low."

"That's not—" Reese blurted, taking a step closer. "It wasn't like that."

Duncan's entire body went stiff. He felt frozen in the twilight realm, or was this an *Alfred Hitchcock Presents*? Either way his reality was shifting into a monster that was preparing to devour him.

"Then tell me what it is," he finally spoke, unable to contain the acrimony swirling around inside. Reese pinched the bridge of her nose, then pressed her lips together. "Tell me." He raised his voice a register.

"Dunc." She swallowed hard. "When I first got here and found out you had purchased my grandmother's inn, I was devastated. Of course I wanted to save Hill House from becoming a youth village. My mother seemed to think we still had a connection and thought it would be a good idea for me to use that for a chance to convince you to sell the inn back." She sighed and a crack ran across his heart. "I couldn't do what they asked, but I pretended mainly because I liked the idea of having a way to be around you without them judging me, again."

Reese needed an excuse to be around him. His legs grew

weak. Somehow he managed to remain strong and stood taller. No matter the decade, elitist views didn't change. They were passed down like her privilege. She would not get the satisfaction of witnessing their sucker punch. "So, it was all a scam?"

"No," she said breathlessly and moved toward him. He threw his arm up to stop her from coming any closer. "The first time I saw you my heart cried out. Then the night we saw each other in the rink and you followed me after I'd fallen, I knew I would never deceive you because I still cared for you. The last month here has made me realize how much I've missed it…you…and what we should've had."

He stared into her eyes. His heart teetered between life and death as his mind attempted a replay of them making love while simultaneously acknowledging her betrayal. He once again had been a fool in love with Chareese Devlin. No more.

"That was in the past. What we had died when you left ten years ago. There's no lost love letter, or long-overdue confessions that will erase what happened then or now." His throat burned. He didn't know what to believe except that she had ruined him for any other woman.

A tear slid down her cheek. "You don't mean that."

"Yes I do. We never discussed a future. We were just having fun, right?" He cocked his head, doing everything in his power to run damage control. "You were going to leave and accept that promotion and travel the world in the name of fashion while I stayed here and made the Shores a better place. I'm guessing that was too simple for you."

"Dunc—"

"Just stop, Chareese," he gritted his teeth. "You used me and then my baby sister."

"Alex told me all about it," Destiny piped back in. "She said I was charity, and that you becoming my mentor made it easier for the Devlins to get back what they wanted. You didn't even believe I should be allowed to participate in the ball."

"That is a lie," Reese shouted.

Duncan's hands formed fists even as he took a deep breath. "We are no one's charity, Destiny. Get out, Chareese."

Reese's heart sank to the devil's pit as she took a step backward. She was losing the man she loved, a girl she believed in thought she was a fraud, and her own sister had betrayed her. All were proof of why she had never wanted to come back. She should've stayed away. "Let me say this before I leave. I have experienced emotional tolls of adhering to elitist standards. And while I, as one person, will never be able to break down the societal hierarchies that have impacted us, I've tried to help."

Her attention went to Destiny because it was too much to look at Duncan right now. The pain in his face latched on to her soul and took her to a place she never wanted to know again. "I did not seek you out to get close to your brother. I was asked to mentor you and tried to refuse because of the past he and I shared. However, there are people that want to see you make a proper debut, and after your brother made me realize the privilege I'd taken for granted, I was determined to help you succeed.

"It is true that helping you allowed me to spend time with your brother, but that isn't why I mentored you. I'm sure Alex has been more than catty. I mean, she tried crashing your first meeting with Xavier. But, hey, you're a smart girl, Destiny. Deep down I believe you know that my sister said those things to get to you because, for once in her spoiled life, she didn't win the prize. You did."

Destiny didn't respond, she simply ran up the stairs. Reese avoided Duncan's penetrating stare and turned to leave. There was no need to offer more words that would fall on deaf ears. She understood he was hurt. She was too.

"And just like that you don't have anything to say to me?" His even tone halted her steps.

Reese had a lot to say to him. She thought this was their second chance and that she would spend the rest of her life telling him how much she loved him. Only, they couldn't seem to escape their past. It was too strong.

"Everything"—she stayed facing the exit door, not yet ready to lay eyes on him—"I said to you earlier was true." She choked back what little pride she had left and finally turned to look at him. "I love you, Duncan. You still doubt that, along with the place you've commanded in this world. You beat the odds, proved everyone wrong, and even reclaimed your family legacy.

"And yet it's not enough for you to accept that a world you've wanted to be a part of for so long is full of mistakes, conflict, and irony. Utopia does not exist in the Shores, but it can feel like it when you're ready to give and receive love without the burdens of our complicated past."

She hurried out of the door and to her car before tears could fall. One day, maybe after another ten years of being away from the Shores, she would find a way to not love Duncan McNeal. For now, she planned to find her dear sister and release her rage. Alex had betrayed their entire family because things had not gone her way.

In no time Reese made it home. She burst inside the house yelling her sister's name as she viciously searched for her. Had Alex been a chick off the street, she might slap her on sight. Like the old church people say, hurt people hurt people, and she was ready to tack a dent in her sister's ass. Right now she blamed Alex for the broken heart caving into pieces within her chest.

"What," Alex snapped as she came in from the lanai drying off. "Why are you calling me like some mad woman? My friends think you're crazy."

Reese peeked outside and saw several debutantes from the most well-to-do families out on the pool deck. She was certain that Destiny had not been invited. Before she could open her mouth to question Alex on her scandalous antics, both her parents entered the family room. Great, this was about to be a full-family meeting.

Time to air all the dirty laundry. "I'm not, but you are."

"You're not what," Genevieve asked.

"Crazy," Reese answered her mother, then turned back to Alex. "You've got some nerve. Why would you tell Destiny that I was *only* helping her to get close to Duncan so we could get Hill House back? That was not true."

Instead of becoming the contrite kid with a hand caught in the cookie jar, Alex deployed a sardonic grin as she wrapped the towel around her body. "It was no big deal, Reese. I needed that little bitch to know her place. She thought she was better than me because Xavier was escorting her."

"No, you thought she was better because she had something you wanted but couldn't have."

"You were way outta line, Alexandria." Genevieve stepped between them. She never used slang when speaking unless she was pissed. Alex had poked a bear. "How dare you go around running your mouth about your sister like some loose-lipped common girl. Do you realize what is at stake?"

"Mom, I stood in Dad's office when you said Reese should all but fuck Duncan to get Hill House bac—"

The crack in the air silenced the room. Her father yanked her mother to his side as Reese watched water well in Alex's eyes. Her sister's hand shook as she lifted it up and cupped her red cheek, obviously still processing the slap across the face she'd just received.

In all her twenty-seven years, Reese had never seen her

mother raise a hand to anyone. For years, Alex got her way through hissy fits and stubbornness. So yes, a part of her deserved to be brought down.

However, it was her mother's fault. Her sister had been conditioned to believe she was the crème-de-la-crème, and if people got too close, you found a way to leave them behind. Had Reese not endured the experience of seeing her father and grandmother berate the McNeals, she could've very well been the same way.

"Your mother is sorry. She didn't mean to hit you, Alex," her father offered.

Alex raised her head with indignation and glared at the three of them. "Then why won't she say it?" she spat, nostrils flaring. Seconds turned to minutes and Genevieve offered nothing. "I don't need an apology. I spoke the truth."

"Your truth is flawed, Alexandria." Her father's tone hardened.

She lowered her hand from her cheek and placed her attention on Reese. "Then so is my sister's. Why don't you tell us all the truth, Reese? The town's been whispering about you and Duncan since you went to the cove. You don't care about Hill House, you want him and he wants you. Everyone can see it. Mom and Dad just won't accept it."

Typical Alex. Just when Reese was starting to feel sorry for her sister, she was reminded why they never shared a true bond. And since today was apparently a confessional, she took a deep breath and met her parents' lingering gaze. The only way to escape the generational cycles of failure that had pitted the Devlins against the McNeals was to find a path forward through love. She would be honest.

"Mom was right...there was an opportunity for me to get close to Duncan, and it was linked to our past. I was nervous to get close to him because I never wanted to hurt him again." She looked directly at her father. "And I wanted Hill House. It was a place that gave me some of my fondest memories.

"From the moment I entered Duncan's orbit I knew I couldn't manipulate him because it would have corrupted my heart. Yet, I continued pretending to all of you that I was spending time with him to change his mind. I didn't want to be judged or accused of not putting family first…but the reality is that I wanted to be with him."

"I forbid it." Her father's hand sliced through the air. "That family is unworthy."

"What made you determine that? Is it the fact that Mr. David and Mom were once in love or that your mother and Duncan's grandmother loved each other?"

Her father began walking away. "When you leave this time, don't worry about coming back if those are the lies you will tell in this town."

"I found Grandma Connie's journal and correspondence between her and Miss Suzette, Dad." He whirled around. "I read their love letters. Miss Suzette and Grandma Constance were in love in an era that did not openly embrace queer women. My grandmother died full of regrets, and she hoped that one day her family would be bold enough to embrace the love that has existed between two families for a very long time. Why can't you accept that?"

"Kent, I've been thinking on this for a while now. Maybe if you can learn to accept who your mother really was, and let go of your grudge against David, you will understand that Reese and Duncan are meant to be." Genevieve went to him and took his hands. Reese was still trying to catch her breath. Her mother had approved of something she wanted. "We fought against this for so long, even at the expense of losing Reese here with us for ten years because you feared the town would spit on your mother's legacy. We can't do that anymore."

Alex stomped her feet and gained everyone's attention. "So, this is why you always find compassion for her? Because she stayed gone. I make one mistake and you slap me."

"You've made a ton of mistakes so be glad that's the first time I've slapped you, Alexandria. Do not ever confuse me with your friends. You will never curse at me and think it's okay to be disrespectful." Genevieve went to Alex, hugged her, and apologized. She then stood in front of Reese.

"I will always believe in the rules and traditions of the old guard, Reese. However, I would be met with great remorse if I allowed them to dictate my relationship with my daughter. I love you, more than you will ever know. I'm sorry for the hurt I've caused, and I sincerely hope you and Duncan can find a way to make things right."

The minute her mother's arms wrapped around her, she felt whole. For so long they had battled around who Reese wanted to be and who she was allowed to love. To have her mother's support was more than she'd bargained to receive this summer. Only, as they came apart, she saw that her father had left the room.

"Give him some time," her mother said. "He's battled preserving his mother's legacy for a long time. It's possible that if your uncle hadn't lost Hill House, he might have been more apt to accepting whom you've chosen to love."

Reese ran her fingers through her hair. "Then I guess Dad and I will be besties again soon. Duncan hates me." She shed a tear. "I don't see how he will ever forgive me."

Thirty-One

LAST NIGHT HAD been brutal. Reese had endured the second worst nightmare of her life, and waking up hadn't allowed her to escape it. Heartache crippled her as she journeyed down the stairs to the rear side of the house. She gazed through the window, admiring how the lake remained constant even as the world around it changed.

Life had been the opposite for her. She had adapted to the demands of her family, college, career, and now the pain of a broken heart, again.

Reese quickly unlocked the door, stepped outside, and breathed in the fresh air. A modicum of solace greeted her as she rushed toward the bank of the lake. The old tree swing her father had built when she was a child caught her eye. She went to it, wiping the wood seat of pollen and debris before tugging the rope to assess its sturdiness. It seemed strong enough, so she sat, wishing the love she and Duncan had for each other could be too.

She sat for a while. Her attention floated from the water up to the pale-blue sky sprinkled with fluffy white clouds, and she prayed for the strength to overcome the pain tearing at her body from the inside out. Reese still couldn't believe her sister's betrayal. She hoped one day soon she could forgive her because she doubted Destiny or Duncan ever would.

"Your father used to push you for what seemed like hours on that swing." Her mother startled her from behind, then came to stand next to her.

Reese adjusted in the seat and looked back out onto the lake. It was beautiful, calm, and everything she wasn't right now. "In the same way he pushed me away yesterday?" She tried hard to fight tears from falling. She lost, closing her eyes to end the burning sensation as tears rolled down her cheek. "I guess maybe I shouldn't be surprised since it was him the last time too."

"Chareese."

"No, Mom, it's true. I spent years being mad at you instead of him. You never walked away from me or avoided hard conversations. You said what you said and meant it…Maybe that's why it seemed easier to talk to him and forgive him for everything that happened all those summers ago." She sniffled. "I'm so sorry, Mom."

Genevieve moved closer and wrapped an arm around Reese's shoulders. "You don't have to apologize, Chareese. I demanded perfection from you then got upset when it wasn't achieved, and that wasn't fair, because nobody is perfect. The many experiences you've had have shaped you into who you are, and I couldn't be more proud. You are more courageous than I ever was at your age, and I envy that."

Silence lingered between them for more than a few minutes as her mom patted her back. And while a part of Reese remained shriveled on the inside, another side was set free by the connection that had been reestablished with her mother.

"You must know," her mother started, "that your father will come around. I just don't know when."

Reese sighed, "Perhaps when I leave. It's best I get back to the city. I have a lot to figure out where my career is concerned, and I need the space to do that."

"But I thought—"

"None of that matters anymore." She gulped back her pain. "Duncan hates me and Hill House is set to become a youth village."

Reese's phone began to ring. She couldn't remember bringing it with her as she hopped off of the swing and began checking her pockets.

"Oh," her mother gasped, pulling the phone from her rear pocket and giving it to Reese. "I was so focused on you that I forgot I had it. This is why I followed you out here. Your phone wouldn't stop ringing. Looks like the girls have been trying to get in touch with you."

Reese took the phone from her mother silently, hoping to see his number. There was not one missed call or text from Duncan. Instead she saw over twenty messages in her group chat with Ava, Carrah, Peyton, and Quinn. She scrolled through the missed messages. "They're trying to plan a pajama party," she mumbled.

"Ha! Wouldn't that be like old times?"

Reese didn't have any party-going spirits about her. She was still stuck on Duncan's dismissal, Destiny's disdain, and her father's contempt. It would be a bad mix of energy to carry over to someone's house where she was expected to be lively and fun. Quinn especially would never forgive her for wasting an evening away drowning them in sorrows. She considered tossing her phone into the mud at the shoreline, the perfect alibi for her avoidance.

Except, she wouldn't be able to ignore everyone forever since the ball was at the end of the week. She slumped back into the swing. "I'm not in the mood to be around people right now."

"It might be what you need to help take your mind off

of things. Friends help us weather storms." Genevieve patted Reese on the head. "I doubt Duncan hates you. He's hurt so you'll need to give him some time. If he knows you the way I think he does, then he will see through your sister's stunt." She kissed Reese on the cheek and then left to go back inside.

A new text from Quinn came through threatening Reese to reply or they were all coming over. Warning bells rang loud; she became panicked, wondering if they had heard about her and Duncan's blowout and were using the pj party as a disguise for an intervention. Who had told them?

Her fingers hovered over the keyboard of her phone. She took a deep breath, not sure of what any of them knew, but decided to reply. Her days left in the Shores were numbered, and her mom was right, she could use a distraction to take her mind off of things. So, she texted back.

> Sorry, was in bed. No need for you to come harass me Quinn.

It's eleven o'clock! Quinn ended the text with a confused face emoji.

And it's summer. Sometimes I sleep late. What's up? They would buy that response. It was well-known that Reese was not an early riser. Besides, she wasn't about to tell them she'd been up since the crack of dawn from a restless night of sleep.

PJ Party tonight?! My House is what Ava texted back.

Somehow, a small smile managed to curve her lips.

> Sounds like old times. What time and do I need to bring anything?

* * *

Later that evening, Reese drove away from lakeshore territory to the midtown area where Ava lived. The mature trees and rolling green hills were hallmarks of the middle-class section of town. While the homes were smaller and built to the scheme of traditional ranch houses, they were still desirable.

Reese slowed down and turned onto Ava's street, which was beautifully canopied by ancient oaks. Unexpectedly, a sliver of happiness emerged within her when she arrived. This was the second time it had happened today and instead of allowing it to leave, she latched on to it. She quickly parked, grabbed her things, and got to the front door.

Before she could knock, Peyton pulled her inside. The moment was nostalgic. The house smelled of popcorn and brownies, the two things they always had regardless of whose house they were crashing at for the night when they were young. And they were all in cute pajamas. Except instead of rainbows and unicorns, or the Victoria's Secret garb they wore as teens, each of her friends had upgraded to high-end designer bedtime threads.

Carrah was glamorous as usual in pink, vintage-inspired pjs trimmed with feathers. Quinn maintained her practicality in a simple, no-frills gray-knit pant set. Romantic sophistication was owned by Peyton in her fancy linen shorts with peachy ruffles, and Ava did not disappoint in her bright, whimsical gown that remained chic. Their choices for the evening dictated much of who they were in real life, which was probably why they all sized Reese up seeing her in plain, dark-colored silks.

Maybe she should've cared a little more while getting dressed. To the fault of her creative brain, Reese often chose her clothes based on mood. Today there was no inspiration, feeling, or light, and her pajamas reflected that sullenness.

"Oh my goodness, I can't believe all of you are here. How

long has it been since you all had a sleepover?" Mrs. Hamilton bounced into the foyer, squeezing each of them into a hug. "Takeout is on the way. In the meantime I've got y'all some popcorn, brownies, and wine"—she winked—"since you're old enough to drink now."

They all erupted in laughter. Mrs. Hamilton had always been the more lax one of their moms, which was why they preferred Ava's house for sleepovers. After thanking Mrs. Hamilton for her hospitality, the girls found their way to the TV room and made quick work laying out their sleeping bags before indulging in the smorgasbord of treats. A lot of talk about town, the families, and ball dominated the first hour or so after they arrived.

Everything changed when Ava asked, "So what's this I hear about you and Duncan getting chummy…again?"

Peyton coughed, eyeing their little circle. Ava burst into laughter along with Quinn. Reese never cracked a smile. She was now reminded of why she hesitated attending tonight.

"Sorry, I don't know what you mean." Reese picked up her glass and gulped down the ginger ale. When she lowered her chin and put the glass down, she found all of them staring at her. "What?"

"It's been like this since we were kids. Why must you always act like you and Dunc are just friends? We weren't blind back then and definitely not now considering the way I saw you in his lap while we were at the cove." Quinn leaned back as if she'd just made a significant play in her game of chess.

"Are you still trying to hide the way you feel about him because of your parents? You're damn near thirty, Reese." Ava stood and went to pour herself more wine. "Guess it's a good thing I've been gone most of the time you've been here because I would've told you this is nonsense."

Reese and Carrah exchanged a look of knowing. This was never a subject she discussed. There was too much judgment, and she was never sure which side her friends would land on since they all grew up in families that shared her parents' mindset, and they also knew Duncan.

"Not all of us had the freedoms you were afforded, Ava. I thought you recognized that."

"Ahh…because I'm a local and all of you simply come for the summer?"

"What the hell, Aves!" Carrah got to her feet, wine spilling out of her glass, and narrowed her eyes. "You know Reese didn't mean it like that."

Reese stood up and grabbed Carrah's arm. She was forever the hot-headed, impulsive one of the group, and Reese didn't want her friend to say anything she couldn't take back. "Ava, have I ever treated you as such? Why would you say that?"

"Because it's the reason you are afraid to be bold…daring even when it comes to Dunc. I watched him come home every summer after you left that last one. He missed you, wanted you…and you never came back. Hell, you didn't come back for any of us, Reese. But then you show up ten years later like we are supposed to pretend as if time hasn't gone by." Ava slammed her glass down. "Social media can never take the place of this." She gestured to all of them, who were now on their feet watching unnecessary drama unfurl. "I missed you, dammit."

"I'm sorry," Reese sobbed. Her fists formed balls. This, coupled with her and Duncan's situation, was emotional overload.

"I missed you too, Reese." Carrah tugged away from her hold.

Quinn and Peyton moved closer to where Reese stood by Carrah. "We all did," Quinn said.

"It never felt right without you." Peyton took her hand and squeezed it tight. "There were no more juicy circle secrets, since you weren't here to report on the ladies' meeting your mother hosted."

"Oh my God, or all the piping hot tea you used to pour us after doing your little duty at Hill House with your grandmother," Ava admitted. She looked like she wanted to say more, but stopped.

Reese walked away from everyone and sank back down onto her sleeping bag on the floor. The room swirled with tension after so many of her faults had been revealed. They were all right and deserved more of her for friendship's sake. "I must confess…" They all scrambled to sit back down in their circle. Reese had uttered the first three words to start the chain of secrets game they used to play. "…I have loved Duncan McNeal since I was thirteen. Maybe longer, but I didn't know it."

Gasps filled the room, but Reese kept going. "This summer I finally told him the same and apologized for that last summer."

She looked around and saw that, with the exception of Carrah, everyone had puzzled faces. She exhaled a long, deep breath and then told them the story of that ill-fated summer from ten years ago. Reese could've hidden her shame. But she didn't stop until after she disclosed the mess of last night.

"Why have you held on to that for so long," Peyton questioned, fingering a tear from the corner of her eye.

"Right," Quinn snapped. "We could've all rebelled against our dates with you. Lord knows I'm good for a protest." She chuckled and so did everyone else because it was true. "Had I known, Reese, you wouldn't have had to go at it alone. I told you before that I've been troubled for a long time over some of the thoughts and views our parents hold."

"Ditto," Carrah whispered.

Ava went to the center of the circle and faced Reese. "I had no idea asking that one question would trigger all this." Ava gave Reese a sheepish grin. "And now, I must confess that after the second summer of your absence, where I witnessed Duncan's hurt and we experienced our own, I wished for you to never come back. I was wrong. Just like we needed you, he does too. I asked what I asked earlier tonight because I heard he was happy. I hope you and him are able to find your way back to each other."

"It's wishful thinking at this point, but me too," Reese admitted.

* * *

Duncan lay awake as the sun rose for the second day since the life he was considering with Reese fell apart. He had tried everything to take his mind off of her. His most recent foray with a bottle of cognac had his head banging as his memory suffered on a constant loop of how things went down the other night.

Ignoring her messages made him feel like the villain. Only, he had to protect his heart. He'd let his guard down with Reese and now he was paying for it.

He groaned, pushing away the covers from his bed, and sat up. Seconds passed before he collapsed back into the pillows. His head was spinning, his body felt hot, and his heart ached so bad he clawed at his chest.

Was this hell? He hoped not, but right now he knew he was far from being where he wanted to be—and that was with Reese. His eyes closed, her pretty face greeted him, and then the world went dark.

Duncan's eyes flew open at the sound of his doorbell ringing like it was giving warning of a fire. He stumbled from bed and hurried downstairs to where he was also greeted by banging. He peeked through the peep hole and saw Gavin along with Tasha, his office assistant.

"What the hell is going on," he growled, opening the door.

"You tell us," Gavin remarked, pushing in so that he and Tasha could enter. Duncan closed the door behind them, then turned to face his best friend and assistant. "You look like shit, bro. Why aren't you answering your phone?"

Gavin walked deeper into the house. Tasha stayed in the foyer twirling her fingers, eyes downcast to avoid looking at Duncan, who was only in lounge pants. He appreciated her modesty but was irritated by the way Gavin sprang up on him…And why was he with Tasha?

"Morning, Tasha," he finally grumbled.

"You mean afternoon," Gavin quipped as he held up the empty bottle of Hennessy. "Late night?"

Duncan left where Tasha stood and went to Gavin. He snatched the bottle from his hand, went to the kitchen, and put it in the trash. Shocked was an understatement. He didn't even remember drinking. Until a slight ache started at his head and forced everything he would've loved to forget back to the surface.

Destiny, Chareese, her betrayal, him drowning his sorrows…"I've had better," he said, sensing Gavin was behind him. "What made you come by, and why did you bring Tasha?"

"This morning made the third day that you weren't returning calls or answering messages. That's not like you. At first, I thought you were just booed up with Reese. Until I heard she was with the girls."

"With the girls?" Duncan asked.

"Ava had some kind of get-together. Which meant she wasn't with you, and then Xavier mentioned that Destiny tol—" Duncan held his hand up while shaking his head. "What happened?" Gavin whispered.

Duncan shrugged; he glanced away for a second before sliding his hands into his pockets. "Nothing." He wasn't yet ready to share the full betrayal. It was still too raw. "It's over…as it should've been after all those summers ago."

Gavin recoiled. His surprise was evident, but still unmatched to Duncan's after hearing Reese admit to needing a reason to be around him. The taste was still bitter, and he didn't know if it could ever be replaced.

Not in the mood to offer up more of his personal life, Duncan strolled from the kitchen with Gavin behind and went to where Tasha had remained in the foyer. "I appreciate the both of you coming by to check on me. I still don't understand why you called Gavin?" He questioned his assistant with a pointed look. "I mean it's only what, a few hours not reaching me if it's the afternoon as Gavin said."

Tasha sighed. "You never no call, no show. I tried you multiple times along with other staff and was worried after not getting you, so, I called Gavin. You usually answer his calls even when you aren't accepting anyone else's."

"I get that, but—" Duncan took a deep breath. He was still exhausted from his last conversation with Reese and didn't have the fire in him today to debate. "I'm taking the rest of the day. I should be in on Monday."

"Kent Devlin came by the office this morning demanding he see you." Tasha stood a little taller, finally justifying her reasons for making contact with Duncan. "I'm sorry, but I don't think you have the luxury of starting your weekend early. He said it was urgent and he needed to discuss the future of Hill House. He's determined to see you today."

Thirty-Two

A WEEK HAD passed since Duncan watched Reese walk out of his life. The only difference now was that he didn't have the urge to chase her like he did when he was eighteen and dumb. Shame on him for falling for her...again.

Duncan glanced down to his phone and scrolled through all the missed calls and texts from her. His mind kept telling him there was nothing left to say. However, his heart said something different. He dared not think of the way his body was feenin' for hers. Besides, according to her father, after tonight she would be gone. She had only come back to see her sister debut.

"Dunc." His mother knocked on his bedroom door. He adjusted the cufflinks on his shirt once more before he left the mirror. A bright smile greeted him. "Destiny is supposed to be there early. She seems too nervous to drive herself so I'm going to head on over."

He gave his mother a quick once-over and noted that only her hair was done. "If you take her, when will you get dressed?"

She shrugged. "It's no big deal. Tonight is about Destiny. I don't have to be there like that."

"Stop. You do." He took a deep breath. He wasn't oblivious to her obvious wayward thinking. Despite the origin story of the ball that included his great-grandmother, his parents still hesitated embracing the legacy Frances McNeal left behind. Years of the effects of class division wouldn't disappear within a few days. Therefore, he understood.

However, Duncan hadn't any doubts. He'd worked hard to get where he was and so had his sister. The recent discovery of his family history affirmed that the McNeal family had always been hardworking stewards of the community regardless of when they thought they weren't.

"You and Dad have to be there. Like you know, sitting inside the actual ballroom where this all takes place for Destiny. You can't look on from the sidelines this time. If you do, then you'll hold regrets for the rest of your life for missing her take this step into the future. Don't let the way these people move deter you from celebrating your daughter."

"Duncan, I'm not like any of those women. I got my dress from a regular department store. I don't have a fancy degree or use big words. I could care less about a tea unless I'm the one that gets to bake the cake. I've worked with my hands all my life."

He stepped closer and took her hands into his. "These working hands raised me and that beautiful girl downstairs I call sister. We are who we've become because of you." He dried a tear that fell from her eyes. "You and Dad have overcome years of being mistreated because of how people viewed Grandma Suzette's choice. Financial hardship could've kept us down, but y'all worked hard and now you have one of the most successful restaurants in the area. Don't you see that you not giving up has become our legacy, one that Destiny and I will carry forward?"

Tears rushed down her cheek before she hugged him tight. "Thank you, son."

"Yes, thank you." Duncan glanced up to see his dad and Destiny standing behind them. "I don't think I could've said it better."

They exchanged a look of knowing. A few days ago, his father wouldn't have agreed. After Duncan told him about the many letters between Constance and Suzette, his father settled into understanding that despite the town's sentiments, Connie wasn't out to ruin Suzette. His father still struggled with the fact that she had made him and his siblings casualties of her affair. Yet, they couldn't change the past.

"Everything that happened has brought us here," his dad said as he stretched his arms out, then gestured for them all to hold hands. Once they were linked, he smiled at each of them. "Our family is stronger than it's ever been. I now find myself blessed that we inherited a legacy I didn't want until now. Thank you for never giving up, Dunc. And for helping me...us find peace with the choices your grandmother made. This path to redemption has not been easy."

"No one ever said it was. At least we had each other." Duncan squeezed his mother's and father's hands.

"Then what about you and Chareese?" his mother asked. "I thought you spoke to her father?"

Duncan dropped their hands and moved away from the circle. He grabbed his coat, adjusted his bow tie, and returned to three bewildered faces. "If you need to be there early, we need to leave now, little sis."

Destiny hesitated, then took off downstairs. His parents remained silent as he headed toward the stairs. Discussions about Reese were off the table. She had stabbed him in the heart again, and this time he couldn't forgive her. So, while his father may have let go of his grudge, Duncan held on with iron fists.

The fact that she'd entertained her parents' schemes so easily revealed how the Devlins still thought their family was better. He would never be the boy from the other side of the tracks again. And he was happy Mr. Devlin had acknowledged that when they met in his office a few days ago. Still, his ambition had brought him too far and love wouldn't cripple him.

"There is a reason why people consider pride a sin, Duncan," his father called. "Don't let it blind you to what could be the best thing for you. People make mistakes. The love for our family makes us do things we never imagine."

"Okay, so what stops it from happening again?" He took a glimpse over his shoulder before heading down.

Duncan and Destiny left for the Lakeside Inn. The car ride was awkwardly quiet, an anomaly considering how much they shared with each other. When Duncan drove into the parking lot of the old hotel, Destiny cleared her throat. He knew she had something to say, he just didn't know what. However, he hoped that she was taking his side and not in agreement with their parents. He needed to feel as though he wasn't being unreasonable in his refusing to accept Reese's apology.

"You know I only did this ball because of you." He turned to look over at her and found she was already staring at him. "You sold me on the experience and connections that would benefit me long after I left home for college. Up until Reese became my mentor, I was skeptical. I had time to think about what she said."

Destiny blew a loud breath as she slumped into her chair. "She was right and I was too hurt after being called a charity case to realize it. Chareese isn't like her mom or, God forbid, her shady sister. She was really nice, sincere, and never treated me that way. She took me around, introduced me to influential people, and willingly gave me everything those other girls had taken years to learn. I could tell she really did want the best for me.

"I'm not sure of everything that happened between you and Reese. The one thing I believe is that she loves you, Dunc. The way she looked at you that night is exactly how I'd look at the man who stole my heart."

He whistled long while punching his fist into his palm. "Do tell, what big-headed boy is vying for your affections. You talkin' real grown, little sis, and you know I don't care that Xavier is my best friend's brother. Y'all just met."

"Ignoring you…Anyways, I should've given Reese more credit. Instead I got caught up in Alex's jealousy. This one time I need you to trust your sixteen-and-a-half-year-old sister. Reese is not like the other women in that crowd, and she doesn't want to be. She could've been like other mentors and gave me tips that I could've researched online. Yet, she took time to make sure I knew what to say, how to bow, waltz, and she introduced me to a guy that I actually like beyond him being my escort." She smirked at the way Duncan side-eyed her.

"I don't think she did all that to get Hill House back. I mean she could've…you know, not left room for Jesus and buttered you up."

"Pause"—he cleared his throat with a chuckle—"not left room for Jesus?"

"Get with the times, big bro. Just another way of saying she could've spent all her time seducing you when she was supposed to be helping me, but she didn't. She invested time in me and made me better. So, when you see me walk out tonight, know that I couldn't have done it without her."

Destiny popped the door handle and exited the car. Duncan joined her at the trunk and helped her unload. The instant they entered the area of the old hotel designated for the debutantes, they were engulfed in an atmosphere of elegance. They both walked a little taller and held their heads higher as they read the meticulously placed calligraphed signs on gold bejeweled easels.

A distinctly rose scent guided them to a small alcove where a group of women in designer dresses and sparkling diamonds awaited them. They again thanked Duncan for his donation, while welcoming him and Destiny with open arms. Their actions reconfirmed why he had been desperate to preserve his reputation, and the affection that passed between his sister and women he'd known all his life as the well-to-do crowd was both shocking and humbling. His reasons for Destiny's participation in the event were again validated when he heard one of the women mention that her husband, a judge in Atlanta, was eager to meet Destiny this evening and discuss her future legal career.

After receiving the key to a dressing suite, they followed directions and continued down a hall. They exchanged glances at the sight of participants with their mothers in tow. As they came to a door with her name upon it, Duncan sensed that his sister wanted their mother. After hanging up her gown she sank into a chair in front of a vanity mirror and closed her eyes.

"I can go get Mom. It won't take long." They made eye contact through the mirror.

She shook her head. "No, it's fine. I've made it this far without her being entrenched in this world. Besides, she'll clam up and it would get all weird. I imagine I can do another few hours."

"You sure you good?"

"Yeah, make sure you cheer me on when I walk in. Not all loud though. Just clap," she giggled.

"Are you seriously attempting an etiquette lesson?" He went to her and gave her shoulders a gentle squeeze. "I'm proud of you. I know you're going to do great."

She sighed, avoiding him. "I hope so."

He kissed her forehead and left. The second he closed the door he removed his phone from his pocket and texted Reese.

* * *

Reese stood looking in the mirror of her sister's dressing suite. She managed to tune out her mother and Alex bickering over lipstick color with the makeup artist, and admired the curve-defining, one-shoulder fuchsia gown that made her glow like gold. Too bad she didn't feel as vibrant on the inside.

Over a week had passed with Duncan ignoring her calls and texts. Her virtual apology was a last resort that also went unanswered. She had hoped to make some sort of amends. But, after days had gone by without any sort of contact, she booked a flight for the morning after the ball. There was no reason to stay after Alex debuted this evening. She would figure out her next steps later since she planned to decline the promotion.

"Pink, Alex. Mom is right, that deep red does not complement your skin tone well. Nor is this the occasion. It's too bold." Reese finally chimed in on the debate that had raised tension in the room.

"You choose now to mentor me"—she smacked her teeth—"what a joke."

Reese whipped away from the mirror and narrowed her eyes at Alex. Lord knows she had been trying to delay this conversation. She hadn't wanted this confrontation to be a part of her sister's memories when she recalled her deb experience. Alex had managed to weasel out of it the day she came home from Duncan's, and then found ways to avoid Reese. Only, Reese couldn't let her behavior endure. It was toxic and demeaning, and it was time for a change.

"Why would I give my time and energy to such a spoiled girl? You've had everything handed to you and still find it hard to appreciate any of it. I'm over your comments with my mentorship. For the record I'd much rather spend time with someone who is receptive to my advice and then works hard to use it to become better."

Alex's hard glare defrosted into an expression Reese hadn't seen since they were much younger. "When is the last time you came to be with us during the summer? Or not been so busy you only had time to drop in for more than two days? I can't think of a time in my teenage life that you've been here for me to ask crazy boy questions or get advice on navigating our crowd of people. So, how do you think it feels to see my sister, fashion girl extraordinaire, out gallivanting with a girl that's my competition?"

"The ball is not about making one girl better than the other, Alexandria." Genevieve's hard tone leveled the room. "This is a time for us to celebrate and build networks with young ladies who are like-minded and will become influential in this world. All of you are introduced to the movers and shakers in society that will at some point assist you on your path to greatness. While I understand some perceive there is competition, I need you to understand that it is not endorsed by the ball committee."

Oh snap! Genevieve had truly done a three-sixty since the other night. She wasn't on her high horse. Reese didn't know if she should be happy or scared. At least she was finally doing her part to rein in the monster Alex had become and save her from being caught up in the luxuries that she had been afforded for far too long.

A sigh escaped Alex. "I thought you wanted me to stand out and be the best. You always talk about how Reese was so celebrated. Everyone compares me to her and never fails to mention that her debut class was the most legendary."

Reese understood the pressure to conform to the expectations of the world they grew up in. It was why she hadn't been back. However, she heard Alex's pain of them lacking a sisterly bond. She took the blame for it not being as strong as it should be. Reese went to her sister, kneeled down, and met her eye to eye. "Of course Mom wants you to be the best. She's made that clear since we were tiny." A bubble of laughter escaped them both.

"In this case, you being the best means ensuring your fellow debs are on their A game too. This ball isn't you versus Destiny. You are each wonderful, beautiful, and created in your own special way. Tonight, display your star power together. I daresay that this is the most legendary debut, since the great-granddaughters of the original founders are debuting."

Reese hugged her sister hard. "I love you, Alex," she whispered. "Sorry if you ever felt like I didn't. My reasons for not being here during the summer have haunted me for a long time. You shouldn't have had to suffer and nor should our relationship. One thing though, can you please stop comparing us or feeling like you have to be better than me? We are two different people. But we are sisters, and that is a bond no one can break."

"I'm sorry too, Reese." Alex hugged her tight.

Her mother's hand rested on her shoulder before she pulled them apart. "Girls, I'm so happy that you two have finally found a way back to each other. However, mind your makeup, Alex, and Chareese, you're already dressed. I don't want anything ruined. Tonight is a big night."

Their mother would never be able to help herself. They all fell into laughter until a knock came across the door and silenced them. Genevieve hurried to open it. She walked back with all signs of humor removed.

"Chareese, Duncan is at the door."

Thirty-Three

FIRST IT WAS one hour, then five, and once it became a whole three days that she had not received a reply from Duncan she'd stopped counting. And now here he was at the door.

"Check your phone." Her mother walked back toward her. "He said he's been trying to reach you."

Reese pulled her phone from the diamond-encrusted clutch that was buried under Alex's stuff. She saw the SOS calls Duncan made in the name of helping Destiny.

"What are you waiting for?" her mom scolded. "There's a handsome young man on the other side of the door."

"Yeah, I know." She palmed her forehead. How was she going to leave her sister to go help Destiny? "Apparently Destiny needs my help. Her mom didn't come."

"Go," Alex said. "I'll send the makeup girl over once she's finished with me." Alex giggled, pointing at Reese's gaping mouth. "We just talked about this. I want her to do good too. I also owe her an apology," Alex mumbled under her breath.

Reese kissed Alex, wished her luck, and then went to the door. She closed her eyes and took about fifty deep breaths before she opened it and saw Duncan. She absolutely wasn't ready to see mister tall, dark, and handsome waiting outside in his tuxedo. The man oozed sex appeal that made her go weak in the knees. Once the dizzying feeling subsided, she found her breath.

"Hey," she said. They were back at square one. Her brain was crossing signals with her heart and she had no idea what to say.

"Hey." His lips pressed together. "I'm not here about us."

Reese nodded and lifted up her phone despite the ache in her chest. "Yeah, I got that. Where's Destiny?"

Duncan turned on his heel and led them down a hall. She knew now wasn't the time to make this about them. She resisted the urge to start small talk and repressed memories of them on his boat, in his bed…She focused as they approached a door with Destiny's name. Duncan knocked, and once they heard Destiny say come in, he turned the knob to enter.

Reese threw her hand atop his, ignoring the desires of her heart that surged out of control the minute her skin met his. "Wait here," she whispered.

"No," he protested. "She's my sister."

"She needs me now. Try to trust me on this." Reese went inside and closed the door without giving him a chance to form a rebuttal.

Destiny was seated at the vanity with her Caboodle flipped open, staring down into it. Reese could not imagine what the girl's loneliness felt like as she prepared for such a big moment alone. When she debuted, her mother, both grandmothers, and the dressmaker were all in her room. Minutes ago, she and her mother and the makeup artist were in Alex's suite fussing over her. This was a gross contrast to that scene, and she hoped she could fill the void.

"Hi, Destiny." Reese walked over to where the teen sat. "I

know I'm the last person you probably want to see right now, but we spent so much time together prepping for this night. I thought it would be nice to check on you and see if you needed help with anything."

Destiny rolled her eyes. "I didn't know my mom was supposed to come. People were looking at me all weird like I had broken the rules."

"Actually," Reese snickered while assessing Destiny to see how much work she had to do to get her ready, "they are the ones who broke the rules. Members of the ball committee and past debutantes usually stay back here and help girls get ready so their debut can be true."

"So, I'm assuming your mom broke her own rules? 'Cause I know Mrs. Devlin's not letting Alex get dressed on her own."

Reese couldn't help laughing. Destiny joined in, and for once since the day began, her spirit felt a little lighter. "Technically, yes, my mom did break the rules. But I'm not here about them, let's get you ready."

Within the hour, Reese had unpinned Destiny's curls, ensured her undergarments were proper for the fit of the dress, and selected a color palette that the makeup artist perfectly executed on the mocha-skinned beauty. Her natural beauty shined like the brightest star in the sky as Reese finger-combed her ringlets until they were beautiful waves cascading down Destiny's back.

The high that usually surrounded Reese when she was at work on set greeted her. She glanced over her shoulder smiling at the pure-white organza gown. The thrill of helping Destiny slip into the formal wear and then seeing her hair, makeup, and accessories come together would subdue the dark clouds of emotions seeking a way to break through.

"Ready to put on—"

"Destiny," an older feminine voice called from the other side of the door, effectively freezing Reese in place before a series of light knocks echoed in the room. "I have a guest for you."

Reese and Destiny looked at each other. Another round of knocks prompted Reese to go to the door. She looked out the peep hole to see Mrs. McNeal standing beside Mrs. Russell.

"It's your mother," she said to Destiny.

"Give me a few minutes, Ma." Destiny spoke loud enough to get an okay from the other side of the door.

In less than ten minutes Reese helped Destiny into her gown. She took a step back, relishing the magic that swirled around them. Destiny had turned into a princess. Without hesitation she went and opened the door for Mrs. McNeal and Mrs. Russell so they too could admire the figure-flattering silhouette of the gown and its flowy skirt that was accented with a small train. More than anything, Reese really liked that Destiny had selected a dress with an elegant boho-chic vibe that embodied her free spirit.

"Oh my goodness, you look so beautiful," Mrs. McNeal gushed all over Destiny. The second she stepped in to wrap her arms around her daughter, Mrs. Russell cut between them, shaking her head, citing risks to the gown. "I want to hug and kiss you, but I'll be good for now so your gown doesn't get ruined. You remind me of those little porcelain dolls people are afraid to touch." Destiny's mother walked around her, unable to contain her pride.

"Thank you for understanding, Mrs. McNeal. You look incredible, young lady." Mrs. Russell inspected Destiny's hair and makeup. "I wouldn't expect anything less. You were mentored by Chareese." The old woman winked at Reese. "Now, let's hurry. The debs are lining up. We'll see all of you inside the ballroom." Mrs. Russell took Destiny and left the room.

"Thank you, Chareese." Mrs. McNeal pulled her into a hug.

"I appreciate you being there for my daughter when I didn't know how to be."

"You're welcome. Destiny is an amazing girl. I'm certain she will do well this evening."

Mrs. McNeal left Reese alone in the room. Before Reese headed upstairs, she drifted into the mirror and freshened up. She then checked the clock on the wall and noted there wasn't much time left before the event was set to start.

With mixed emotions she made her way up to the main level outside of where the ballroom was located. This would be her last night in the Shores, and she was leaving the same way she had all those years ago, lonely and brokenhearted…and no one was allowed to know. So, for appearances' sake, she curved her lips into one of her fake smiles and turned on the Devlin charm as she began rubbing elbows.

She passed through raised laughter, politicking and eavesdropping on gossip, all the while subliminally searching for him. Although, she wasn't surprised by his absence. He'd probably found his way inside the ballroom, since he'd developed a distaste over the years for many of the people present. Still, with every greeting made and handshake offered, Reese had hoped Duncan was on the other side.

From afar she spotted her father and began moving through the crowd to be with him. As she moved closer, the people that were congregated in front of her dad left the reception area and proceeded to the ballroom. It allowed her to see that the man he appeared to be in deep conversation with was Duncan.

Reese's body went still and her heart slowed to a crawling pace. Her eyes locked with Duncan's, but before she could walk off, her father glanced over his shoulder and saw her. He beckoned her to come forward as though he were oblivious to their current situation.

She debated next steps. Duncan had rejected all of her attempts to apologize. Even this evening he made a point to disregard any mention of them. As she continued on to where they stood he didn't seem pleased.

"Dad, Duncan." She acknowledged them, then looked away to avoid the heartache that hit her whenever she looked at Duncan.

"Reese"—her father patted her on the back—"I see why you like him. I'm sorry it's taken me this long to understand."

Her head snapped up to her father and then Duncan. What in the matrix was happening? The last she checked, Kent Devlin cared not to engage in conversations with his enemy.

"This long to understand what, exactly?" she asked, regaining her confidence despite Duncan being present. She was done with cryptic meanings and half-ass truths. She needed to understand precisely what he meant and what it could mean for her.

"That my views of the McNeal family were biased and ill-informed. I uhh…visited Hill House and had a chance to review the correspondence you mentioned along with your grandmother's journal. To ignore her words would further dis-appoint her memory and I cannot do that any longer." He puffed his chest out a bit and glanced over at Duncan. "I also spent some time with Duncan. This young man has done a lot for the community. He saved the house from certain ruin by commercial investors, and plans to do more. Instead of fighting him, I will be supporting his efforts."

She pinched herself and both men chuckled. She didn't join in. She was pleased that it seemed the rifts between the Devlins and McNeals could finally enter a phase of healing. However, while everyone else had been playing nice, she was left to keep misery's company.

Had she known her dad was learning to accept their family's

secrets and her feelings for Duncan, she wouldn't have been walking on eggshells at home. Likewise, if Duncan had found it in his angry mind to forgive her father, why couldn't he do the same for her?

"Wow." Humorless sarcasm dripped from her. "This is the best thing I've heard since I've been here."

* * *

Duncan recoiled at first, then launched forward the second she pivoted on her heel to walk away from them. He thought she would be happy. He was. "Wait, Reese." He caught her by the hand. "Why are you leaving?"

"Because I've spent over a week trying to find a way back to you." She whipped to her dad. "You walked away from me after I gave you our family's truths and haven't said a single word to me until mere seconds ago. And now you both want me to be happy that you've had some sort of guy talk and things are good?"

"It took me some time to process everything, Chareese. It is an ugly past that should have been confronted a long time ago. You're right, I'm sorry," her father admitted, then placed a kiss at her temple.

"I'm not." Duncan's face remained firm. He could see peripherally that Mr. Devlin may have been second-guessing his judgment of him. He didn't care. For Reese it may have been days. For him it had been ten years. "What does a week matter if I'm looking for a lifetime with you?"

"I think I should leave the two of you to talk." Mr. Devlin shook Duncan's hand and then proceeded into the ballroom.

"Maybe we should go somewhere else?"

Duncan shook his head. He didn't care about appearances,

and he needed to know that she felt the same. They could only escape the past that had held their families hostage if she was able to let go and embrace the future. "Here is fine."

She sighed and glanced around. There were still a number of people in the vicinity. He silently prayed she would live up to being the woman he believed her to be and not cower under the pressure. This moment was for them.

Reese fingered the corner of her eye. "So, you accept my apology?"

"No." Duncan reached up and pushed the tear sliding down her cheek away. "Because I was never upset that you wanted to change my mind on Hill House. It hurt that you needed a reason to be around me for their benefit. I was reminded of that night ten years ago when you lied about what we were to each other because they believed I wasn't good enough for you."

"I'm sorry, Duncan." She closed the gap between them and cupped his face. "You're right. I shouldn't have needed an excuse to be with you. Not when you've been the only man I've ever loved."

His heart almost beat out of his chest. He'd loved this woman his entire life. He would not refuse this second chance. "I tried to run from this love for fear of being hurt again, but I can't ignore how you make me feel. No one else will do, so I guess that means I'm going to have to accept your apology, Chareese Devlin."

He released a sexy chuckle as a grin popped onto her face. He wrapped his arms around her, holding her tight as their noses played before she leaned in and pressed her lips against his. He didn't hold back. A week had been too long, and he was starved of her affections. There was no limit to the love he was ready to give.

Reese broke the kiss and stared into his face. "Before

everything happened, I asked you to be my date here tonight. Will you escort me in?"

"You don't have to ask me that." He dropped another kiss upon her lips.

"I do." She was breathless. "Us walking into that room together will symbolize much more than you might be prepared to handle."

Duncan paused. He hadn't exactly thought this far ahead. Unlike Reese, he had not been trained to view actions as signals within the world of the Black elite. "Explain."

"Let me put it this way, your sister isn't the only one from the McNeal family making a debut tonight." Her smile was wide and almost contagious.

He wasn't sure if he wanted to be in a world that treated people differently because of their lineage, generational wealth, or social affiliations. However, if becoming part of this circle he had lived alongside for so long would grant him additional resources to pave paths for others to move forward, then maybe he should go.

"Are you okay?" she asked, obviously sensing his hesitation. "It's not all bad, Dunc. There are advantages. The rift that has existed between our families will appear resolved. Friends of the Devlins will become friends of the McNeals. The status you've rightfully earned will be given, and last but most important, everyone will know that you're mine." She winked at him.

Since they were old enough to chase each other in the backyard of Hill House, he had wanted her. He would learn to navigate this new space he was entering without compromising the man he had become.

"I've always wanted to be yours." He stepped to her side and bent his elbow at an angle. Reese then slid her hand under his arm and looped it around. "Shall we?"

Thirty-Four

A SEA OF at least five hundred people had already congregated in the ballroom. The social fanfare and the elaborate décor that were hallmarks of the event proved to be slightly overwhelming as together, they took steps into their future. Heads turned as they walked down the aisle. Smiles and nods of approval from Gavin, Quinn, Ava, Carrah, Peyton, Chris, and others whom they'd known all their lives gave them a boost of confidence as they closed in on the Devlins' table.

"Mom, Dad." Reese glanced up at Duncan and then back down to her parents, who were seated at the table next to the mayor, her husband, Judge Caldwell, and his wife. He could tell she was nervous. Hell, he was a little bit too. Her father had been cool in the lobby, but things could be different in front of their *friends*. "Is there room for *us*?"

Reese's fingers laced between his. She had already explained what walking in together meant, so sitting at her parents' table must be another level of validation, and Duncan cared not to entertain shit that hadn't helped him get anywhere in life. However, he vowed to be the change the upper crust feared.

He then peeked over his shoulder, searching for his parents. He finally spotted them sitting at a table with a few empty seats. "It's fine, Reese," he whispered. "There's room for me at my parents' table."

"Is there a seat for me too?" Her hand gripped his harder.

"Always."

Before they could leave, Genevieve grabbed hold of both their hands. Mr. Devlin stood behind her. "Please take your seats at this table. I will go and invite David and Pearl to sit here with us as well. There is much to celebrate tonight." She kissed Reese on the cheek and darted off.

Mr. Devlin smiled and gestured for them to take their seats, then acquainted everyone with each other. As Duncan was introducing himself for the first time to Judge Caldwell and his wife, his parents came over and claimed the empty chairs. In no time the entire table had found some hot topic to latch on to as they waited for the evening to start.

Duncan took in a deep breath. He scanned the room and his table, and then his eyes landed on the girl of his dreams. Life was almost full circle.

"Reese." She paused her conversation with his mother and turned to face him. "Are you still leaving tomorrow?" The question had been on his mind since he laid eyes on her tonight. And her father had confirmed it while they were speaking. He had just been too afraid to ask because he didn't want to be selfish. She had a life and an accomplished career before returning to the Shores for the summer.

"I was," she teased. "However, you've changed my mind. I think I will extend my trip."

The lights in the room dimmed, signaling the start. He had to get this out or he'd be sitting on pins and needles the whole night. Reese deserved to know where he stood with Hill House and the youth village project. After all, it was what had brought them to where they were now.

"What if I told you I'm still moving forward with the youth village?"

Her big, brown eyes scanned him. She glanced down to her empty hands and then looked back at him. "Disappointed, but I understand. It's a business decision and the community needs it. I'm still extending my trip."

He leaned back in his chair, massaging his goatee. "Good, then you can assist me with selecting a new building for the youth village. Also if you're up to it, you did mention something about changing curtains and revamping the inn. I'd love for you to explore your talents in interiors and help oversee my firm's restoration for the reopening of Hill House."

Reese shot out of her chair and threw her arms around him. Somehow she ended in his lap. "You mean that! You're saving Hill House?"

"Sit down, Chareese," her mother scolded. "You're making a scene."

Reese slid back down in her seat, unable to stay still. Her smile lit up the room and filled his heart with a joy he had searched for, for ten long years. Duncan would live every day to see her happy like this.

"Are you going to answer the lady's question?" his father asked.

Duncan looked around the table, and it seemed as though everyone was waiting on his answer. The night he made love to Reese in the old house changed his mind about the purpose of Hill House. The day he read those letters between his and Reese's grandmothers was when he knew without a doubt that the old house was not meant to be a youth village.

It was meant to be a place where people could unwind, reconnect, and fall in love. He had, twice with the same woman.

"I'm not sure if I saved it or if it saved me," he confessed to Reese. He tuned out a few cheers and focused on her. "The time we've spent together over the last month has revealed so much. I saw what Hill House meant to you and what it could mean again for us. It's worth saving, and hopefully with the restoration other people will have a chance to enjoy a place that has made the Shores special."

* * *

Water welled in Reese's eyes. It seemed she had spent the last few days crying, but at least this time it was happy tears. Surprisingly, it wasn't because Hill House would remain a bed and breakfast. It was because the man sitting across from her had done the one thing no one in their families had been able to do in decades.

Duncan had been unselfish in his decision and allowed the love that was within the walls of her grandmother's old inn to rule his decision. A decision that would help to heal their families and honor the love that Constance and Suzette had when they worked together at the bed and breakfast.

Reese grabbed him by the face, not caring about her mother's social niceties, and kissed him hard. She pulled back, unable to resist his contagious smile even as their mothers muttered disapproval.

"So, I guess I need to quit my job."

"What?" He chuckled.

"Well, yeah. I had been thinking about taking a few classes in interior design. Maybe shadow friends in the industry. Brush up on skills for furniture textiles. I have to help you make sure the restoration and your venture with the inn is successful."

"Our inn," he corrected her.

A cough came from across the table. She looked over at her parents and couldn't believe her mother was shedding tears.

"Our inn," she repeated, and he nodded.

"If you agree, I'd like to place your name on the deed with mine. Didn't I hear you mention something about being the lady of Hill House?" He gave that panty-teasing smile as she swatted at him, and she knew she was going to rock his world tonight.

Her father gave a hearty chuckle. "I'll help you, Chareese."

"And so will I," offered Miss Pearl.

Her father's face became serious. "Been a long time since the four of us supported something together." He smiled at Pearl and David before leaning in and kissing Genevieve at her temple.

"Mama and Miss Connie would be proud." David nodded to Kent. "I'm certainly upset it took so long, but happy that we honored the hope and love between them."

Miss Pearl sat dabbing a handkerchief at her eyes. "Yes, they would."

Genevieve extended her hands. She grabbed her husband's on one side and Pearl's on the other. Pearl then grabbed David's and connected to Reese and Duncan. "I never thought I would see a day like this. It's been a long road to get here." Her mother's pleasant smile communicated pride, joy, and love.

All of which Reese felt sitting next to Duncan. There would never be another day that she was without him.

"I love you, Duncan. Thank you for giving Hill House, and me, a second chance."

"You gave us one." He sat up and pecked her lips. "Some things are just meant to be. I love you, Chareese."

Acknowledgments

There will never be enough words to express how thankful I am for my family and their unwavering support and encouragement. To Mark, my love—you are my strength, my light. I couldn't do this life without you. To my Marz, you keep me thinking of new ways to create witty-strong heroines. Love you, Girlie-pop! To my B-Man, you remind me to be gentle and kind— You are my SONshine. To my daddy, thanks for helping me define the strength of Black Men between these pages. To my mama, you gave me such a vision. To my baby sis, you keep me reaching for the stars and daring to put my characters in bold colors. To my brother, Horace, you speak to me from heaven daily and tell me to get my ass up and write— I miss you. To my aunts Carolyn and Vivian, thank you for the random sweet notes that keep me encouraged. To Diana Neal, I love going down your rabbit holes. To LaQuette, I gave you Southern drama and you said, write it because there are Black Dynasties. To Paula McGhee, thanks for always checking in on me.

To my agent, the fabulous Latoya Smith, thank you for finding and opening doors. But most of all for having my back—you are a true ride or die. Looking forward to what comes next.

To Kirsiah Depp, the sweetest editor a girl could ask for,

thank you for diving into this world, believing in it, and making it better. We are challenging the status quo and it feels good to bring everyone to the Shores.

To all the beautifully talented women writing romance featuring Black Heroines and Heroes—keep writing! The world deserves to see our excellence as we defy stereotypes and show that everyone is worthy of a Happily Ever After.

To my readers, thank you. I hope you enjoyed the Shores. Be on the lookout for the next HEA set in this charming town.

About the Author

C. Chilove is the past secretary for Romance Writers of America (RWA) and past president of Cultural, Interracial, Multicultural chapter of RWA. She is a Southern girl writing sexy, thought-provoking romance that explores the human condition while proving love transcends societal clichés. Her characters are strong, witty, and prove that diversity is beautiful. When she's not writing, she's living out her personal happily-ever-after by rockin' the stands for her volleyball star, cheering on her future MLB slugger, or celebrating date night with her hubby.